THE ACCLAIMED TALTOS NOVELS
BY STEVEN BRUST

Enter the spellbinding world of an assassin-for-hire . . . and his reptile companions.

JHEREG

. . . in which young Vlad, bound for adventure, finds a faithful reptile companion.

YENDI

. . . in which Vlad and his jhereg learn that a woman's love can scald a killer's blood.

TECKLA

. . . in which two jhereg are better than one, especially during a revolution.

TALTOS

. . . in which Vlad and company walk on the wild side, the Path of the Dead.

"Lightning-paced . . . a fun, enjoyable read!"   *—OtherRealms*

"A breath of fresh chilly air."   —Ed Bryant, *Mile High Futures*

PHOENIX

. . . in which the Demon Goddess makes Vlad an offer he can't refuse.

"Involving, captivating . . . highly recommended!"
—The Midwest Book Review

"A fine, enjoyable novel . . . emotionally powerful . . . a wry sense of humor."   *—OtherRealms*

ATHYRA

. . . in which Vlad learns there are very few benefits for a retired assassin.

"Newly amazing . . . compelling."   *—Locus*

ALSO BY STEVEN BRUST . . .

COWBOY FENG'S SPACE BAR AND GRILLE

"A great writer!"   *—OtherRealms*

"Flashes of brilliance . . . a good swift plot!"   *—Locus*

STEVEN BRUST

ACE BOOKS, NEW YORK

This book is an Ace original edition,
and has never been previously published.

ORCA

An Ace Book / published by arrangement with
the author

PRINTING HISTORY
Ace edition / March 1996

All rights reserved.
Copyright © 1996 by Steven Brust.
Cover art by Ciruelo Cabral.
This book may not be reproduced in whole or in part,
by mimeograph or any other means, without permission.
For information address: The Berkley Publishing Group,
200 Madison Avenue, New York, NY 10016.

The Putman Berkley World Wide Web site address is
http://www.berkley.com

ISBN: 0-441-00196-3

ACE®
Ace Books are published by the Berkley Publishing Group,
200 Madison Avenue, New York, NY 10016.
ACE and the "A" design are trademarks
belonging to Charter Communications, Inc.

PRINTED IN THE UNITED STATES OF AMERICA

10 9 8 7 6 5 4 3

ACKNOWLEDGMENTS

My thanks to the Scribblies: Emma Bull, Pamela Dean, and Will Shetterly for their help with this one, and also to Terri Windling, Susan Allison, and Fred A. Levy Haskell. Thanks as well to Teresa Nielsen Hayden, who recommended a book that turned out to be vital; to David Green, for sharing some theories; and, as always, to Adrian Charles Morgan.

And to the fan who actually suggested the whole thing in the first place: Thanks, Mom.

In memory of my brother,
Leo Brust, 1954–1994

PROLOGUE

My Dear Cawti:

   I'm sorry it has taken me so long to answer your letter, but the gods of Coincidence make bad correspondents of us all; I am not unaware that the passing of a few weeks to you is a long time—as long as the passing of years is to me, and this is long indeed when one is uncertain—so I will plead the excuse that I found your note when I returned from traveling, and will answer your question at once: Yes, I have seen your husband, or the man who used to be your husband, or however you would describe him. Yes, I have seen Vlad—and that is why it has taken me so long to write back to you; I was just visiting him in response to his request for assistance in a small matter.

   I can understand your concern for him, Cawti; indeed, I will not try to pretend that he isn't still in danger from the Organization with which we are both, one way or another, still associated. They want him, and I fear someday they will get him, but as of now he is alive and, I can even say, well.

I don't pretend that I think this knowledge will satisfy you.

You will want the details, or at least those details I can divulge. Very well, I consent, both for the sake of our friendship and because we share a concern for the mustached fellow with reptiles on his shoulders. We will arrange a time and a place; I will be there and tell you what I can—in person, because some things are better heard face-to-face than page-to-eye. And, no, I will not tell you everything, because, just as there are things that you wouldn't want me to tell him, there are things he wouldn't want me to tell you—and, come to that, there are things I don't want to tell you, either. It is a mark of my love for you both that I keep these secrets, and trust you with those I can, so don't be angry!

Come, dear Cawti, write back at once (you remember that I prefer not to communicate psychically), and we will arrange to be alone and I will tell you enough—I hope—for your peace of mind. I look forward to seeing you and yours again, and, until that time, I remain,

Faithfully,

Kiera

Chapter One

VLAD KNEW ALMOST at once that I was in disguise, because I told him so. When he called out my name, I said, "Dammit, Vlad, I'm in disguise."

He looked me over in that way of his—eyes flicking here and there apparently at random—then said, "Me, too."

He was wearing brown leather, rather than the grey and black of the House of the Jhereg he'd been wearing when I last saw him; but he was still an Easterner, still had his mustache, and still had a pair of jhereg on his shoulders. He was, I assumed, letting me know that my disguise wasn't terribly effective. I didn't press the issue, but said, "Who's the boy?"

"My catamite," he said, deadpan. He faced him then and said, "Savn, meet Kiera the Thief."

The boy made no response at all—didn't even seem to hear—which was a bit creepy.

I said, "You're joking, right?"

He smiled sadly and said, "Yes, Kiera, I'm joking."

Loiosh, the male jhereg, shifted its weight and was probably laughing at me. I held out my arm to it; it flew across the four feet that separated us and allowed me to scratch its snakelike chin. The female, Rocza, watched us closely but made no move; perhaps she didn't remember me.

"Why the disguise?" he said.

"Why do you think?"

"You don't want to be seen with me?"

I shrugged.

He said, "Well, in any case, our disguises match." He was referring to the fact that I was wearing a green blouse and white pants, rather than the same black and grey he'd once worn. My hair was also different—I'd brushed it forward to conceal my noble's point so I'd look more like a peasant. But perhaps he didn't notice that; for an assassin, he can be amazingly unobservant sometimes. Still, you wear a disguise, first, from the inside, and perhaps that can in part explain the fact that my disguise didn't fool Vlad; I've always trusted him, even before I had reason to.

"It's been a long time, Vlad," I said, because I knew that to him, who could only expect to live sixty or seventy years, it would have seemed like a long time.

"Yes, it has," he agreed. "How odd that we should just happen to run into each other."

"You haven't changed."

"There's less of me," he said, holding up his left hand and showing me that the last finger was missing.

"What happened?"

"A very heavy weight."

I winced in sympathy. "Is there someplace we can talk?" I said.

He looked around. We were in Northport, quite a distance from Adrilankha, but it was the same ocean, and the docks, if older, were pretty much the same. There was a small, two-masted cargo ship unloading about fifty yards away, and there was a fishermen's market nearby; between them, on the very edge of the ocean, we were in plain view of hundreds of people, but no one was near us. "What's wrong with here?"

"You don't trust me," I said, feeling a bit hurt.

I could see a snappy answer get as far as his teeth and stop there. Vlad and I had a great deal of history; none of it should have given him any reason to be suspicious of me. "Last I heard," he said, "the Organization wanted very badly to kill me; you still work for the Organization. Excuse me if I'm a bit jumpy."

"Oh, yes," I agreed. "They want you very badly indeed."

The water lapped and gurgled against the dock that had stood since the end of the Interregnum; I could feel the spells that kept the wood from rotting. The air was thick with the smell of ocean: salt water and dead fish; I've never really liked either.

"Who *is* the boy?" I asked him, as much to give him time to think as because I wanted to know. Savn, as Vlad had called him, seemed to be a handsome Teckla youth, probably not more than ninety years old. He still had that look of strength and energy that begins to diminish during one's second century, and his hair was the same dusky brown as his eyes. It annoyed me that I could conceive of him as a catamite. He still hadn't responded to me or to anything else.

"A debt of honor," said Vlad, in the tone he uses when he is trying to be ironic. I realized that I'd missed him. I waited for him to continue. He said, "Savn was damaged, I guess you'd say, saving my life."

"Damaged?"

"Oh, the usual—he used a Morganti weapon to kill an undead wizard."

"When was this?"

"Last year. Does it matter?"

"I suppose not."

"I'm glad you got my message, and I'm glad you came."

"You're still psychically invisible, you know."

"I know. Phoenix Stone."

"Yes."

"How is Aibynn?"

Aibynn was one of the last people Vlad wanted to ask about; he knew it and I knew it. "Fine as far as I know. I don't see him much."

He nodded. We watched the bay for a while, but it didn't do much. I turned back to Vlad and said, "Well? I'm here. What is it?"

He smiled. "Maybe I've come up with a way to get the Organization to forgive and forget."

I laughed. "My dear Vlad, if you managed to loot the Dragon Treasury to the last orb and deposited it all at the feet of the Council they wouldn't forgive you."

His smile disappeared. "There's that."

"Well then?"

He shrugged. He wasn't ready to talk about it yet. That was all right, I can be a very patient woman. "You know," I said, "there aren't all that many Easterners who walk around with a pair of jhereg on their shoulders; are you quite certain you aren't too conspicuous?"

"Yeah. No professional would try anything in a place like this, and any amateur who wants to is welcome to take a shot. And by the time word gets around so someone who knows his business can set up something, I'll be gone."

"But they'll know where you are."

"I don't plan on being here for more than a few days."

I nodded.

He said hesitantly, "Any news from home?"

"None I can tell you."

"Excuse me?"

"You're asking about Cawti."

"Well—"

"I've promised not to say anything except that she's fine."

"Oh." I watched his mind work, but he didn't say anything else. I very badly wanted to tell him what was going on, but a promise is a promise, even to a thief. Especially to a thief.

I said, "How have you been getting by?"

"It's been harder since I acquired the boy, but I've managed."

"How?"

"I mostly stay away from towns, and you know the forests are filled with bandits of one sort or another."

"You've become one?"

"No, I rob them."

I laughed. "That sounds like you."

"It's a living."

"That sounds like you, too."

He shifted his weight as if his feet were causing him pain; it made me think about the amount of walking he must have been doing in these past three years and more. I said, "Do you want to sit down?"

"You don't miss much," he said. "No, I'm fine. Ever heard of a man named Fyres?"

"Yes. He died a couple of weeks ago."

"Other than that, what do you know about him?"

"He had a great deal of money."

"Yes. What else?"

"He was, what, a baron? House of the, uh, Chreotha?"

"Orca."

"All right. Then that tells you what I know about him."

Vlad didn't answer, which meant that I was supposed to ask him a question. I thought over a number of things I'd have liked to know, then settled on, "How did he die?"

"They've found no evidence of murder."

"That's not— Wait. You?"

He shook his head. "I don't do that sort of thing anymore."

"All right," I said. Vlad has always had the ability to make me believe him, even though I know what a liar he is. "Then what do you think happened?"

His eyes were in constant motion, and the jhereg, too, never stopped looking around. "I don't know," he said, "and I have to find out."

"Why?"

For just an instant he looked embarrassed, and "Oh ho!" passed through my head, but I sent it on its way—Vlad could be embarrassed by the oddest things. "It doesn't matter," he said. "Let me tell you what I'd like you to do."

"I'm listening."

One thing I like about Vlad is that he understands details. He not only gave me every detail of every alarm I was likely to encounter but also told me how he found out, so I could do my own checking. He told me where the stuff was likely to be and why he thought so, and the other places it might be located if he was wrong. He gave me the schedules of the patrols in the area and explained exactly what he hadn't been able to discover. It took about an hour, at the end of which time I knew the job would be well within my capabilities—not that there are many jobs that aren't, if they involve stealing.

I said, "There will be a price."

"Of course," he said, trying to hide that I'd hurt his feelings.

"You have to tell me why you want it."

He bit his lip and looked at me carefully; I kept my face expressionless, because I didn't want him learning too much. He nodded abruptly, and the deal was made.

It took me two days to check everything Vlad had told me—two days that I spent working out of a reasonably comfortable room in a hotel in the middle of Northport; on the third I went to work. The place I was to burgle was situated a couple of miles east of Northport, and the walk there was the most chancy part of the operation—if anyone saw me and saw through my disguise as easily as Vlad had, it would arouse curiosity, and that would lead to investigations and that would lead to this and that. I solved the problem by staying off the roads and sticking as much as I could to the thin-wooded areas to the side. I didn't get lost, but it was several hours before I reached the bottom of a small hill, with Fyres's mansion looming above me.

I spent a couple of hours walking a wide circuit around it, taking a long, slow look at the place. One of the things Vlad hadn't given me was a set of blueprints, but with this newer work you can almost create the inside by seeing the outside; for some reason post-Interregnum architects object to having rooms without windows, which means the dimensions indicate the layout. You can also identify windowed corridors because (again, I don't know why) the windows are invariably smaller than those in rooms. By the time I'd finished my walk, I pretty much knew what it looked like, and I'd found the most obvious places for an office.

I spent the last hours of daylight watching for any signs of activity. There were none, which was as it should be—Fyres's family (a wife and three children) didn't live there, his mistress had abandoned the place, the staff were, no doubt, ensconced within, and all of the remaining protec-

tion was sorcerous and automatic. I took out a few of the
devices I use to identify such things and set to work.

Darkness came as it always does, with shadows becoming dusk—shadows that were a bit sharper here than in
Adrilankha, I suppose because the westerly winds thin out
the overcast, so the Furnace is more apparent. Everything is
brighter in the west of the Empire, as it is in the far east; all
of which makes the darkness seem even darker.

The protections weren't bad, but not as thorough as I
would have expected. The first was very general and nearly
useless—all you had to do was pretend you belonged there
and it would let you burn down the place without raising a
fuss. The recognition spell was only marginally trickier, re-
quiring me to cause it to bend around and past me; but there
was no spell monitoring whether the recognition spell was
being bent, so, really, they might as well not have bothered
with it. There were the usual integrity detectors on the
doors and windows, but these are easily defeated by trans-
ferring the one you want to pass to another door or window.
These, in fact, did have monitor spells to watch for just this,
but they'd been cast almost as an afterthought and without
anything to let the security people know the monitor had
been removed—I could take it down just by identifying the
energy committed to that spell and absorbing it into a working of my own.

I considered the significance of how poorly the mansion
was protected. It might mean that since the place was abandoned and its owner was dead, no one felt the need to use
high-level protections. It might also mean that the Orca
weren't as sophisticated as the Jhereg. Or it might mean
that there were some traps concealed that I hadn't found
yet. That possibility was worth an extra hour of checking,
and I took it.

I went through enough gear to stock a small sorcery shop

and found fertility spells that had probably been placed on the ground before the mansion was built, spells that kept the latrines from smelling, spells that kept the mansion from sinking into the ground, spells that kept the stonework from crumbling, and spells to make the row of rednut trees that flanked the road grow just so—but nothing else that had anything to do with security. I even used a blue stone I'd picked from the pocket of Vlad's friend Aliera, but the only signs of elder sorcery were distant echoes from the explosion that had dissolved Dragaera City at the start of the Interregnum.

I was satisfied. I climbed the hill slowly, keeping my eyes open for more mundane traps, although I didn't expect to find any, and I didn't. I eventually reached the edge of the mansion, which, I suppose I should have mentioned, demonstrated the sort of post-Interregnum aesthetic that thinks monoliths attractive for their own sake, producing big blocks of stone with the occasional bit of decoration, usually a wrought-iron animal, sticking out as an afterthought. Buildings like this are exceedingly easy to burglarize, because you know exactly where everything is relative to everything else, and because the regularity of the construction makes those who live there believe that it is difficult to conceal oneself while climbing up a wall, which is silly—I once challenged three friends to try to spot me while I scaled three stories of a blank wall, after telling them which wall I was going up and when I was going to do it. They couldn't find me. So much for the difficulty of concealment.

It took me about ten seconds to levitate up to the level of the window; I rested on the ledge and considered that idiotic spell I already mentioned that was supposed to make certain the integrity of the window wasn't broken. There was, indeed, nothing fancy about it, but I was careful and spent some time circumventing the alarm. The window, by the way, was filled in, as were all of them, with a solid sheet of glass cunningly worked into slots in a wood and leather contrivance that, in turn, fitted snugly into the window; a silly luxury that would need to be replaced in a hundred years or so, even if the fragile thing weren't broken in the meantime.

I broke it carefully, first covering it with a large sheet of paper smeared with an extremely tacky gel and then pushing slowly until the glass gave and the shards stuck to the paper rather than falling and making noise. There were jagged bits of the stuff all around the wooden frame so I had to be careful entering the room, but I was able to enter without cutting myself; then I hung the paper in the window where the glass had been so I could illuminate the room without the light appearing to anyone outside (if there was, by chance, someone outside).

I used another several seconds sensing for spells in the room, then lit a candle, squinted against the glare, and glanced around quickly. No matter how many times you've been through this, you always half expect to see someone sitting in the room waiting for you with all sorts of arguments to hand. It has never happened, and it didn't this time, but it's one of those things that pass through your mind.

I closed my eyes and stood very still for a while, listening for anyone moving around and for whatever creaks and groans might be usual for this building. After a minute, I opened my eyes and took a good look.

Office or study, said that part of my brain that wants to rush in and categorize before all of the details are individually assimilated. I let it have its way, ignored its opinion, and made some mental notes.

The room was dominated by two large cabinets against

the far wall, both of some dark wood, probably cherry, and showing signs of careful but uninspired construction. In front of them was a small desk, facing the room's other window, with a chair behind it. From the chair, the occupant, presumably Fyres, could reach back to either cabinet. On top of the desk were a set of books that would probably reward some study, several sheets of paper, blotter, inkwell, and quill; several other quills were all set in a row to one side, as if awaiting their call. The desk and the room were neither unusually tidy nor remarkably messy, except for between one and four weeks' worth of dust over everything, which would be about right if no one had been in here since his death. Why would no one have been in his office since his death? No, questions later.

I checked all the desk drawers and cabinets and found both sorcerous alarms on each. None of them were terribly complicated and I wasn't in a big hurry, so I took my time disabling them (unnecessarily in all probability—they were almost certainly keyed directly to Fyres, who wouldn't be receiving any messages—but it is always best to be certain). I also looked for more mundane sorts of alarms—easily identified by thin wires hidden against desk legs or along walls—but there weren't any. It occurs to me now, as I relate this, that it may seem as if Fyres took insufficient precautions against theft, and I ought to correct this impression; most of his precautions probably involved guards, and, chances are, the guard schedule had been obliterated with Fyres's life. And the magical alarms were really quite good; it's just that I'm better.

It took maybe two minutes to assure myself that there were no secret drawers in the desk, another ten to be certain about the cabinets. The rest of the room took an hour, which is a long time to be on the scene, but I didn't think the risk was too great.

Once I was certain I hadn't missed anything, I began going through his papers, looking for anything that seemed like what Vlad was after. The longer I sat there, the harder it was to make myself go slowly and be careful not to miss anything, but, after four hours or so, I was pretty sure I had the information. It made a neat little bundle, which I tied up and slung over my back. I still had an hour or so before dawn.

I restored order to the papers and books I'd messed up, then slipped across the hall to the master bedroom. Everything was very still, and I could hear—or maybe I just imagined it—servants breathing from their quarters above me. The bed was made, the clothes were neatly arranged in the wardrobe, and, unlike the office, everything was freshly dusted—obviously the staff had been given orders to stay out of the other room, and they were still scrupulously following them. I opened drawers and scattered things about as if a thief had been looking for valuables. I did, in fact, find a safe, so I spent a few minutes marking it up as if I'd attempted to open it, then I went back to the study, out the window, and down.

I was back in town before the first light. I found my hotel and climbed into my second-story window so I wouldn't have to go past the desk clerk. I put the booty under my pillow and slept for nine hours.

My rendezvous with Vlad took place in one of those dockside inns that feature thick beer and harshly spiced fish stew. Vlad availed himself of the latter; I abstained. It was too early in the day for there to be much business; only a table or two was filled. Neither of us attracted much attention. I've always wondered how Vlad (even with a jhereg on his shoulder—only one today) managed to avoid making himself conspicuous wherever he went.

"Where's the boy?"

"With friends."

"You have friends?" I said, not entirely being sarcastic.

He gave me a brief smile and said, "Rocza is watching him."

He accepted the bundle of ledgers and papers, trying not to look eager. I made faces at Loiosh while he perused them; at last he looked up and nodded. "This is what I'm after," he said. "Thanks."

"What do they mean?"

"I haven't any idea."

"Then how do you know—?"

"From the notations at the top of the columns."

"I see," I lied. "Well, then—"

"What am I after?"

"Yes."

He looked at me. I'd seen Vlad happy, sad, frightened, angry, and hurt; but I'd never before seen him look uncomfortable. At last he said, "All right," and began speaking.

Chapter Two

ON THE WALL of a small hostelry just outside of Northport someone had written in black, sloppy letters: "When the water is clean, you see the bottom; when the water is dirty, you see yourself."

"Deep philosophy," I remarked to Loiosh. *"Probably a brothel."*

He didn't laugh. Call me superstitious, but I decided to find another place. I nodded to the boy to follow. I'm not sure when he started responding to nonverbal cues; I hadn't been paying that much attention. But it was a good sign. On the other hand, that had been the only improvement in the year he'd been with me and that was a bad sign.

Wait for it, Kiera; wait for it. I've done this before. I know how to tell a Verra-be-damned story, okay?

So I kept walking, getting closer to Northport. I'd come to Northport because Northport is the biggest city in the world—okay, in the Empire—that doesn't have any sort of university. No, I have nothing against universities, but you must know how they work—they act like magnets to pull in the best brains in an area, as well as the richest and most pretentious. They are seats of great learning and all that. Now I had a problem that required someone of great, or maybe not-so-great learning, but walking into a university, well, I didn't like the idea. I don't know how to go about it, and that means I don't know how to go about it without getting caught. For example, what happens if I go to, say, Candletown, and inquire at Lady Brindlegate's University, and someone is rude to me, and I have to drop him? Then what? It makes a big stink, and the wrong people hear about it, and there I am running again.

But I figured, what if I find a place with a lot of people but no institution to suck up the talented ones? It means it's going to be a place with a lot of hedge-wizards, and wise old men, and greatwives. And that's just what I was look-ing for—what I had been looking for for most of a year, and not finding, until I hit on this idea.

I'll get to it, I'll get to it. Trust me.

I got a little closer to town, stopped at an inn, and—look, you don't need to hear all this. I stayed out of a fight, lis-tened to gossip, pumped a few people, went to another inn, did the same, repeat, repeat, and finally found myself at a little blue cottage in the woods. Yes, blue—a blue lump of house standing out from all the greens of the woods sur-rounding Northport. It was one of the ugliest objects I've ever seen.

The first thing that happened was a dog came running out toward us. I was stepping in front of Savn and reaching for a knife before Loiosh said, *"His tail is wagging, boss."*

"Right. I knew that."

It was some indeterminate breed with a bit of hound in it—the sleek build of a lyorn with the sort of long, curly, reddish hair that needed cleaning and combing, a long nose,

and floppy ears. It didn't come up to my waist, and it gen-
erally seemed pretty nonthreatening. It stopped in front of
me and started sniffing. I held out my left hand, which it
approved, then it gave a half-jump up toward Loiosh, then
one toward Rocza, went down on its front legs, barked
twice, and stood in front of me waiting and wagging. Rocza
hissed; Loiosh refused to dignify it by responding.

The door opened, and a woman called, "Buddy!" The
dog looked back at her, turned in a circle, and ran up to her,
then rose on its hind legs and stayed there for a moment.
The woman was old and a foot and a half taller than me.
She had grey hair and an expression that would sour your
favorite dairy product. She said, "You're an Easterner," in a
surprisingly flutelike voice.

"Yes," I said. "And your house is painted blue."

She let that go. "Who's the boy?"

"The reason I'm here."

"He's human."

"And to think I hadn't noticed."

Loiosh chuckled in my head; the woman didn't. "Don't
be saucy," she said. "No doubt you've come for help with
something; you ought to be polite." The dog sat down next
to her and watched us, his tongue out.

I tried to figure out what House she was and decided it
was most likely Tsalmoth, to judge by her complexion and
the shape of her nose—her green shawl, dirty white blouse,
and green skirt were too generic to tell me anything.

"Why do you care?" said Loiosh.

"Good question."

"Okay," I said. "I'll be polite. You're a—do you find the
term 'hedge-wizard' objectionable?"

"Yes," she said, biting out the word.

"What do you prefer?"

"Sorcerer."

She was a sorcerer the way I was a flip-dancer. "All right. I've heard you are a sorcerer, and that you are skilled in problems of the mind."

"I can sometimes help, yes."

"The boy has brain fever."

She made a harrumphing sound. "There is no such thing."

I shrugged.

She looked at him, but still didn't step out of her door, nor ask us to approach. I expected her to ask more questions about his condition, but instead she said, "What do you have to offer me?"

"Gold."

"Not interested."

That caught me by surprise. "You're not interested in gold?"

"I have enough to get by."

"Then what do you want?"

"Offer her her life, boss."

"Grow up, Loiosh."

She said, "There isn't anything I want that you could give me."

"You'd be surprised," I said.

She studied me as if measuring me for a bier and said, "I haven't known many Easterners." The dog scratched its ear, stood, walked around in a circle, sat down in the same place it had been, and scratched itself again.

"If you're asking if you can trust me," I said, "there's no good answer I can give you."

"That isn't the question."

"Then—"

"Come in."

I did, Savn following along dutifully, the dog last. The inside was worse than the outside. I don't mean it was dirty—on the contrary, everything was neat, clean, and polished, and there wasn't a speck of dust; no mean trick in a wood cottage. But it was filled with all sorts of magnificently polished wood carvings—magnificent and tasteless. Oil lamps, chairs, cupboards, and buffets were all of dark hardwood, all gleaming with polish, and all of them horribly overdone, like someone wanted to put extra decorations on them just to show that it could be done. It almost made it worse that the wood nearly matched the color of the dog, who turned around in place three times before curling up in front of the door.

I studied the overdone mantelpiece, the tasteless candelabra, and the rest. I said, "Your own work?"

"No. My husband was a wood-carver."

"A quite skillful one," I said truthfully.

She nodded. "This place means a lot to me," she said. "I don't want to leave."

I waited.

"I'm being asked to leave—I've been given six months."

Rocza shifted uneasily on my right shoulder. Loiosh, on my left, said, *"I don't believe this, boss. The widow being kicked out of her house? Come on."*

"By whom?"

"The owner of the land."

"Who owns the land?"

"I don't know."

"Why does he want you to leave?"

"I don't know."

"Have you been offered compensation?"

"Eh?"

"Did he say he'd pay you?"

"Oh. Yes." She sniffed. "A pittance."

"I see. How is it you don't know who owns the land?"

"It belongs to some, I don't know, organization, or something."

I instantly thought, *the Jhereg,* and felt a little queasy. "What organization?"

"A business of some kind. A big one."

"What House?"

"Orca."

I relaxed. "Who told you you have to move?"

"A young woman I'd never seen before, who worked for it. She was an Orca, too, I think."

"What was her name?"

"I don't know."

"And you don't know the name of the organization she works for?"

"No."

"How do you know she really worked for them?"

The old woman sniffed. "She was very convincing."

"Do you have an advocate?"

She sniffed again, which seemed to pass for a "no."

"Then finding a good one is probably where we should start."

"I don't trust advocates."

"Mmmm. Well, in any case, we're going to have to find out who holds the lease to your land. How do you pay it, anyway?"

"My husband paid it through the next sixty years."

"But—"

"The woman said I'd be getting money back."

"Isn't there a land office or something?"

"I don't know. I have the deed somewhere in the attic with my papers; it should be there." Her eyes narrowed. "You think you can help me?"

"Yes."

"Sit down."

I did. I helped Savn to a chair, then found one myself. It was ugly but comfortable. The dog's tail thumped twice against the floor, then it put its head on its paws.

"Tell me about the boy," she said.

I nodded. "Have you ever encountered the undead?"

Her eyes widened and she nodded once.

"Have you ever fought an Athyra wizard? An undead Athyra wizard with a Morganti weapon?"

Now she looked skeptical. "You have?"

"The boy has. The boy killed one."

"I don't believe it."

"Look at him."

She did. He sat there, staring at the wall across from him.

"And he's been like this ever since?"

"Ever since he woke up. Actually, he's improved a little—he follows me now without being told, and if I put food in front of him, he eats it."

"Does he keep himself—?"

"Yes, as long as I remember to tell him to every once in a while."

She shook her head. "I don't know."

"He took a bash on the head at the same time. That may be part of the problem."

"When did it happen?"

"About a year ago."

"You've been wandering around with him for a year?"

"Yeah. I've been looking for someone who could cure him. I haven't found anyone." I didn't tell her how hard I'd been looking for someone willing and able to help; I spared her the details of disappointments, dead ends, aimless searches, and trying to balance my need to help him with my need to stay away from anywhere big enough for the Jhereg to be a danger—anywhere like Northport, say. I didn't tell her, in other words, that I was getting desperate.

"Why haven't you gone to a *real* sorcerer?" There was more than a hint of bitterness there.

"I'm on the run."

"From whom?"

"None of your business."

"What did you do?"

"I helped the boy kill an undead Athyra wizard."

"Why did he kill him?"

"To save my life."

"Why was the wizard trying to kill you?"

"You ask too many questions."

She frowned, then said, "We'll begin by looking at his head wound."

"All right. And tomorrow I'll start on your problem."

She spread out a few blankets on the floor for us, and that's where we slept. I woke up once toward morning and saw that the dog had curled up next to Savn. I hoped it didn't have fleas.

A few hours later I woke up for real and got to work. The old woman was already awake and holding a candle up to Savn's eyes, either to see if he'd respond to the light or to look into his mind, or for some other reason. Rocza was on the mantel, looking down anxiously; she'd developed a fondness for Savn and I think was feeling protective. The dog lay there watching the procedure and thumping its tail whenever the old woman moved.

I said, "Where are the papers?"

She turned to me and said, "If you'd like coffee first, help yourself."

"Do you have klava?"

"You can make it. The deed and the rest of my papers are in boxes up there." She gestured toward the ceiling above the kitchen, where I noticed a square door.

I made the klava and filled two cups. Then I found a ladder and a lamp, and took myself up to a large attic filled—I mean *filled*—with wooden crates, all of which were filled with junk, most of the junk being papers of one sort or another.

I grabbed a crate at random, brought it back down, and started going through it.

In the course of my career, Kiera, I've done a few odd things here and there. I mean, there was the time I spent half a day under a pile of refuse because it was the only place to hide. There was the time I took a job selling fish in the market. Once I ended up impersonating a corporal in the Imperial Guard and had to arrest someone for creating a disturbance in a public place. But I hope I never have to spend another week going through a thousand or more years' worth of an old lady's private papers and letters, just to find the name of her landlord, so I could sweet-talk, threaten, or intimidate him into letting her stay on the land, so she'd be willing to cure— Oh, skip it. It was a long week, and it was odd finding bits of nine-hundred-year-old love letters, or scraps of advice on curing hypothermia, or how to tell if an ingrown toenail is the result of a curse.

I spent about fourteen hours a day grabbing a crate, going through the papers in it, arranging them neatly, then bringing the crate back up to the attic and setting it in the stack of those I'd finished while getting another. I discovered to my surprise that it was curiously satisfying work, and that I was going to be disappointed when I found what I was looking for and would have to leave the rest of the papers unsorted.

Sometimes locals would show up, no doubt with some problem or another, and on those occasions I'd leave them alone and go walking around outside, which helped to clear my head from all the paperwork. If any of her customers had a problem with the boy or the jhereg, I never heard about it, and I enjoyed the walks. I got so I knew the area pretty well, but there isn't much there worth knowing. One day when I got back after a long walk the old woman was standing in front of the fireplace holding a crumpled-up piece of paper. I said, "Is that it?"

She threw the paper into the fire. "No," she said. She didn't face me.

I said, "Is there something wrong?"

"Let's get back to our respective work, shall we?"

I said, "If it turns out the lease isn't in any of these boxes—"

"You'll find it," she said.

"Heh."

But I did find it at last, late on the fifth day after going through about two-thirds of the crates: a neat little scroll tied up with green ribbon, and stating the terms of the lease, with the rent payable to something called Westman, Niece, and Nephew Land Holding Company.

"I found it," I announced.

The old woman, who turned out to have some strange Kanefthali name that sounded like someone sneezing, said, "Good."

"I'll go visit them tomorrow morning. Any progress?"

She glared at me, then said, "Don't rush me."

"I'm just asking."

She nodded and went back to what she was doing, which was testing Savn's reflexes by tapping a stick against his knee, while watching his eyes.

Buddy watched us both somberly and decided there was nothing that had to be done right away. He got up and padded over to his water bowl, drank with doglike enthusiasm, and nosed open the door.

"Are we going to kill someone tomorrow, boss?"

"I doubt it. Why? Bored?"

"Something like that."

"Exercise patience."

Loiosh and I went outside and tasted the air. He flew around while I sat on the ground. Buddy came up, nosed me, and scratched at the door. The old woman let him in. Loiosh landed on my shoulder.

"Worried about Savn, boss?"

"Some. But if this doesn't work, we'll try something else, that's all."

"Right."

I started to get cold. A small animal moved around in the woods near the house. I realized with something of a start not only that I'd come outside without my sword but that I didn't even have a dagger on me. The idea made me uncomfortable, so I went back inside and sat in front of the fire. A little later I went to bed.

I'd been to Northport a few years before, and I'd been hanging around the edges these last few days, but that next morning was really the first time I'd seen it. It's a funny town—sort of a miniature Adrilankha, the way it's built in the center of those three hills the way Adrilankha is built between the cliffs, and both of them jutting up against the sea. Northport has its own personality, though. One gets the impression, looking at the three-story inns and the five-story Lumber Exchange Building and the streets that start out wide and straight and end up narrow and twisting, that someone wanted it to be a big city but it never made it. The first section I came to was one of the new parts, with a lot of wood houses where tradesmen lived and had shops, but as I got closer to the docks the buildings got smaller and older, and were made of good, solid stonework. And the people of Northport seem to have this attitude—I'm sure you've noticed it, too—that wants to convince you what a great place they're living in. They spend so much time talking about how easygoing everyone is that it gets on your nerves pretty quickly. They talk so much about how it's only around Northport that you can find the redfin or the fatfish that you end up not wanting to taste them just to spite the populace, you know what I mean?

It was harder to find Westman than it should have been, because there was no address in the city hall for a Westman company. They did exist, they just didn't have an address registered. I thought that was odd, but the clerk didn't; I guess he'd run into that sort of thing before. The owner was listed, though, and his name wasn't Westman. It was something called Brugan Exchange. Did Brugan Exchange have an address? No. Was there an owner listed? Yeah. Northport Securities. What does Northport Securities do? I have no idea. You understand that the clerk didn't kill himself being helpful—he just pointed to where I should look and left it up to me, and it took three imperials before he was willing to do that. So I dug through musty old papers; I'd been doing that a lot lately.

Northport Securities didn't have an owner listed. Nothing. Just a blank space where the Articles of Embodiment asked for the owner's name, and an illegible scrawl for a signature. But, wonder of wonders, it did have an address—it was listed as number 31 in the Fyres Building.

Ah. I see your eyes light up. We have found our connection with Fyres, you think. Sort of.

I found the Fyres Building without any trouble—the clerk told me where it was, after giving me a look that indicated I must be an idiot for needing to ask. It was at the edge of Shroud Hill, which means it was almost out of town, and it was high enough so that it had a nice view. A very nice view, from the top—it was six stories high, Kiera, and reeked of money from the polished marble of the base to the glass windows on the top floor. The thought of walking into the place made me nervous, if you can believe it—it was like the first time I went to Castle Black; not as strong, maybe, but the same feeling of being in someone's seat of power.

Loiosh said, *"What's the problem, boss?"* I couldn't answer him, but the question was reassuring, in a way. There was a single wooden door in front, with no seal on it, but above the doorway "FYRES" was carved into the stonework, along with the symbol of the House of the Orca.

Once inside, there was nothing and no one to tell me where to go. There were individual rooms, all of them marked with real doors and all of which had informative signs like "Cutter and Cutter." I walked around the entire floor, which was laid out in a square with an open stairway at the far end. "I said, *"Loiosh."*

"On my way, boss."

I waited by the stairs. A few well-dressed citizens, Orca, Chreotha, and a Lyorn, came down or up the stairs and glanced at me briefly, decided that they didn't know what to make of the shabbily dressed Easterner, and went on without saying anything. One woman, an Orca, asked if I needed anything. When I said I didn't, she went on her way. Presently Loiosh returned.

"Well?"

"The offices are smaller on the next floor, and they keep getting smaller as you go up, all the way until the sixth, which I couldn't get into."

"Door?"

"Yeah. Locked."

"Ah ha."

"Number thirty-one is on the fifth floor."

"Okay. Let's go."

We went up five flights, and Loiosh led the way to a tacked-up number 31, which hung above a curtained doorway. Also above the doorway was a plain black-lettered sign that read, "Brownberry Insurance." I entered without clapping.

There was a man at the desk, a very pale Lyorn, who was going over a ledger of some sort while checking it against the contents of a small box filled with cards. He looked up, and his eyes widened just a little. He said, "May I be of service to you?"

"Maybe," I said. "Is your name Brownberry?"

"No, but I do business as Brownberry Insurance. May I help you?"

He volunteered no more information, but kept a polite smile of inquiry fixed in my direction. He kept glancing at Loiosh, then returning his gaze to me.

I said, "I was actually looking for Northport Securities."

"Ah," he said. "Well, I can help you there, as well."

"Excellent."

The office was small, but there was another curtained doorway behind it—no doubt there was another room with another desk, perhaps with another Lyorn looking over another ledger.

"I understand," I said carefully, "that Northport Securities owns Brugan Exchange."

He frowned. "Brugan Exchange? I'm afraid I've never heard of it. What do they do?"

"They own Westman, Niece, and Nephew Land Holding Company."

He shook his head. "I'm afraid I don't know anything about that."

The curtain moved and a woman poked her head out, then walked around to stand next to the desk. Definitely an Orca; and I'd put her at about seven hundred years. Not bad if you like Dragaerans. She wore blue pants and a simple white blouse with blue trim, and had short hair pulled back severely. "Westman Holding?" she said.

"Yes."

The man said, "It's one of yours, Leen?"

"Yes." And to me, "How may I help you?"

"You hold the lease for a lady named, uh, Hujaanra, or something like that?"

"Yes. I was just out to see her about it. Are you her advocate?"

"Something like that."

"Please come back here and sit down. I'm called Leen. And you?"

"Padraic," I said. I followed her into a tiny office with just barely room for me, her, her desk, and a filing cabinet. Her desk was clean except for some writing gear and a couple large black books, probably ledgers. I sat on a wooden stool.

"What may I do for you?" she said. She was certainly the most polite Orca I'd ever encountered.

"I'd like to understand why my client has to leave her land."

She nodded as if she'd been expecting the question. "Instructions from the parent company," she said. "I'm afraid I can't tell you exactly why. We think the offer we made is quite reasonable—"

"That isn't the issue," I said.

She seemed a bit surprised. Perhaps she wasn't used to being interrupted by an Easterner, perhaps she wasn't used to being interrupted by an advocate, perhaps she wasn't used to people who weren't interested in money. "What exactly is the issue?" she said in the tone of someone trying to remain polite in the face of provocation.

"She doesn't want to leave her land."

"I'm afraid she must. The parent company—"

"Then can I speak to someone in the parent company?"

She studied me for a moment, then said, "I don't see why not." She scratched out a name and address on a small piece of paper, blew on it until the ink dried, and gave it to me.

"Thank you," I said.

"You are most welcome, Sir Padraic."

I nodded to the man in the office, who was too absorbed in his ledger to notice, then stopped past the door, looked at the card, and laughed. It said, "Lady Cepra, Cepra Holding Company, room 20." No building, which, of course, meant it was this very building. I shook my head and went down the stairs, sending Loiosh ahead of me.

He was back in about a minute. *"Third floor,"* he said.

"Good."

So I headed down to the third floor.

Do you get the idea, Kiera? Good. Then there's no need to go into the rest of the day, it was more of the same. I never met any resistance, and everyone was very polite, and eventually I got my answer—sort of.

It was well after dark when I returned to the cottage. Buddy greeted me with a tail wag that got his whole back half moving. It was nice to be missed.

"As long as you aren't fussy about the source."

"Shut up, Loiosh."

I walked in the door and saw Savn was asleep on his pile of blankets. The old woman was sitting in front of the fire, drinking tea. She didn't turn around when I came in. Loiosh flew over and greeted Rocza, who was curled up next to Savn.

I said, "What did you learn about the boy?"

"I don't know enough yet. I can tell you that there's more wrong with him than a bump on the head, but the bump on the head triggered it. I'll know more soon, I hope."

"What about curing him?"

"I have to find out what's wrong first."

"All right."

"What about you?"

"I'm fine, thanks."

She turned and glared at me. "What did you find out?"

I sat down at what passed for a kitchen table. "You," I said, "are a tiny, tiny cog in the great big machine."

"What does that mean?"

"A man named Fyres died."

"So I heard. What of it?"

"He owned a whole lot of companies. When he died, it turned out that most of them had no assets to speak of, except for office furnishings and that sort of thing."

"I heard something of that, too."

"Your land is owned by a company that's in surrender of debts, and has to sell it before the court orders it sold. What we have to do is buy the place ourselves. You said you have money—"

"Well, I don't," she snapped.

"Excuse me?"

"I thought I did, but I was wrong."

"I don't understand."

She turned back to the fire and didn't speak for several minutes. Then she said, "All of my money was in a bank. Two days ago, while you were out, a messenger showed up with information that—"

"Oh," I said. "The bank was another one? Fyres owned it?"

"Yes."

"So it's all gone."

"I might be lucky enough to get two orbs for each imperial."

"Oh," I said again.

I sat thinking for a long time. At last I said, "All right, that makes it harder, but not much. I have money."

She looked at me once more, her lined face all but expressionless. I said, "Somewhere there's someone who owns this land, and somewhere there's someone who is responsible for that bank—"

"Fyres," she said. "And he's dead."

"No. Someone is taking charge of these things. Someone is handling the estate. And, more important, there's some very wealthy son of a bitch who just needs the right sort of pressure put on him in order to make the right piece of paper say the right thing. It shouldn't disrupt anything—there are advantages to being a small cog in a big machine."

"How are you going to find this mythical rich man?"

"I don't know exactly. But the first step is to start tracing the lines of power from the top."

"I don't think that information is public," she said.

"Neither do I." I closed my eyes, thinking of several days' worth of my least favorite sort of work: digging into plans, tracing guard routes, finagling trivial information out of people without letting them know I was doing it, and all that just so we could perhaps get a start on how to address the problem. I shook my head in self-pity.

"Well?" said the old woman when she'd waited long enough and decided I wasn't going to say any more. "What are you going to do? Steal Fyres's private papers?"

"Do I look like a thief?"

"Yes."

"Thank you," I said.

She sniffed.

"Unfortunately," I added, "I'm not."

"Well, then?"

"I do, however, know one."

INTERLUDE

"I suppose, if one must lose a finger—"

"Yes. And it had healed cleanly."

"It hurts to think about it. I wonder what fell on it?"

"I don't know."

"You didn't ask?"

"He didn't seem inclined to talk about it. You know how he gets when there's something he doesn't want to talk about."

"Yes. A lot like you."

"Meaning?"

"There's a lot you aren't telling me, isn't there?"

"I suppose. Not deliberately—at least not yet. Later, there may be things I'd sooner not discuss. But if I told you everything I remember as I remember it, we'd still be here—"

"I understand. Hmmm."

"What is it?"

"I was just thinking how pleased he'd be if he knew we were spending a whole afternoon just talking about him."

"I shan't tell him."

"It doesn't matter."

"Should I go on?"

"Let's order some more tea first."

"Very well."

Chapter Three

I LOOKED AT him after he'd finished speaking, struck by several things but not sure what to say or to ask. For one thing, I'd forgotten that when Vlad starts telling a story, you had best get yourself a tall glass of something and settle in for the duration. I thought this over, and all that he'd told me, and finally said, "Who did the boy kill?"

"A fellow named Loraan."

I controlled my reaction, stared at Vlad, and waited. He said, "I take it you know who he was?"

"Yes. I follow your career, you know. I'd thought he was pretty permanently dead."

Vlad shrugged. "Take it up with Morrolan. Or rather with Blackwand."

I nodded. "The boy saved your life?"

"The simple answer is yes. The more complicated answer would take a week."

"But you owe him."

"Yes."

"I see. What happened while you were waiting for me?"

"I learned everything about Fyres that was public knowledge, and a little that wasn't."

"What did you learn?"

"Not much. He liked being talked about, he liked owning things, he didn't like anyone knowing what he was up to. The accountants are going to be hard at work to figure out exactly what he owed and what he was worth—I imagine his heirs are pretty nervous."

"It'll be harder without those papers."

"Yeah. But I'll probably return them when I'm done. I'm in more of a hurry than they are."

"What else has happened?"

"Who do you mean?"

"With the boy."

"Oh. Nothing. She's still trying to figure it out. I guess it isn't easy to know what's going on in someone's head."

That, of course, was the understatement of Vlad's life.

"What's she done?"

"Stared into his eyes a lot."

"Notice any sorcery?"

"No."

I thought for a minute, then, "Take me to the cottage," I said. "I want to see it, and I want to meet this woman, and we can go over the information there as well as anywhere else."

"We?"

"Yes."

"All right."

We struck out for the cottage, walking. I like walking; I don't do enough of it. It was about four miles, deep in the woods, and the cottage really was painted bright blue so that it showed against the greens of the woods to a truly horrifying effect.

As we approached, a reddish dog ran out the door and stood in front of us, wagging its tail and letting its tongue hang out. It sniffed me, backed away with its head cocked, barked twice, and sniffed me again. After consulting with its canine sensibilities, it decided I was provisionally all right and asked us if we wanted to play. When we took too long to decide, it ran back toward the house. The door opened again, and a matron came out.

Vlad said, "This is my friend, Kiera. I'm not going to try to pronounce your name."

She looked at me, then nodded. "Hwdf'rjaanci," she said.

"Hwdf'rjaanci," I repeated.

"Kiera," she said. "You look like a Jhereg."

I could feel Vlad not looking at me and not grinning. I shrugged.

She said, "Call me Mother; everyone around here does."

"All right, Mother."

She asked Vlad, "Did you learn anything?"

"Not yet." He held up the parcel I'd given him. "We're just going to look things over now."

"Come in, then."

We did, the dog following behind. The inside was even worse than Vlad had described it. I didn't comment. Savn was sitting on a stool with his back to the fire, staring straight ahead. It was creepy. It was sad. "Battle shock," I murmured under my breath.

"What?" said the old woman.

I shook my head. Savn wasn't a bad-looking young man, for a Teckla—thin, maybe a bit wan, but good bones. Hwdf'rjaanci was sitting next to him, stroking the back of his neck while watching his face.

Hwdf'rjaanci said, "Will you be staying here?"

"I have a place in town."

"All right."

Vlad went over to the table, took out the papers, and began studying them. I knelt down in front of the boy and looked into his eyes; saw my own reflection and nothing else. His pupils were a bit large, but the room was dark, and they were the same size. A bit of spell-casting tempted me, but I stayed away from it. Thinking along those lines, I realized that there wasn't much of an air of sorcery in the room; a few simple spells to keep the dust and insects away, and the dog had a ward against vermin, but that was about it.

I felt the woman watching. I kept looking into the boy's eyes, though I couldn't say what I was looking for. The woman said, "So you're a thief, are you?"

"That's what they say."

"I was robbed twice. The first time was years ago. During the Interregnum. You look too young to remember the Interregnum."

"Thank you."

She gave a little laugh. "The second time was more recent. I didn't enjoy being robbed," she added.

"I should think not."

"They beat my husband—almost killed him."

"I don't beat people, Mother."

"You just break into their homes?"

I said, "When you're working with the mentally sick, do you ever worry about being caught in the disease?"

"Always," she said. "That's why I have to be careful. I can't do anyone any good if I tangle my own mind instead of untangling my patient's."

"That makes sense. I take it you've done a great deal of this?"

"Some."

"How much?"

"Some."

"You have to go into his mind, don't you?"

"Yes."

I looked at her. "You're frightened, aren't you?"

She looked away.

"I would be, too," I told her. "Breaking into homes is much less frightening than breaking into minds.

"More profitable, too," I added after a moment.

I felt Vlad looking at me, and looked back. He'd overheard the conversation and seemed to be trying to decide if he wanted to get angry. After a moment, he returned to looking at the papers.

I stood up, went over to the dog, and got acquainted. It still seemed a bit suspicious of me, but was willing to give me the benefit of the doubt. Presently Hwdf'rjaanci said, "All right. I'll start tomorrow."

By the time I got there the next morning, Vlad had covered the table with a large piece of paper—I'm not sure where he got it—which was covered with scrawls and arrows. I stood over him for a moment, then said, "Where's the boy?"

"He and the woman went out for a walk. They took Rocza and the dog with them."

"Loiosh?"

"Flying around outside trying to remember if he knows how to hunt."

He got that look on his face that told me he'd communicated that remark to Loiosh, too, and was pleased with himself.

I said, "Any progress?"

He shrugged. "Fyres didn't like to tell his people much."

"So you said."

"Even less than I'd thought."

"Catch me up."

"Fyres and Company is a shipping company that employs about two hundred people. That's all, as far as I can tell. Most of the rest of what he owned isn't related to the shipping company at all, but he owned it through relatives—his wife, his son, his daughters, his sister, and a few friends. And most of those are in surrender of debts and have never really been solvent—it's all been a big fraud from the beginning, when he conned banks into letting him take out loans, and used the loans to make his companies look big so that he could take out more loans. That's how he operated."

"You know this?"

"Yeah."

"You aren't even an accountant."

"Yeah, but I don't have to prove it—I've learned it because I've found out what companies he was keeping track of and looked at the ownership and read his notes. There's nothing incriminating about it, but it gives the picture pretty clearly if you're looking for it."

"How big?"

"I can't tell. Big enough, I suppose."

"What's the legal status?"

"I have no idea. I'm sure the Empire will try to sort it all out, but that'll take years."

"And in the meantime?"

"I don't know. I'm going to have to do something, but I don't know what."

Savn and Hwdf'rjaanci returned then and sat down on the floor near the fire. The woman's look discouraged questions as she took Savn's hands in hers and began rubbing them. Vlad watched; I could feel his tension.

I said, "You have to do something soon, don't you?"

He gave me a half-smile. "It would be nice. But this isn't the sort of thing I can stumble into. I should know what I'm doing first. That makes it trickier." Then he said, "Why are you helping me, anyway?"

I said, "I assume you've been making a list of all the companies you know about and who their owners are."

"Yeah. They've gotten to know my face real well at City Hall."

"That may be a problem later on."

"Maybe. I hope not to be around here long enough for it to matter."

"Good idea."

"Yes."

"No help for it, I suppose. Do you think it might be wise to pick one of these players and pay a visit?"

"Sure, if I knew what to ask. I need to figure out who really owns this land and—"

Loiosh and I reacted at once to the presence of sorcery in the room, Vlad just an instant later. Our heads turned toward Hwdf'rjaanci, who was holding Savn's shoulders and speaking under her breath. We watched for maybe a minute, but there was no point in talking about it. I cleared my throat. "What were you saying?"

Vlad turned back to me, looking blank. Then he said, "I don't remember."

"Something about needing to find out who really owns this land."

"Oh, right." I could see him mentally shaking himself. "Yeah. What I really want is to get the picture of this thing as it's going to emerge when the Empire finishes its investigations, say two hundred years from now. But I can't wait that long."

"I might be able to learn something."

"How?"

"The Jhereg."

Vlad frowned. "How would the Jhereg be involved?"

"I don't know that we are. But if what Fyres was doing was illegal, and it was making a lot of money, there's a good chance for a Jhereg connection somewhere along the line."

"Good point," said Vlad.

Loiosh was still staring at the woman and the boy. Vlad was silent for a moment; I wondered what Vlad and Loiosh were saying to each other. I wondered if they spoke in words, or if it was some sort of communication that didn't translate. I've never had a familiar, but then, I'm not a witch. Vlad said, "You have local connections?"

"Yes."

"All right," he said. "Do it. I'll keep trying to put this thing together."

The woman said, "Cold. So cold. Cold."

Vlad and I looked at her. She wasn't shivering or anything, and the cottage was quite warm. Her hands were still on Savn's shoulders and she was staring at him.

"Can't keep it away," she said. "Can't keep it away. Find the cold spot. Can't keep it away." After that she fell silent.

I looked at Vlad and turned my palms up. "I might as well go now," I said.

He nodded, and went back to his paperwork. I headed out the door. The dog gave its tail a half-wag and put its head down between its paws again.

It was over two or three miles to Northport, but I had been there often enough to learn a couple of teleport points, so I went ahead and put myself into an alley that ran past the back of a pawnbroker's shop, startling a couple of local urchins when I appeared. They stared at me for a second, then went back to urchining, or whatever it is they do. I walked around the corner and into the dark little shop. The middle-aged man behind the counter looked up at me, but before he could say a word I said, "Sorry to disappoint you, Dor."

"What, you don't have anything for me?"

"Nope. I just want to see the upstairs man."

"For a minute there—"

"Next time."

He shrugged. "You know the way."

Poor Dor. Usually when I come into his place it's because I have something that's too hot to unload in Adrilankha, which means he's going to get something good for
a great price. But not today. I walked past him into the rear
of the shop, up the stairs, and into a nice, plain room where
a couple of toughs waited. One, a very dark fellow with a
pointy head, like someone had tried to fit him through a
funnel, was sitting in front of the room's other door; the
other one had arms that hung out like a mockman and he
looked about as intelligent, although looks can be deceiv-
ing; he was leaning against a wall. They didn't seem to recognize me.

I said, "Is Stony in?"

"Who wants to know?" said Funnel-head.

I smiled brightly. "Why, I do."

He scowled.

I said, "Tell him it's Kiera."

Their eyes grew just a little bit wider. That always happens. It is very satisfying. The one stood up, moved his
chair, opened the door, and stuck his head into the other
room. I heard him speaking softly, then I heard Stony say,
"Really? Well, send her in." There was a little more conversation, followed by, "I said send her in."

The tough turned back to me and stood aside. I dipped
him a curtsy as I stepped in past him—a curtsy looks silly
when you're wearing trousers, but I couldn't resist. He
stayed well back from me, as if he were afraid I'd steal his
purse as I walked by. Why are people who will walk into
potentially lethal situations without breaking a sweat so

often frightened around someone who just steals things? Is it the humiliation? Is it just that they don't know how I do it? I've never figured that out. Many people have that reaction. It makes me want to steal their purses.

Stony's office was deceptively small. I say deceptive because he was a lot bigger in the Organization than most people thought—even his own employees didn't know; he felt safer that way. I'd only found out by accident and guesswork, starting when someone had hired me to lighten one of Stony's button men and I'd come across pieces of his security system. Stony himself was pretty deceptive, too. He looked, and acted, like the sort of big, mean, stupid, and brutal thug that the Left Hand thinks we all are. In fact, I'd never known him to do anything that wasn't calculated—even his famous rages always seemed to result in just the right people disappearing, and no more. Over the years, I'd tried to puzzle him out, and my opinion at the moment was that he wasn't in this for the power, or for the pleasure of putting things over on the Guard, or anything else—he wanted to acquire a great deal of money, and a great deal of security, and then he planned to retire. I couldn't prove it, I reflected, but I wouldn't be at all surprised if someday he just packed up and vanished, and spent the rest of his life collecting seashells or something on some tiny island he owned.

Over the years, I had gradually let him know that I knew where he stood in the Organization, and he had gradually stopped pretending otherwise when we were alone. It was possible that he liked having someone with whom he could drop the game a little, but I doubt it.

All of this flashed through my mind as I sat in the only other chair in the room—the room just big enough to contain my chair, his chair, and the desk. He said, "Must be something big, for you to come here." His voice was rough and harsh, and fitted the personality he pretended to; I assumed it was contrived, but I've never heard him break out of it.

"Yes and no," I said.

"There a problem?"

"In a way."

"You need help?"

"Something like that."

He shook his head. "That's what I like about you, Kiera. Your way of explaining everything so clearly."

"My part isn't big, and what I need isn't big, but it's part of something big. I didn't want to ask you to meet me somewhere because I'm asking for a favor, and you don't get anything from it, so I didn't want to put you out. But it isn't a favor for me, it's for someone else."

He nodded. "That makes everything completely clear, then."

"What do you know of Fyres?"

That startled him a little. "The Orca?"

"Yes."

"He's dead."

"Uh-huh."

"He owned a whole lot of stuff."

"Yeah."

"Most of it will end up in surrender of debts."

"That's what I like about you, Stony. The way you have of reeling out information no one else knows."

He made a loose fist with his right hand and drummed his fingernails on the desk while looking at me. "What exactly do you want to know?"

"The Organization's interest in him and his businesses."

"What's your interest?"

"I told you, a favor for a friend."

"Yeah."

"Is it some big secret, Stony?"

"Yes," he said. "It is."

"It goes up pretty high?"

"Yeah, and there's a lot of money involved."

"And you're trying to decide how much to tell me just as a favor."

"Right."

I waited. Nothing I could say would help make up his mind for him.

"Okay," he said finally. "I'll tell you this much. A lot of people had paper on the guy. Shards. *Everybody* had paper on the guy. There are going to be some big banks going down, and there are going to be some Organization people taking sudden vacations. It isn't just me, but we're in it."

"How about you?"

"I'm not directly involved, so I may be all right."

"If you need anything—"

"Yeah. Thanks."

"How did he die?"

Stony spread his hands. "He was out on his Verra-be-damned boat and he slipped and hit his head on a railing."

I raised an eyebrow at him.

He shook his head. "No one wanted him dead, Kiera. I mean, the only chance most of us had to ever see our investment back was if his stuff earned out, and with him dead there's no way of it ever earning out."

"You sure?"

"Who can be sure of anything? I didn't want him dead. I don't know anyone who wanted him dead. The Empire sent their best investigators, and they think it was an accident."

"All right," I said. "What was he like?"

"You think I knew him?"

"You lent him money, or at least thought about it; you knew him."

He smiled, then the smile went away and he looked thoughtful—an expression I doubt most people would ever have seen. "He was all surface, you know?"

"No."

"It was like he made himself act the way he thought he should—you could never get past it."

"That sounds familiar."

He ignored that. "He tried to be polished, professional, calculating—he wanted you to believe he was the perfect bourgeois. And he wanted to impress you—he always wanted to impress you."

"With how rich he was?"

Stony nodded. "Yeah, that. And with all the people he knew, and with how good he was at what he did. I think that part of it—being impressive—was more important to him than the money."

I nodded encouragingly. He smiled. "You want more?"

"Yeah."

"Then I'd better know why."

"It's a little embarrassing," I said.

"Embarrassing?" He looked at me the way I must have been looking at Vlad when I realized that *he* was embarrassed.

"I have this friend—"

"Right."

I laughed. "Okay, skip it. I owe someone a favor," I amended untruthfully. "She's an old woman who is about to be kicked off her land because everybody is selling off everything to stave off surrender of debts because of this mess with Fyres."

"An old woman being foreclosed on? Are you kidding?"

"No."

"I don't believe it."

"Would I make up something like that?"

He shook his head, chuckling to himself. "No, I suppose not. So what do you plan to do about it?"

"I don't know yet. Just find out what I can and then think about it." Or, at any rate, if Vlad had had any other plan, he hadn't mentioned it to me. "What else can you tell me?"

"Well, he was about fourteen hundred years old. No one heard of him before the Interregnum, but he rose pretty quickly after it ended."

"How quickly?"

"He was a very wealthy man by the end of the first century."

"That is quick."

"Yeah. And then he lost it all forty or fifty years later."

"Lost it all?"

"Yep."

"And came back?"

"Twice more. Each time bigger, each time the collapse was worse."

"Same problem? Same sort of paper castles?"

"Yep."

"Shipping?"

"Yep. And shipbuilding. Those have been his foundations all along."

"You'd think people would learn."

"Is there an implied criticism there, Kiera?" His look got just the least bit hard.

"No. Curiosity. I know you aren't stupid. Most of the people he'd be borrowing from aren't, either. How did he do it?"

Stony relaxed. "You'd have to have seen him work."

"What do you mean? Good salesman?"

"That, and more. Even when he was down, you'd never know it. Of course, when someone that rich goes down, it doesn't have much effect on how he lives—he'll still have his mansion, and he'll still be at all the clubs, and he'll still have his private boat and his big carriages."

"Sure."

"So he'd trade on those things. You get to talking with him for five minutes, and you forget that he'd just taken a fall. And then his secretaries would keep running in with papers for him to sign, or with questions about some big deal or another, and it looked like he was on top of the world." Stony shrugged. "I don't know. I've wondered if he didn't have those secretaries pull that sort of thing just to look good; but it worked. You'd always end up convinced that he was in some sort of great position and you might as well jump on the horse and ride it yourself before someone else did."

"And there were a lot of us on the horse."

"A lot of Jhereg? Yeah."

"And in deep."

"Yeah."

"That isn't good for my investigation."

"You worried you might bump into the Organization? Is that it?"

"That's part of it."

"It might happen," he said.

"All right."

"What if it does?"

"I don't know."

He shook his head. "I don't want to see you get hurt, Kiera."

"Neither do I," I said. "How far beyond Northport does this thing go?"

"Hard to say. It's all centered here, but he'd begun spreading out. He has offices other places, of course—you have to if you're in shipping. But I can't say how much else."

"What was going on before he died?"

"What do you mean?"

"I have the impression things were getting shaky for him."

"Very. He was scrabbling. You wouldn't know it to look at him, but there were rumors that he'd stepped too far out and it was all going to crumble."

"Hmmm."

"Still wondering if someone put a shine on him?"

"Seems like quite a coincidence."

"I know. But I don't think so. As I said, I never heard any whispers, and the Empire investigated; they're awfully good at this sort of thing."

I nodded. That much was certainly true. "Okay," I said. "Thanks for your help."

"No problem. If there's anything else, let me know."

"I will." I stood up.

"Oh, by the way."

"Yes?"

He leaned back in his chair and looked at the ceiling. "Seen anything of that Easterner you used to hang around with?"

"You mean Vlad Taltos? The guy who screwed up the Organization representative to the Empire? The guy everyone wants to put over the Falls? The guy with so much gold on his head that his hair is sparkling? The guy the Organization wants so bad that anyone seen with him is likely to disappear for a long session of question and answer with the best information-extraction specialists the Organization can find? Him?"

"Yep."

"Nope."

"I hadn't thought so. See you around, Kiera."

"See you around, Stony."

Chapter Four

MY FIRST STEP was to fill Vlad in on what I'd learned; but I took a long, circuitous route back just in case I was being followed, so it took me almost until evening to get back to the cottage. When I turned the last corner of the path, Vlad was waiting for me, on the path, about fifty meters from the cottage. That startled me just a bit, as I'm not used to being seen so quickly even when I'm not trying to sneak, until I realized that Loiosh must have spotted me. I must remember to be careful if I ever have to sneak up on that Easterner.

He stood clothed only in pants and boots, his upper body naked and full of curly hairs, and he was sweating heavily, although he didn't seem to be breathing hard.

"Nice evening," I told him.

He nodded.

I said, "What have you been doing?"

"Practicing," he said, pointing at a tree some distance away. I noticed several knives sticking out of it. Then he touched his rapier, sheathed at his side, and said, "I've also punctured my shadow several times."

"Did it hurt?"

"Only when I missed."

"Did it get any cuts in?"

"No. But almost."

"Good to see you're keeping your hand in."

"Actually, I haven't been lately, but I thought it might be time to again."

"Hmmm."

"Besides, I needed to get out."

"Oh?"

"It's ugly in there," he said, gesturing toward the cottage.

"Oh?" I said again.

"The old woman is doing what she promised."

"And?"

He shook his head.

"Tell me," I said.

"He's all screwed up."

"That's news?"

Vlad looked at me.

"Sorry," I said.

"He keeps thinking he killed his sister, or he has to save her, or something."

"Sister?"

"Yeah, she was involved, too. He feels guilty about her."

"What else?"

"Well, he's a Teckla, and Loraan was his lord, and if you're a peasant, you don't do what he did. Deathgate, Kiera. Even touching a Morganti weapon—"

"Right."

"So if he didn't kill Loraan, he must have killed his sister."

I said, "I don't follow that."

"I'm not sure I do, either," said Vlad. "But that's what we're seeing. Or what we think we're seeing. It isn't too clear, and we've been doing a lot of guesswork, but that's how it looks at the moment. And then there's the bash on the head."

"What did that do?"

"She thinks there may be a partial memory loss that's contributing to the whole thing."

"Better and better."

"Yeah."

"What now?"

"I don't know. The old woman thinks we have to find some way of communicating with him, but she doesn't know how."

"Does he hear us when we talk? See us?"

"Oh, sure. But we're like dream images, so what we say isn't important."

"What *is* important? I mean, she probed him, right? What's he doing in there?"

He shrugged. "Trying to keep his sister away from me, or away from Loraan, or something like that."

"A constant nightmare."

"Right."

"Ugly."

"Yes."

"And there's nothing you can do."

"Nothing I can do about that, anyway."

"If you could go in there yourself, I mean, into his mind—"

"Sure, I'd do it. In a minute."

I nodded. "Then I might as well tell you what I learned today."

"Do."

"Do you want to go inside?"

"No."

"All right." He put his shirt on and nodded to me and I told him. He was a good listener; he stood completely still, leaning against a tree; his only motion was to nod slightly every once in a while; and he was spare with his questions, just asking me to amplify a point every now and then. Loiosh settled on his left shoulder, and even the jhereg appeared to be listening. It's always nice to have an audience.

When I was finished, Vlad said, "Well. That's interesting. Surprising, too."

"That the Organization is involved?"

"No, no. Not that."

"What?"

He shook his head and appeared to be lost in thought— like I'd told him more than I thought I had, which was certainly possible. So I gave him a decent interval, then said, "What is it?"

He shook his head again. I felt a little irritated but I didn't say anything. He said, "It doesn't make sense, that's all."

"What doesn't?"

"How well do you know Stony?"

"Quite."

"Would he lie to you?"

"Certainly."

"Maybe that's it, then. In any case, *someone* lied, somewhere along the line."

"What do you mean?"

"Let me think about this, all right? And do some checking on my own. I want to follow something up; I'll tell you about it tomorrow."

I shrugged. There's no reasoning with Vlad when he gets a mood on him. "Okay," I said. "I'll be back in the morning."

He nodded. Then he said, "Kiera?"

"Yes?"

"Thanks."

"You're welcome."

I slept late the next day, because there was no reason not to. It was around noon when I got to the cottage, and no one was there except the dog. It shuffled away from me. I devoted some effort to making friends with it, and of course I succeeded. I talked to it for a while. Most cat owners talk to their cats, but all dog owners talk to their dogs; I don't now why that is.

I'd been there an hour or so when the dog jumped up suddenly and bolted out the door, and a minute or so later Hwdf'rjaanci returned with Savn. I said, "Good day, Mother. I hope you don't mind that I let myself in. I've made some klava."

She nodded and had the boy sit down, then she closed the shutters. I realized that each time I'd been there during the day the windows had been shut. I got her some klava, which she drank bitter.

I said, "What have you learned, Mother?"

"Not as much as I wish," she said. I waited. She said, "I think the two biggest problems are the bump on the head and the sister."

"Can't the bump be healed?"

"It has healed, on the outside. But there was some damage to his brain."

"No, I mean, can't the damage be healed? I know there are sorcerers—"

"Not yet. Not until I'm sure that, if I heal him, I won't be sealing in the problem."

"I think I understand. What about the sister?"

"He feels guilty about her—about her being exposed to whatever it was that happened."

She nodded. "That's the real problem. I think he's somehow using guilt about his sister to keep from facing that. He creates fantasies of rescuing her, but always shies away from what he's rescuing her from. And then he loses control of the fantasies and they turn into nightmares. It's worse, I think, because he used to be apprenticed to a physicker, so he's even more tormented about what he did than most peasant boys would be."

I nodded. Speaking like this, she'd changed somehow— she wasn't an old woman in a cottage full of ugly polished wood carvings, she was a sorcerer and a skilled physicker of the mind. It now seemed entirely reasonable that, as Vlad had told me, the locals would come by from time to time to consult with her on whatever their problems might be.

"Do you have a plan?"

"No. There's too much I don't understand. If I just go blundering in, I might destroy him—and myself."

"I understand." I opened my mouth and closed it again. I said, "What are the walks for?"

"I think he's used to walking. He gets restless when he's sitting for too long."

"And the closed shutters? Are they for him, or do you just like it that way?"

"For him. He's had too much experience, there have been too many things for him to see and hear and feel all at once—I want to limit them."

"Limit them? But if he's trapped in his head, won't it help to give him things outside his head to respond to?"

"You'd think so, and you may even turn out to be right. But more often than not, it works best the other way. It's as if he's trying to escape from pressure, and everything he perceives adds to the pressure. If I was more certain, I'd create a field around him that shut him off from the world entirely. It may yet come to that."

"You've had cases like this before?"

"You mean people who were so pulled into themselves that they were out of touch with the world? Yes, a few. Some of them worse than Savn."

"Were you able to help them?"

"There were two I was able to help. Three I couldn't." Her voice was carefully neutral.

One way of looking at it was that the odds were against success. Another way was that she was due to win one. Neither was terribly productive, so I said, "How did you proceed?"

"I tried to learn as much as I could about how they got that way, I healed any physical damage when there was some, and then, when I thought they were ready, I took them on a dreamwalk."

"Ah."

"You know about dreamwalking?"

"Yes. What sort of dreams did you give them?"

"I tried to guide them through whatever choice they made that put them in a place they couldn't get out of, and give them another choice instead."

"And in three cases it didn't work."

"Yes. In at least one of those, it was because I didn't know enough when I went in."

"That sounds dangerous."

"It was. I almost lost my mind, and the patient became worse. He lost the ability to eat or drink, even with assistance, and he soon died."

I kept my face expressionless, which took some effort. What a horrible way to die, and what a horrible knowledge to carry around with you, if you were the one who had tried to cure him. "What had happened to him?"

"He'd been badly beaten by robbers."

"I see." I almost asked the next obvious question, but then I decided not to. "That must not be an easy thing to live with."

"Better for me than for him."

"Not necessarily," I said, thinking of Deathgate Falls.

"Maybe you're right."

"In any case, I understand why you want to be careful."

"Yes."

She went over and sat down in front of Savn once again, staring at him and holding his shoulders. In a little while she said, "He seems to be a nice young man, somewhere inside. I think you'd like him."

"I probably would," I said. "I like most people."

"Even the ones you steal from?"

"Especially the ones I steal from."

She didn't laugh. Instead she said, "How do you know I won't turn you over to the Empire?"

That startled me, although I don't know why it should have. "Will you?" I said.

"Maybe."

"Maybe you shouldn't be telling me that."

She shook her head. "You aren't a killer," she said.

"You know that?"

"Yes." She added, "The other one, the Easterner, he's a killer."

I shrugged. "What could you tell the Empire, anyway? That I'm a thief? They know that; they've heard of me. That I stole something? They'll ask what I stole. You'll tell them, by which time Vlad will have hidden it, or maybe even returned it. Then what? Do you expect them to be grateful?"

She glared at me. "I wasn't actually going to tell them, anyway."

I nodded.

A few minutes later she said, "You can't have known the Easterner long—they don't live long enough. Yet you treat him as a friend."

"He is a friend."

"Why?"

"He doesn't know, either," I said.

"But—"

"What you're asking," I said, "is whether he can really do what he says he can do."

"And whether he will," she agreed.

"Right. I think he can; he's good at putting things together. In any case, I know that he'll try. In fact, knowing Vlad . . ."

"Yes?"

"He might very well try so hard he gets himself killed."

She didn't have anything to say to that, so she turned her attention back to Savn. Thinking about Savn didn't help me any, and thinking about Vlad getting killed was worse, so I went out and took a walk. Buddy came along, either because he liked my company or because he didn't trust me and wanted to keep an eye on me.

Good dog, either way.

By the time we returned, it was getting dark, and Vlad was sitting at the kitchen table, with a bandage wrapped around his left forearm and no hair growing above his lip. I'm not sure which surprised me more. I think it was the lack of hair.

There was some blood leaking through the bandage, but Vlad didn't seem to be weak or even greatly disturbed. Buddy bounded up to him, asked him to play, sniffed at his wound, and looked hurt when Vlad pulled his arm out of reach. Loiosh watched the display with what I would have guessed to be disdain if I ever knew what jhereg were thinking.

He saw me looking at him and said, "Don't worry. It'll grow back."

"Well," I said. "You seem to have been busy."

"Yes."

"How long since you've returned?"

"Not long. Half an hour or so."

"Learn anything?"

"Yes."

I sat down opposite him. Savn was on the floor, resting. The old woman sat beside him, watching us.

"Shall we start at the beginning?"

"I'd like a glass of water first."

The old woman started to get up, but I motioned her to sit, went outside to the well, filled a pitcher, brought it in, filled a cup, and gave it to Vlad. He drank it all, slowly and carefully.

"More?" I said.

"Please."

I brought him more; he drank some of it, wiped his mouth on the back of his hand, and nodded to me.

I said, "Well?"

He shrugged. "The beginning was your own story."

"Go on."

He said, "It didn't make sense."

"So I gathered at the time. What part of it didn't make sense?"

He frowned and said, "Kiera, have you ever been involved in investigating someone's death—in trying to determine cause of death?"

"No, I can't say I have. Have you?"

"No, but I've been concerned with several, if you know what I mean."

"I know what you mean. And I have an idea of what's involved in an investigation like that." I shrugged. "What about it?"

"How long does it take to decide that someone wasn't murdered?"

"*Wasn't* murdered?"

"Yes."

"I don't know. Looking at the body—"

"Takes a day, maybe two, if he *was* murdered."

"Well, yes, but to prove a negative—"

"Exactly."

"They'd have to go over him pretty carefully, I suppose."

"Yes. Very carefully. And they look at everything else, too—such as if he was the sort of person likely to be murdered, or if there is anything suspicious in the timing of his death, or—"

"Exactly the sort of circumstances that surrounded Fyres's death."

"Yes. Fyres's death would set off every alarm they have. If you were the chief investigator, wouldn't you want to be extra careful before putting your chop on a report that stated he died of mischance attributable to no human agency, or however they put it?"

"What are you getting at?"

"Your friend the Jhereg told you that the Imperial investigators had determined the cause of death to be accidental."

"And?"

"And when did Fyres die?"

"A few weeks ago."

He nodded. "Exactly. A few weeks ago. Kiera, they *can't* have decided that this quickly. The only thing they could know this quickly is if it *was* a murder."

"I see your point. What's your conclusion?"

"That either your friend Stony lied to you or—"

"Or someone lied to Stony."

"Yes. And who would lie to Stony about something like this? Of those, who would he believe?"

"No one."

"Tsk."

"He's a naturally suspicious fellow."

"Well, but who would he believe?"

I shrugged. "The Empire, I suppose."

"Exactly."

"But the Empire wouldn't lie."

Vlad raised his eyebrows eloquently.

I shook my head. "You can't be implying that the Imperial investigators—"

"Yep."

"No."

"You don't believe it?"

"Why would they? How could they hope to get away with it? How many of them would have to be bought off, and how much would it cost? And consider how closely their report is going to be looked at, and think about the risks they run. They'd have to know they'd get caught eventually."

Vlad nodded. "Certainly valid points, Kiera. That's exactly what was bothering me yesterday when you told me about your conversation with Stony."

"Well, then—"

"Kiera, how about if I just tell you what I've been up to, and you form your own conclusions?"

I nodded. "Okay, I'm listening. No, wait a minute." I helped myself to a glass of water, set the pitcher next to me, sat down, and stretched out. "Okay," I said. "Go ahead."

Vlad took another drink of water, closed his eyes for a moment, then opened them and began speaking.

Chapter Five

FIRST, OF COURSE, I had to find out who had carried out the investigation. I was afraid that the Empire had brought people in from Adrilankha and that these people had already returned, which meant a teleport to our beloved capital, about which idea I was less than thrilled, as you can imagine.

But one step at a time. I could have found a minstrel—I have an arrangement with their Guild—but news travels in both directions by that source, so I tried something different.

I made the tentative assumption that some things are universal, so I walked around until I found the seediest-looking barbershop in the area. Barbershops are more common in the East and in the Easterners' section of Adrilankha—barbers cut whiskers as well as head hair—but they exist everywhere. I'll bet you'd never thought of that, Kiera; whiskers aren't just a distinguishing feature; they have to be tended to. Fortunately, I have sharp enough blades that I don't have to go to barbershops for my own whiskers, but most Easterners don't have knives that sharp. But even in the East, Noish-pa tells me, barbershops are pretty much the same as they are here.

The barber, who seemed to be a Vallista, and a particularly ugly one at that, looked at me, looked at Loiosh, looked at my rapier, and opened his mouth—probably to explain that he didn't serve Easterners—but Loiosh hissed at him before he had a chance to say anything. While he was trying to come up with an answer for Loiosh, I walked over to the chairs where customers waited. There was a little table next to them, and I found what I was looking for in about two seconds.

It had a title, *Rutter's Rag,* in big, hand-scrawled letters along the top, and it was mostly full of nasty remarks about city officials I'd never heard of, and it asked the Empire questions about its tax policy, implying that certain pirates were taking lessons from the Empire. It had a list of the banks that had closed suddenly—I assume it included the one our hostess used—and suggested that they were having a race to see which of them could clear out and vanish quickest, while wondering if the Empire, which allowed them to shut their doors on people who had their life savings in them, was really incompetent enough not to have known they were going under, or if this was now to be considered official Imperial policy.

It also, interestingly enough, made some ironic comments about Fyres's death—suggesting that those who had invested in his companies had gotten what they deserved. But that wasn't what I was after. Of course, it didn't give the real name of whoever produced it, but that didn't matter.

"What do you want?" said the barber.

"I want to know who delivers this to you."

That confused him, because I didn't look like a Guardsman, and, besides, they don't really care about sheets like this. But printing it was technically illegal, and those involved in it certainly wouldn't want to be known, so I knew I was going to have to persuade him. I tossed an imperial his way just as he was starting to shake his head. He caught it, opened his mouth, closed it, and started to toss it back. I put a couple of knives into the wall on either side of his head. Good thing I'd been practicing or I might have cut his hair. In any case, I do believe I frightened the man, judging by the squeaks he made.

He said, "A kid named Tip."

"Where can I find him?"

"I don't know."

I pulled another throwing knife (my last one, actually— I'd just recently bought them) and waited.

"He lives around here somewhere," squeaked the barber. "Ask around. You'll find him."

"If I don't," I said, "when do you expect him to deliver another one of these?"

"A couple of weeks," he said. "But I don't know exactly when. I never know when they'll show up."

"Good enough," I said. I took a step toward him and he moved away, but I was only going to get my knives. I put them away and walked back out, turned right at random, and stepped into the first alley I got to. And there they were—another eight urchins, mixed sexes, mixed Houses. Street kids don't seem to care much what your House is. There may be a moral there, but probably not.

I walked up to them and waited a moment to give them a good look. They studied me with a lot of suspicion, a little curiosity, but not much fear. I mean, I was only an Easterner, and maybe I had a sword, but there were still eight of them. Then I said, "Do any of you know Tip?"

A girl, who seemed to be about seventy and might have been the leader and might have been a Tiassa, said, "Maybe."

A boy said, "What you want him for? He in trouble?"

Someone else said, "You a bird?"

Someone else asked to see my sword.

"Yeah," I said. "I'm a bird. I'm going to arrest him as a threat to Imperial security, and then I'm going to haul him away and torture him. Any other questions?"

There were a few chuckles.

"Who are you?" said the girl.

I shrugged and took out an imperial. "A rich man who wants to spread his wealth around. Who are you?"

They all turned to look at the girl. Yes, she was definitely in charge. "Laache," she said. "Is that thing your pet?" she asked.

"Go ahead, explain it, boss."

"Shut up, Loiosh."

"His name is Loiosh," I said. "He's my friend. He flies around and looks at things for me."

"What does he look at?"

"For example, if I were to give this imperial to someone to bring Tip back, he'd fly around and make sure whoever I gave it to didn't scoot off with it. If someone took this imperial and told me where Tip could be found, Loiosh would wait with that person until I was certain I hadn't been fooled."

One of the boys said, "He can't really tell you where someone went, can he?"

Laache grinned at me. "You think we'd do something like that?"

"Nope."

"What reason do I give Tip for showing up?"

I brought forth another imperial. "For him," I said.

"You sure he isn't in trouble?"

"No. I've never seen him before. For all I know, he might have robbed the Imperial Treasury."

She gave me a very adultlike smile and held out her hand; I gave her one of the coins.

"Wait here," she said.

"I'm not going anywhere."

When she left, Loiosh flew off and followed her, which elicited a gasp from the assembled urchinhood.

With her gone, the mood changed—the rest of them seemed suddenly uncomfortable, like they didn't know quite what to do with me. That worked out all right, because I didn't know what to do with them, either. I leaned against a wall and tried to look self-assured; they clumped together and held quiet conversations and pretended they were ignoring me.

After about fifteen minutes, Loiosh said, *"She's found someone, boss. She's talking to him."*

"And . . . ?"

"Okay, they're coming."

"Hooray. Where are they now?"

"Just around the corner."

I said, "Laache and Tip will be here soon."

They looked at me, and one of them said, "How d'you—" and cut himself off. I smiled enigmatically, noticing the looks of respect and fear. Sort of the way my employees used to look at me, way back when. I wondered if I'd come down in the world. If I handled things just right, I could maybe take the gang over from Laache. Vlad Taltos—toughest little kid on the block. I was the youngest, too.

They appeared then—Laache with a young man who seemed to be about the same age as her, and who I'd have guessed to be an Orca—a bit squat for a Dragaeran, with a pale complexion, light brown hair, and blue eyes. Old memories of being harassed by Orca just about his age came up to annoy me, but I ignored them—what was I going to do, beat him up?

He was looking a bit leery and keeping his distance. Before he could say anything, I flipped him an imperial. He made it vanish.

"What do you want?" he said.

"You're Tip?"

"What if I am?"

"Let us walk together and talk together, one with the other, out of range of the eager ears of those who would thwart our intentions."

"Huh?"

"Come here a minute, I want to ask you something."

"Ask me what?"

"I'd rather not say out here where everyone can hear me."

Someone whispered something, and someone else giggled. Tip scowled and said, "All right."

I walked up to him and we walked down the alley about twenty yards, and I said, "I'll give you another imperial if you'll take me to the man who prints *Rutter's Rag*," and he was off down the alley as fast as his feet could carry him. He turned the corner and was gone.

"You know what to do, Loiosh."

"Yeah, yeah. On my way, boss."

I turned back and the kids were all looking at me—and looking at Loiosh flying off into the city.

"Thanks for your help," I called to them. "See you again, maybe."

I strolled on down the alley. It was, of course, possible that Laache had told Tip about Loiosh, but, as we followed him, he didn't seem to be watching above him.

He stayed with the alleys and finally, after looking around him carefully, stepped into a little door. Loiosh returned to me and guided me along the same path he'd taken, and to the door. It wasn't locked.

It seemed to be a storeroom of some sort; a quick check revealed that what was stored included a great deal of paper and drums of what had to be ink, judging by the smell coming off them and filling up the room.

"Ah ha," I told Loiosh.

"Lucky," he said.

"Clever," I suggested.

"Lucky."

"Shut up."

I heard voices coming from my right, where there was a narrow, dark stairway. I took the stairs either silently or carefully—they tend to be the same thing. But you know that, Kiera. When I reached the bottom, I saw them, illuminated by a small lamp. One was Tip, the other was an old man who seemed to be a Tsalmoth, to judge from the ruddiness of his complexion and his build. I couldn't see what colors he wore. He didn't see me at all. The man was seated in front of a desk that was filled with desk things. Tip was standing next to him, saying, "I'm sure he was an Easterner. I know an Easterner when I see one," which was too good an entrance line for me to ignore.

I said, "Judge for yourself," and had the satisfaction of seeing them both jump.

I gave them my warmest smile, and the Tsalmoth scrabbled around in a drawer in his desk and came out with a narrow rod that, no doubt, had been prepared with some terrible, nasty killing thing. I said, "Don't be stupid," and took my own advice by allowing Spellbreaker to fall into my hand.

He pointed the rod at me and said, "What do you want?"

"Don't blame the boy," I said. "I'm very hard to lose when I want to follow someone."

"What do you want?" he said again. His dialogue seemed pretty limited.

"Actually," I said, "not very much. It won't even be inconvenient, and I'll pay you for it. But if you don't put that thing down, I'm likely to become frightened, and then I'm likely to hurt you."

He looked at me, then looked at Spellbreaker, which to all appearances is just a length of gold-colored chain, and said, "I think I'll keep it in hand, if you don't mind."

"I mind," I said.

He looked at me some more. I waited. He put the rod down. I wrapped Spellbreaker back around my left wrist.

"What is it, then?"

"Perhaps the boy should take a walk."

He nodded to Tip, who seemed a little nervous about walking past me, so I stepped to the side. He almost ran to the stairs, stopping just long enough to take the imperial I threw to him. "Don't squander it," I said as he raced past me.

There was another chair near the desk, so I sat down in it, crossed my legs, and said, "My name is Padraic." Quit laughing, Kiera; it's a perfectly reasonable Eastern name, and no Dragaeran in the world is going to look at me and decide I don't look right. Where was I? Oh, yeah. I said, "My name is Padraic."

He grunted and said, "My name is Tollar, but you might as well call me Rutter; there's no point in my denying it, I suppose."

He was a frightened man trying to be brave; I've always had a certain amount of sympathy for that type. From this close, he didn't seem as old as I'd first thought him, but he didn't seem especially healthy, either, and his hair was thin and sort of wispy—you could see his scalp in places, like an Easterner who is just beginning to go bald.

He said, "You have me at a disadvantage."

"Sure," I said. "But there's no need to worry about it. I just need to find out a couple of things, and I took the easiest method I could think of."

"What do you mean?"

"I mean I ask you a couple of questions that you have no reason not to answer, and then I'm going to give you a couple of imperials for your trouble, and then I'm going to go away. And that's it."

"Yeah?" He seemed skeptical. "What sort of questions, and why are you asking me?"

"Because you have that rag of yours. That means you hear things. You pick up gossip. You have ways of finding out things."

He started to relax a little. "Well, yeah. Some things. Where should I start?"

I shrugged. "Oh, I don't know. What's the good gossip since the last rag came out?"

"Local?"

"Or Imperial."

"The Empress is missing."

"Again?"

"Yeah. Rumor is she's off with her lover."

"That's four times in three years, isn't it?"

"Yeah."

"But she always comes back."

"First time it was for three days, second time for nine days, the third time for six days."

"What else?"

"Imperial?"

"Yeah."

"Someone high up in the Empire dipped his hand into the war chest during the Elde Island war. No one knows who, and probably not for very much, but the Empress is a bit steamed about it."

"I can imagine."

"More?"

"Please."

"I'm better on local things."

"Know anything that's both local and Imperial?"

"Well, the whole Fyres thing."

"What do you know about that?"

"Not much, really. There's confirmation that his death was accidental."

"Oh, yeah?"

"That's what I hear."

"I hear the Empire is investigating his death."

He snorted. "Who doesn't know that?"

"Right. Who's doing the investigating?"

He looked at me, and I could see him going, "Ah ha!" just like me. He said, "You mean, their names?"

"Yeah."

"I have no idea."

I looked at him. He didn't seem to be lying. I said, "Where are they working out of?"

"You mean, where do they meet?"

"Right."

"City Hall."

"Where in City Hall?"

"Third floor."

"The whole floor?"

"No, no. The third floor is where the officers of the Phoenix Guard are stationed. There are a couple of rooms set aside for any senior officials who might show up. They're using those."

"Which rooms?"

"Two rooms at the east end of the building, one on each side of the hall."

"And they haven't gone back to Adrilankha yet?"

"No, no. They're still hard at it."

"How could they still be hard at it if they already know what the answer is?"

"I don't know," he said. "I imagine they're just tying up loose ends and doing their final checking. But that's just a guess."

"Which wouldn't stop you from printing it as a fact."

He shrugged.

I said, "Heard anything about their schedule?"

"What do you mean?"

"I mean when they expect to be finished."

"Oh. No, I haven't."

"Okay." I dug out three imperials and handed them to him. "See?" I said. "That wasn't so bad, was it?"

He wasn't worried anymore. He said, "Why is it you want to know all of this?"

I shook my head. "That's a dangerous question."

"Oh?"

"If you ask it, I might answer it. And if I answered it, the answer might appear as gossip in your lovely little sheet. And if that happened, I would have to kill you."

He looked at me and seemed like a frightened old man again. I stood up and walked out without a backward glance.

I told you they were getting tired of seeing me at City Hall, which was another problem, so I tried out a disguise. The first problem was my mustache, so it went. It took a lot of time, too, because even after you shave it off, you have to scrape quite a bit at the whiskers to make sure they don't show at all. The next problem was my height. I found a cobbler who sold me some boots which he then put about eight extra inches on, leaving me about Aliera's height, which I hoped would be good enough. Then I had to practice walking in them and taking long strides. Have you ever tried walking in boots with eight extra inches of sole? Don't. Then I broke into a theater to steal a wig with a noble's point and get some powder to hide the traces of whiskers, then I bought some new clothes, including trousers long enough to hide the shoes but not long enough to trip on. I practiced swaggering just a bit. Kiera, this was not easy—I had to keep my balance, take strides long enough so it wouldn't look funny with my height, and *swagger,* for the love of Verra. I felt like a complete idiot. On the other hand, I didn't draw any funny looks while I was walking around, so I figured I had a chance of pulling it off.

I hid my clothes and my blade behind a handy public house half a mile or so from City Hall. So I did all that, dressing myself up like a Chreotha so people would feel free to push me around. You can learn a lot letting people push you around, and it's always nice knowing that you can push back whenever you want.

I told Loiosh to wait for me outside, which he didn't like but was unavoidable. Then I walked into the place like I knew my business, went up a flight of stairs to take me past the nice Lyorn who'd been helping me so far, found another flight of stairs, turned right, and looked down to the end of the hall. There were three or four people sitting on plain wooden chairs in the hall. Three men, one woman, all of them Orca except for one poor fellow who seemed to be a Teckla.

I leaned against a wall and watched for a while, until the right-hand door opened and a middle-aged Orca walked out. A moment later, as she was walking past me, one of those waiting went in. I walked past and entered the door to the left.

There was a sharp-looking young Dragonlord sitting at a desk. He said, "Good day, my lord."

How long was I a Jhereg, Kiera? Hard to say, I suppose; it depends when you start counting and when you stop. But a long time, anyway, and that's a long time spent getting so you can smell authority—so you know you're looking at an officer of the Guard before you really know how you know. Well, I walked through that door, and I knew.

He was, as I said, a Dragonlord, and one who worked for the Phoenix Guards, or for the Empire; yet he was dressed in plain black pants and shirt with only the least bit of silver; his hair was very short, his complexion just a bit dark, his nose just a bit aquiline; he rather looked like Morrolan, now that I think of it. But I've never seen Morrolan's eyes look quite that cold and that calculating; I've never seen anyone look like that except for an assassin named Ishtvan, who I used a couple of times and killed not long ago. It took me about a quarter of a second to decide that I didn't want to go up against this guy if I could avoid it.

I said, "My lord, you are looking into the death of Lord Fyres?"

"That's right. Who called you in?"

"No one, my lord," I said, trying to sound humble.

"No one?"

"I came on my own, when I heard about it."

"Heard about what?"

"The investigation."

"How did you hear?"

I had no idea how to answer that one, so I shrugged helplessly.

He was starting to look very hard at me. "What's your name?" he said. I was no longer his lord.

"Kaldor," I said.

"Where do you live, Kaldor?"

"Number six Coattail Bend, my lord."

"That's here in Northport?"

"Yes, my lord, in the city."

He wrote something down on a piece of paper and said, "My name is Loftis. Wait in the hall; we'll call you."

"Yes, my lord."

I gave him a very humble bow and stepped back into the hall, feeling nervous. I'm a good actor, and I'm okay with disguises, but that guy scared me. I guess I'd been working on the assumption that the Imperial investigators were on the take, and I'd gone from there to the assumption that they must be pretty lousy investigators. Actually, that was stupid; I know from my own dealings with the Guard that just because one of them is on the take doesn't mean he can't do his job, but I hadn't thought it through, and now I was worried; Loftis didn't seem to be someone I could put much over on, at least not without a lot more work than I'd put in.

So, of course, I listened. I assumed that they'd be able to detect sorcery, but I doubted they'd be looking for witchcraft, so I took the black Phoenix Stone off and slipped it into my pouch—hoping, of course, that the Jhereg wouldn't pick that moment to attempt a psychic location spell. I leaned my head back against the wall, closed my eyes, and concentrated on sending my hearing through the wall. It took some work, and it took some time, but soon I could hear voices, and after a bit I could distinguish words.

"Who do you think sent him?" I wasn't sure if that was Loftis.

"Don't be stupid." *That* was Loftis.

"What, you're saying it was the Candlestick?"

"In the first place, Domm, when you're around me, you'll be respectful when speaking of Her Majesty."

"Oh, well pardon my feet for touching the ground."

"And in the second place, no. I mean we have no way of knowing who sent him, and if we're going to do this—"

"We're going to do this."

"—we should at least be careful about it. And being careful means finding out."

"He could have given us his right address."

"Sure. And he could be the King of Elde Island, too. You follow him, Domm. And don't let him pick up on you."

"You want to put those orders in writing, *Lieutenant*?"

"Would you like to eat nine inches of steel, *Lieutenant*?"

"Don't push me, Loftis."

"Or we could just dump the whole thing on Papa-cat's lap and let him decide our next step. Want to do that? How do you think he'd feel about it?"

"I could tell him it was your idea."

"Sure. Do it. I'm sure he'll believe you, too. You know as sure as Verra's tits I'll roll on this as soon as I have a good excuse. Go ahead. My protests are down in writing, Domm. How about you? Did you just shrug and say, 'Hey, sure, sounds like fun'? Probably. So go ahead."

"Lieutenant, sir, with all respect, my lord, you tire me."

"Tough. You've got your orders, my lord lieutenant. Carry them out."

"All right, all right. You know how much I love legwork, and I know how much you care about what I love. I'll wait until his interview is over, then pick him up. Should I bring some backup?"

"Yeah. Take Timmer; she's good at tailing, and she hasn't stirred her butt since she's been here."

"Okay. What should I tell Birdie about the interview?"

"Play it straight, see what he has to say, and try to keep the bell ringing."

"Huh?"

"Battle of Waterford Landing, Domm. Tenth Cycle, early Dragon Reign. A border skirmish between a couple of Lyorn over rights to—"

"Oh, now that's extremely useful, Loftis. Thanks. Why don't you skip the history, and the obscure references, and just tell me what you want Birdie to do."

"I mean Birdie should try to get him talking, and then just keep drawing him out until there isn't anything left to draw."

"And if he won't *be* drawn?"

"Then that'll tell us something, too."

"Okay."

"You got to admit this is better than just sitting here day after day pretending. At least it's doing something."

"I suppose. Mind if I put him in front of the queue so I don't have to wait all night?"

"Yeah, I mind. Nothing to make him suspicious. You can put him in front of the Teckla if you want."

"Okay. Hey, Loftis."

"Yeah?"

"You ever wonder why?"

"Why what? Why we got the word?"

"Yeah."

"That's a laugh. I haven't been doing anything *but* wondering why for the last two weeks."

"Yeah."

They stopped talking. I moved my head forward, replaced the Phoenix Stone around my neck, and didn't look as someone I didn't recognize walked out of the door and across the hall. An instant later he came back. I watched him, as did all of the others who were waiting, but he didn't look at me at all. Assuming that was Domm, my opinion of him went up a bit—it isn't easy to avoid taking even a quick glance at someone you're going to be following in a few minutes. I got the uncomfortable feeling that I was dealing with professionals here.

I sat there trying to decide if I should skip out now, which would mean I wouldn't have to worry about losing the tail and would give them something to wonder about, or if I should go ahead and let them interview me, and hope to pick up more information that way. I decided to gamble, because, now that I had a better idea of what was going on, as well as how they were going to handle me, I felt like I could maybe learn a bit. I was glad Domm had demanded the explanation for "keep ringing the bell," because it would have been a mistake to have asked Loftis myself.

Someone else showed up, went into the room I'd just come out of, then emerged and took a seat next to me. We didn't speak. None of us had so much as made eye contact with any of the others. But as I sat there waiting for about an hour and a half planning what kind of story I was going to tell them, I didn't get any less nervous.

When they finally called out "Kaldor," it took me a moment to realize that was the name I'd given them. I tell you, Kiera, I'm not made for a life of deception. But I shuffled into the office, still taking long strides and swaggering, but shuffling, too, if you can imagine it, where sat a fairly young, competent-looking Lyorn behind yet another desk. I've been seeing a great number of desks lately—it makes me miss my own. I don't know what it is about a desk that gives one a feeling of power—perhaps it is that, when you are facing someone behind a desk, you don't know what is concealed within it; the contents of a desk can be worse than a nest of yendi.

The chair he pointed me to was another of the inevitable

plain, wooden chairs—there's something about those, too, now that I think of it.

He said, "I am the Baron of Daythiefnest. You are Kaldor?"

Daythiefnest? Birdie. I didn't laugh. "Yes, my lord."

"Number three Coattail Bend?"

"Number six, my lord." Heh. Caught that one, at least.

"Right, sorry. And you have come in on your own?"

"Yes, my lord."

"Why?"

"My lord?"

"What brought you here?"

"The investigation, my lord. I have information."

"Ah. You have information about Fyres's death?"

"Yes, my lord."

He studied me carefully, but, as far as intimidation went, he was nothing compared to Loftis. Of course, it wouldn't do to tell him so; it might hurt his feelings.

"And what is this information?"

"Well, my lord, after work—"

"What sort of work do you do, Kaldor?"

"I mend things, my lord. That is, I mend clothes, and sometimes I mend pots and pans, except my tools got took, which I reported to the Guard, my lord, and I mend sails for sailors sometimes, and—"

"Yes, I understand. Go on."

"I know that you aren't the gentlemen who are going to get my tools back, that's a different outfit."

"Yes. Go on."

"Go on?"

"After work . . ."

"Oh, right. Well, after work, on the days I have work, I like to go into the Riversend. Do you know where that is?"

"I can find it."

"Oh, it's right nearby. You just take Kelp down to where it curves—"

"Yes, yes. Go on."

"Right, my lord. Well, I was in there having a nice glass of ale—"

"When was this?"

"Last Marketday, my lord."

"Very well."

"Well, I'd been drinking a fair bit, and I'd gotten a kind of early start, so before I knew it I was seeing the room go spinning around me, the way it does when you know you've had more than maybe you should?"

"Yes. You were drunk."

"That's it, my lord. I was drunk. And then the room spun, and then I must have fallen asleep."

"Passed out."

"Yes, my lord."

"Well?"

"Yes, my lord?"

"Get on with it."

"Oh. Yes, my lord. I must have been sleeping five, six hours, because when I woke up, needing to relieve myself, you understand, I wasn't nearly so drunk, and I was lying on one of the benches they have in back, and the place was almost empty—there was Trim, the host, who was in the far corner cleaning up, and there was me, and there were these two gentlemen sitting at a table right next to me, and they were talking kind of quiet, but I could hear them, you know, my lord? And it was pretty dark, and I wasn't moving, so I don't think they knew I was there."

"Well, go on."

"One of them said, 'If you ask me, they didn't get anything.' And the other one said, 'Oh, no? Well, I'll tell you something, they got a lot, and it's going on the market next week,' and the first one said, 'What's it going for?' and the other one said, 'A lot. It has to be a lot. If someone is going to lighten Fyres, especially after he's dead, and not take anything but a bunch of papers, they must be important.' And the first one said, 'Maybe that's what he was killed for?' And the other one said, 'Killed? Naw, he just fell and hit his head.' And then, my lord, I sort of figured out what they were saying, even though I was still maybe a bit woozy, and I knew I didn't want to hear any more, so I moaned like I was just waking up, and they saw me, and they stopped talking right then. And I tumbled out of there, singing to myself like I was even drunker than I was, and I went out the back way and I beat it for home as quick as I could, and I didn't even settle up with Trim until the next day. But, as I was walking out, just at the last minute, I took a quick look at the two gentlemen. I couldn't see their faces too well, but I could see their colors, and they were both Jhereg. I'll swear it. And that's what I have, my lord."

"That's what you have?"

"Yes, my lord."

He stared at me like I was a rotten pear and he'd just bit into me, and he thought for a while. "Why did you come and see us now, and not two weeks ago?"

"Well, because I heard of the reward, and I was thinking about my tools that got stole, and—"

"What reward?"

"The reward for anyone who gives evidence about how Fyres died."

"There's no reward."

"There's no reward?"

"Not at all. Where did you hear such a thing?"

"Why, just yesterday, down at the Riversend, a lady told me that she'd heard—"

"She was deceived, my friend. And so were you."

"My lord?"

"There isn't any reward for anything. We're just trying to find out what happened."

"Oh." I tried to look disappointed.

He said, "How did you learn to come here, by the way?"

"How, my lord?"

"Yes."

"Why, the lady, she was a Tsalmoth, and she told me."

"I see. Who was this lady?"

"Well, I don't know, my lord. I'd never seen her before, but she was—" I squinted as if I was trying to remember. "Oh, she was about eight hundred, and sort of tall, and her hair curled, and she was, you know, a Tsalmoth."

"Yes," he said, nodding. "Well, I'm sorry to disappoint you, but there isn't any reward."

I looked disappointed but said, "Well, that's all right, my lord; I'm just glad to have done the right thing."

"Yes, indeed. Well, we know where to reach you if we have any more questions."

I stood up and bowed. "Yes, my lord. Thank you."

"Thank you," he said, and that was it for the interview.

I walked out the door without seeing anyone except those who were waiting for their turn, and I took my time going down the stairs. As I went, I said, *"Loiosh?"*

"Right here, boss."

"I'm going to be followed, so stay back for a while."

"Okay. Who's going to follow you, boss?"

"I don't know, but I think the enemy."

"Oh, we have an enemy now?"

"I think so. Maybe."

"It's nice to have an enemy, boss. Where are you taking them?"

"Good question," I said. *"I'll let you know when we get there."*

Chapter Six

I STOOD ON the street, just outside City Hall, not looking behind me and trying to stay in character while figuring out
where to go and what to do. You don't get tailed all that
often, at least when you know it's happening, and an opportunity like that ought not to be wasted.

"I've spotted 'em, boss. Two of 'em. Pros."

"What are they doing?"

"Waiting for you to do something."

"Good. Let them wait."

I'd done what I actually set out to do, of course—it was
easy to fill in the missing pieces of Loftis's conversation
with Domm, and the missing pieces said that they were fak-
ing their way through the investigation and putting out the
results they were told to, and that was confirmed by the
way the other one, Daythiefnest, had been more concerned
with how I knew enough to find them and why I wanted to
than with the information itself. But what now? Knowing
the investigation was faked brought up the possibility (al-

though not the certainty by any means) that Fyres was, in fact, murdered, but it got me no closer to learning who was pulling the financial strings, or who in the next few months and years would be.

But more than that, Kiera, I was bothered, just as you were when I first suggested it. Why would the Empire do something like that? I'd never heard of it being done, and it would take, well, someone very highly placed in the Empire, and a very strong need, to attempt it. The question was who—who in the Empire and who in Fyres's world? And I didn't know anyone who inhabited either realm.

I mentally ran through the notes I'd made when reading the files you lightened Fyres of. Based on what I picked up from the files, and based on what your friend Stony told you, I'd guess that Fyres's children were somewhere near the center of things—that is, he was certainly going to leave his kids in charge of as much as possible, divided up according to his best guess about who could handle what and how much. He had a wife, one son, and two daughters, as well as a few other scattered relatives.

The wife, I heard somewhere, used to be third mate in a man-o'-war, which might indicate leadership qualities, but according to the files, he never seemed to trust her; and she never had anything to do with his business. There was just enough gossip floating around about his son for me to get the idea that everything he touched turned to mud; over the years, Fyres trusted him with less and less. If I had to guess about the will, I'd say Fyres left him with a house or two, a bunch of cash, and nothing else.

That left the daughters: the younger, Baroness of Reega, and the older, the Countess of Endra. It seemed from Fyres's notes that, as time went on, he was giving them more and more responsibility and working them into his businesses. Right then, Kiera, I really wished I had my old organization, because I could have made one remark to Kragar—how's he doing, by the way?—and in two days I would know everything possible about them. I hate doing the legwork myself, and, more important, I just didn't have time to do it.

Well, if all I could do was blunder about, I might as well get to it, I decided, and I turned around and back into City Hall I went. I didn't see those tailing me scramble out of my way; in fact, I didn't see them at all.

The nice Lyorn didn't recognize me and were far more helpful to Kaldor the Chreotha than they'd been to Padraic the Easterner—what they would have thought of Vlad the Jhereg I don't even want to think about. Oh, and they weren't all Lyorn, either, just for the record—but the ones who weren't looked like they wanted to be. Enough said.

In two minutes I was in front of the collection of city maps, and it took me about half an hour to determine that neither a barony of Reega nor a county of Endra could be found in the area. So I puttered around some more and found out that neither one actually existed—they were titles without places to go with them, which I suppose I should have expected of Orca. I then dug into the citizen rolls, which took a fair bit of time. I could have done it faster by asking for help, but then, no doubt, my shadows would have been able to find out what I was up to and I wasn't sure that was a good idea.

Endra—that is, the person—lived high on Vantage Hill, overlooking a little town called Harper on the outskirts of Northport. It was, I calculated, only an hour's walk, and I liked the idea of Domm and Timmer getting blisters on their feet; besides, you know how I feel about horses. So I set out. The day was nice, with a mild breeze blowing in from the sea. As I walked, I made a few minor but important adjustments to my costume—you know, I turned up the

collar, I fixed my hair, I straightened my buttons, and, gen-
erally, I made myself appear more prosperous, because I
figured I had to reach a certain social level before I'd have
a chance that Endra—or, more likely, whoever answered
the door for her—would even consider letting me see her.

One thing I'd forgotten when I set out was that, since I
was still in my disguise, I was wearing the platform boots
that didn't fit me very well; about halfway there I started
calling myself names, and Loiosh, trailing behind to keep
an eye on my shadows, starting laughing at me. And I was
a bit worried about not having my sword with me. And it
made me nervous to know there were two people following
me. In other words, I was not in a good mood by the time I
reached Vantage Hill.

Endra's place was pretty simple, actually. It was a plain
house, standing by itself on a little hillock, but it was certainly well built, and it struck me as comfortable. The
grounds were well manicured with some nicely behaved
trees in a neat row and trimmed grass and patches of gar-
den, but not molded and tended like the Imperial Palace, or
like The Demon's place, if you've ever been to— Oh, of
course you've been there. Sorry.

I don't know. As I approached it, I was thinking that
maybe I'd been spoiled by Castle Black and Dzur Mountain, but I had expected something more—I guess ostentatious is the word. But then I remembered your description
of Fyres's place—the one he actually lived in as opposed to
one of the places he used to impress people—and it wasn't
as big and impressive as it could have been either, was it? I
figured maybe it's a family trait. It was also interesting that
there seemed to be no guards patrolling the area. Fyres's
place had had plenty, but did one generation cause that big
a drop-off in the need for security? I hate dealing with
things I don't understand.

I pulled the door clapper and waited. Presently someone opened the door and frowned at me. I bowed and gave him Kaldor as a name, and asked if it would be possible for his mistress to spare me a few minutes of conversation.

He stared at me for a moment, as if he wasn't sure he'd heard me correctly. Then he said, "May I ask what your business is with the Countess?"

"I'm afraid it's private," I said.

He looked doubtful. I tried to look like I knew my business, which wasn't as easy as a Chreotha as it would have been in my usual guise, nor was he responding as well as I'd have expected when I looked like myself; I'm not certain why that is. Maybe there's more shock value in seeing an Easterner at one's door. Maybe I'd have been better off pretending to be a Dragonlord, but then I probably wouldn't have learned as much from the Imperial investigators.

Eventually, however, he let me in, and bid me wait while he found out if the Countess was available. I did what everyone has always done in that situation—I looked around. It was big, and it was impressive, and the stairway was white marble that swept up in a gracious curve and complemented the white, white walls broken by—ah, Kiera, my dear, if you'd been there, you'd still be drooling. I don't have the disposition of a thief, but I was tempted. There were gold plates on the wall, marble busts, crystal sculpture, a tapestry made of bloody damn pearls that would have made you cry. Stained glass embedded with gems. The place didn't speak of wealth, it screamed it. All of the ostentation I'd looked for on the outside was reserved for the inside, where it destroyed all my little notions about what a plain, simple, unassuming lifestyle this family chose. It was very strange, Kiera, and I couldn't help wondering at the sort of mind that had produced it.

And then it occurred to me that there was a similarity between the outside and the inside—and that was how little they said. I mean, sure, they screamed money, but what else? You can tell a lot about someone by seeing his home, right? Well, not these people. The place said nothing, really, except that she was rich. Was that because she was shallow, or because she didn't want anyone to know anything about her?

The servant appeared as I was considering this and said, "The Countess can spare you a few moments. She's in the library. Please follow me."

I did so.

The library. Yeah.

Remember those traps Morrolan has in his library? Oh, I imagine you do. Did you ever fall for them? No, I withdraw the question; sorry. But, yeah, everything in the library looked like Morrolan's traps—great huge tomes with jewel-encrusted covers chained to pedestals. Well, okay, so I'm overstating it a bit. But that was how the library felt—everything *looked* good, but it didn't give you the feeling you wanted to sit down and *read* anything. The library wasn't for reading, it was for meeting people in an atmosphere that tried to be intellectual. Or that's how it struck me, at any rate. I don't know. Maybe I've just never known enough rich people to have an opinion—maybe they have their own rules, or maybe they're trying to make up with money what they've been denied by birth; I don't know. I'm just giving it to you as it hit me at the time.

She was sitting at a table—not a desk, for a change—and reading a book, or pretending to. She looked up as I came in and gave me a quizzical half-smile, then rose to greet me; she was quite thin and had very short, light-colored straight hair—a "warrior's cut," in fact, which went oddly with her dress, which was a flowing blue gown. She had the Orca eyebrows—almost invisible—a largish mouth and thin lips, narrow, wide-set eyes, and a strong chin.

Her voice had a bit of the twang of the region, but not as much as our hostess has, or most of the people we've been running into around here, and it was quite musical sounding. She said, "Your name again was—?"

"Kaldor, my lady."

"You wished to speak to me?"

"Yes, my lady, if I may have a few moments."

"You may. Please sit. Here. What is your business?"

And here, Kiera, is where I paid the price of deceit. Maybe. Because it occurred to me that I might just be able to come out and ask her if she'd be willing to let us buy this land, or at least plead the case. But if she said no, and she was then questioned by Domm, they'd have no trouble tracing me back, and that could be unhealthy.

I said, "My condolences, my lady, on the death of your father."

She raised an eyebrow—it looked like a practiced maneuver—and said, "Yes, certainly."

I said, "It is the death of your father that brings me here."

She nodded again.

I said, "I have reason to believe the Empire is not looking into his death as seriously as they should."

"That's absurd."

"I don't think so, my lady."

"Why?"

"I can't tell you exactly."

"You can't tell me?"

I shook my head. I said, "If you would like, though, a friend of mine who knows something about it will come by, and he can tell you more—he just wanted me to find out if you cared."

"I care," she said. "But I don't believe it."

"But will you talk to my friend?"

She stared at me very hard, then said, "All right. When can I expect him?"

"I'm not sure."

"What's his name?"

"I'm not to say, my lady. He'll identify himself as my friend, though."

She looked at me for quite a while, then nodded and said, "All right."

I stood up and bowed. "I've taken enough of your time, I think."

She stood, which was a courtesy I hadn't expected, and as I left, the servant came and escorted me to the door. I left the way I'd come and began walking back to town.

What had I accomplished? I'm not certain, but I had left a way open for me to return in some other guise, even as myself, if it seemed appropriate.

I considered the matter as I walked. The day was still young, and I had a long way to go to reach the Baroness of Reega, and my feet were killing me.

Reega lived on a hill—I guess the rich always live on hills, maybe because the aristocrats do—called Winteroak, which was on the northern edge of Northport, overlooking the Kanefthali River Valley. It was quite a hike, so as soon as I was out of sight of Endra's place I sat down long enough to remove the black Phoenix Stone and perform a quick spell to make my feet feel better. I couldn't do a whole lot without letting the watchers know what I was up to, but it helped. I put the Phoenix Stone back on and continued. If they were like me when I was following someone, they would have noticed at once that they couldn't locate me either psychically or sorcerously, and they'd wonder about that, but my luck would have to be awfully bad for them to pick that moment to try again. Sometimes it's worth a certain amount of risk to alleviate discomfort.

This is a funny part of the world, Kiera. Have you noticed it? The landscape, I mean. Maybe it's because we're so far north of the equator, or because the Kanefthali Mountains start only a few hundred miles away—though I don't see how that can have anything to do with it. But it seems odd to me that you can walk from the east side of Northport to the west, or from hills overlooking the docks straight north, and you'll have four completely different landscapes. I mean, along the coast, it might as well be Adrilankha—you've got the same kind of ugly red cliffs and the sort of dirt that makes you think nothing could ever grow there no matter what you did. But just a little ways to the east you have these prairies that look like the area around Castle Black and west of Dzur Mountain, and there's lots of water and it looks like it might be good farmland. And the country around Endra's is all rocky and hard and pretty in the same way the southern tip of Suntra is pretty—unforgiving, but attractive, anyway. So you head north, along the river to where Reega lives, and it's like the big forests to the east of Dzur Mountain, almost jungle, only they've been cut back because there are a lot of people there, but it isn't hard to imagine running into a dzur or a tiassa prowling around. Isn't that strange? I wonder if there's some magic about it, or if it just happened that way.

But sorry, I've wandered away from the point. Reega's place was nestled in among a lot of trees and stuff, and looked completely untended—there were a good number of other houses in the area, so I had to ask directions a few times to figure out which it was. It was nice, Kiera. I mean it was smaller than Fyres's or Endra's, though still quite a bit bigger than this place, but it seemed to want to be a house, instead of a mansion that wanted to be a castle.

Looking at it, I figured that when I clapped she'd answer the door herself, and, as a matter of fact, that's just what happened.

She was a bit shorter and a bit heavier than her sister, and her hair was longer and curled quite a bit, but they had pretty much the same face. She looked at me the way someone who lived in a house like that ought to look at you, as if she was a bit curious about why someone would want to talk to her—by which I mean, not like the daughter of someone as rich as Fyres ought to look at you. I wondered if I was at the wrong place. I said, "Baroness Reega?"

"That's right," she said. "And you are—?"

"Kaldor. May I speak to you for a moment?"

"Concerning what?" she asked. She still seemed polite and friendly, but she hadn't invited me in.

"Your father."

"My father?"

"You are the daughter of Lord Fyres, aren't you?"

"Why, yes I am."

"Well, then, what I have to say concerns you."

She gave me a contemplative look and said, "What is it, then?"

It seemed odd to be discussing this standing outside of her house, but it was her choice. I said, "I have reason to believe that the Empire is not looking into his death as thoroughly as they ought to be."

Her eyes narrowed to slits, and she studied me, and I was suddenly not at all sure of my disguise. She said, "Oh you do, do you?"

"Yes, my lady."

"And what business is that of yours?"

Ah ha. If you've been counting, Kiera, that was the third "ah ha" of the day.

"My lady?"

"Why do you care?"

"Well, I was hoping, you know, that . . . uh . . ."

"That there would be a reward in it for you?"

"Well—"

She gestured with her hand toward the road behind me. "You may leave now."

I couldn't think of anything else to do, so I bowed and left. It had been a long walk for a short conversation, but no walk is wasted if there's an "Ah ha" at the end of it. I shared this thought with Loiosh, who suggested that he could supply me with as many "ah ha's" as I wanted. I didn't have an answer handy, so I just headed back to town.

My next stop was the Riversend, because I figured that would give my story some verisimilitude with my shadows, and because it had a back door in case I wanted to use it, and because I had my clothes and my weapons stashed there. If I needed to visit the son and the widow, I figured it would wait, because evening was coming on and my feet were hurting like blazes, and I wanted a good meal and a drink, which was another reason to stop at the Riversend.

But first things first. I asked Loiosh what my shadows were up to. He said, *"One's going around to the back, boss."*

"Is the other one coming in?"

"No."

"Okay."

I walked through the tavern, opened up the back door, moved a few empty crates, recovered the bundle that I'd made of my possessions, recovered my sword from behind the garbage pile, and slipped back inside before Timmer or Domm or whoever it was got there. The inn wasn't very crowded, but no one particularly noticed me, anyway.

I sat down at a table and caused the host (whose name really is Trim, by the way) to bring me some wine, a bowl of fish soup, and whatever fowl they had roasting away over the spit and producing those amazing smells. They were apparently basting it with some sort of honey and lemon mixture that made the fire dance very prettily and made my stomach growl like a dzur.

Trim's service was very fast, and his food was very good; I hoped that they wouldn't question the poor bastard, or if they did, that they were nice about it.

I ate, drank, rested, and tried to figure out my next step. The last was the hard part, the others come pretty easy if you practice long enough. Loiosh was getting hungry, too, which I felt bad about, but I needed him to keep watching, so my meal was accompanied by his running complaints. I didn't allow this to detract from the food, however.

Then Loiosh said, *"Boss, the guy's coming inside."*

"Okay," I said, and I placed the sword against the wall behind me, resting it against a support beam where it would be, if not hidden, at least not horribly obvious. I made sure I had a dagger near to hand, then I finished sopping up the meal with the remains of the bread—a good black bread made with seeds of some kind.

In fact, they both came in—the man and the woman—and planted themselves in front of me; no doubt they'd received instructions from headquarters. I looked up at them with an expression of profound innocence, to which I tried to mix in a certain amount of alarm.

"Lord Kaldor?" said the man.

I nodded.

"May we speak with you for a moment?"

I nodded again.

"I'm Lieutenant Domm, this is Ensign Timmer, of Her Imperial Majesty's Guard."

I nodded for the third time. I was getting good at it.

They sat down, even though I hadn't invited them to; I think they felt that standing while I sat would make it harder for them to intimidate me. Meanwhile, I tried to act like I was intimidated but trying to act like I wasn't. I don't think I did very well—it's a lot easier to pretend to be tough when you're scared than to pretend to be scared when you're tough. Or, at least, it is for me.

"Need any help, boss?"

"Not yet, Loiosh."

"We'd just like to ask you some questions. We understand that you've been telling people that we're not conducting a thorough investigation into a certain matter. We'd like to know why you think so."

I was betting on Reega over Endra, so I said, "My lord, I went over to the city hall today, where they're—you're—talking to everyone, and I told them what I knew, and they didn't care, so I figured that must mean—"

"Bullshit," said Timmer, opening her mouth for the first time. "What's the real reason?"

"That's the only—"

She turned to Domm and said, "Let's take him back and work on him for a while. We don't have time for this."

"Be patient," said Domm. "I think he'll talk to us."

"Why bother? We can peel him like an onion."

Domm shook his head. "Not unless we have to. The big guy doesn't like us destroying people's brains unless there's no other choice."

"So who's going to tell him?"

"Let's try it my way first."

"Okay. You're the boss."

He nodded and turned back to me. It was becoming harder and harder to try to look frightened. People all around us in the inn had now moved away and Trim was giving us uneasy glances. A reassuring wave, I thought, would probably not be a good idea. Domm leaned over the table to bring his face right up to mine.

"Who are you, what do you know, how do you know it, and what are you after?"

I sank back into the chair and made my eyes get wide, which is as good as I can do at pretending to be afraid. I tried to figure out if there was any way to talk my way out of this without giving them anything. Nothing came instantly to mind. Domm said, "Am I going to have to let Timmer here work on you? It isn't how I like to do things, but if you don't give me any choice, I'm going to have to give you to her."

It suddenly occurred to me that, if they believed I was a professional, they wouldn't be trying to pull stuff like that on me—I was in a better position than I'd thought I was.

"Okay," I said. "I'll tell you what I know."

Domm sat down again and waited, but kept his eyes fixed on me. I'll bet he's pretty good at telling when people are lying. But then, I'm pretty good at lying.

I said, "There was this man." He asked me if I wanted to make some money—fifty imperials, he said, to go to a room in the city hall, say all these things, then walk around to a couple of places and say some more things. He told me what to say."

"Who is he?" snapped Timmer.

"I don't know. I'd never seen him before."

"Where did you meet him?"

"Here—right here."

Domm said, "How did he know to talk to you?" He was good, this guy.

"I don't know," I said.

"Oh, come on. You can do better than that. Do you expect us to believe he just walked in here and picked the first guy he saw to make this offer to?"

I shook my head. "I don't know."

Domm said, "What House was he?"

"Orca," I said. They looked at each other, which gave me the impression I'd scored a hit, although it was a pretty obvious thing to say.

Timmer said, "What did he look like?"

I started to make something up, then decided that Kaldor wasn't all that observant, and they could work for what they got. "I don't know, he was just, you know, just someone."

"How old do you think he is?"

"I don't know. Not too old. Twelve hundred or so."

"Tall? Short?"

"I don't know."

"Taller than you?"

"Oh, yes. Everyone's taller than me."

Domm stood up. "Taller than me?"

"Uh, I think so."

He sat down again. "Heavy-set?"

"No, no. Skinny."

"Long hair? Short hair? Straight? Curly?"

And so on. Eventually they got a pretty good description of the nonexistent Orca, and I told them I hadn't realized I was so observant.

"All right," said Domm, nodding slowly after I'd finished. Then he paused, as if thinking things over, then he said, "Now let's have the rest of it."

"Huh?" I said, pretending to be startled.

"Who are you, and why did he come to you?"

Okay, this was the tricky part. As far as they were concerned, they'd gotten me beat, and it was just a matter of squeezing a little to get everything out of me. So I had to keep letting them think that, while still trying to pull my own game. This was, of course, made more difficult by the fact that I didn't know what my own game *was*—I was still trying to find out as much as I could about what was going on.

I gave a sigh, let my lips droop, and covered my face with my hands. "None of that," snapped Domm. "You know who we are, and you know what we can do to you. You have one chance to make this easy on yourself, and that's by telling us everything, right now."

I nodded into my hands. "Okay," I said to the table.

"Start with your name."

I looked up and, trying to make my voice small, I said, "What's going to happen to me?"

"If you tell us the truth, nothing. We may take you in for more questioning, and we'll need to know where we can reach you, but that'll be all—*if* you tell us the truth and the whole truth."

I gave Timmer a suspicious look.

"She won't do anything," said Domm.

"I want to hear her say it."

She smiled just a bit and said, "I stand by what the lieutenant said. *If* you tell us the truth."

Lying bastards, both of them. I gave them a suspicious look. "What about your commander? Will he go for it?"

Domm started to look impatient, but Timmer said, "If we give him the answers, he won't care how we got them."

"Is that the one I first talked to? What was his name, Loftis?"

"Yeah. He'll go for it."

I nodded, as if I was satisfied. I could feel them relax. "I should never have done this," I said in the tones of a man about to spill his guts. "I'm just a thief, you know? I mean, I've never hurt anyone. I know a couple of Jhereg who buy what I steal, but—wait a minute. You don't have to know the names of the Jhereg, do you?"

"I doubt it," said Domm.

"They'll kill me."

"It shouldn't be necessary," said Timmer comfortingly. "And we can protect you, anyway," she lied.

"All right," I said. "Anyway, it was stupid. I should have known better. But *fifty* imperials!"

"Tempting," said Domm.

"That's the truth," I said. "Anyway, my real name is Vaan. I was named after my uncle, who built—But you don't want to hear about that. Right?" I stopped and shook my head sadly. "I'm really in trouble, aren't I?"

"Yes," said Timmer.

"But you can get out of it," said Domm.

"Do you do this a lot? I mean, track people down and question them?"

They shrugged.

"That must be fun."

Domm permitted himself a half-smile. "You were saying?"

"Uh, right." I remembered I had a glass with some wine still in it, so I drank some and wiped my face with the back of my hand. "You got onto me from the locals, didn't you? I mean, you're from Adrilankha—anyone can hear it from your voice—but you checked on me with the locals and they told you about me."

They grunted, which could mean anything, except that Timmer let slip a look that said they'd rather die than have anything to do with the locals. That was important, although it wasn't the big thing I wanted to find out. But I had them going now. They'd broken me, and they knew that I would tell them everything I knew about everything if they handled me right, and handling me right meant letting me talk, only nudging me if I got too far off course. So now

I had to stay almost on course, and let them drift with me just for a bit.

I said, "The local Guards had me in once or twice, you know. They let me go because they could never be sure, but they know about me. They beat me once, too—they thought I knew something about some big job or another, but I didn't know anything about it. I never know anything about big jobs. Big jobs scare me. This one scared me, and I guess I was right to be scared." I drank some more wine and risked a look at them. They were relaxed now, and not paying all that strict attention—in other words, set up.

I shook my head. "I should have listened to my instincts, you know? I was telling some friends of mine just the other day that I had a bad feeling—"

All of a sudden Domm was no longer relaxed. "What friends?" he snapped. "What did you tell them?" Then he caught himself and looked at Timmer, who was looking at him and frowning. And that made the fourth "Ah ha" of the day, which I decided would have to be enough, especially because one of the things I learned from this one was that they—or at least Domm—had no intention of leaving me alive.

I reached back, grabbed my sword, and nailed Domm in the side of the head with the flat, trying to knock him both out and into Timmer, but I couldn't get quite enough power for either to work with my thin little blade. Timmer was fast. *Really* fast. She was up, weapon out, and coming at me before I'd stood up, and I had to squeeze into the corner and parry with both hands or she'd have spitted me; as it was she did violence to my arm, which I resented. But before she could withdraw her steel I cut at her forearm, then sliced up at her head, and—because of one move or the other—her blade fell to the floor. She bent over to pick up her weapon while I reached down and got my parcel of clothes from next to my chair. Among other things, it had my boots in it.

Domm was shaking his head—I'd at least slowed him down. Timmer came at me again, but I knocked her sword aside with my parcel, then hit *her* with the parcel, and I came up over the table and on the way by I thumped Domm's head with the pommel of my rapier. As I came over the table it tipped and I was able to put it between me and Timmer for a second, which then I used to turn and dash out the back door. I couldn't go as fast as I'd have liked, because of those Verra-be-damned boots, but I made it before they caught up with me.

I'd had an escape route planned, but I hadn't intended to be bleeding when I took it. I headed out of the alley and into another one while sheathing my weapon. I heard footsteps and I knew that Timmer was behind me. I wasn't terribly keen on killing her—you know as well as I do what sort of heat it brings to kill a Guardsman—but I was even less keen on her killing me, and there was no way I could escape her by running—not in those boots. And if I teleported, of course, she'd just trace the teleport; no future in that.

I was just considering where I should make a stand when I got lucky. I turned a corner and someone vanished—some guy had just stepped out of some shop and teleported home with his purchases. If I hadn't been wearing the black Phoenix Stone, which prevents Devine contact, I would have given a prayer of thanks to Verra; as it was, I ran right through the spot where he'd teleported from, held my arm against the parcel of clothes in the hopes that I wouldn't drip any more blood, and ran another twenty feet and through the curtained entrance to the shop.

It turned out to be a clothier, and there were a couple of customers in it. The man behind the counter—a real

Chreotha—said, "May I be of some service to you, my lord?"

"Yes," I said, trying to catch my breath. "Do you have something in red?"

"You're bleeding!" said one of the customers.

"Yes," I said. "It's the fashion, you know."

"My dear sir—" said the proprietor.

"A moment," I said, and I pulled the curtain aside just a hair, just enough to see the end of Timmer's teleport. "Never mind," I said. "I think I like the pattern it's making. Good day."

I went back into the alley, and then to another one, and did my best not to leave a trail of blood. With any luck at all I had a good couple of minutes before Timmer realized that she'd followed the wrong man, and, I hoped, Domm was too far out of it to be a problem.

"Well, Loiosh?"

"You're in the clear for the moment, boss."

"Okay. Hang on for another minute, then join me."

I found a little nook I'd noticed before, and spent a minute and a half becoming a bleeding Easterner instead of a bleeding Chreotha. I put the remains of the Chreotha disguise in the bag, took off the gold Phoenix Stone, and teleported the bag to a spot I knew well just off the coast of Adrilankha, where it went to join a couple of bodies who wouldn't mind the intrusion. Loiosh arrived on my shoulder with a few choice words about how clever I thought I was compared to what a fool I'd been acting like. I thanked him for sharing his opinion with me.

Since I'd taken the chain off, anyway, there was no reason not to teleport back here, so I arrived at a point I'd memorized a little ways away into the wood, and here I am, Kiera, happy to see you as always, and has anyone ever told you that you're lovely when you're disgusted?

INTERLUDE

"I'VE NEVER HEARD of that Stony you talked to. If he's just sort of midlevel in Northport, what made you think he'd know anything about Fyres?"

"That's one of the things I can't tell you."

"Oh. There are a lot of things like that, aren't there?"

"I told you there would be, Cawti."

"Yes, I know. I've never known Vlad to use disguises before."

"Neither had I. It was probably something he picked up while traveling."

"What about the old woman? How was she taking all of this?"

"I suspect it bothered her a great deal, but she never let on. In fact, the whole time she had an attitude like none of it had anything to do with her."

"I can't blame her, I guess. It would be strange."

"Yes."

"It's funny, you're summarizing for me Vlad's report to

you about his conversations with others, which is three steps removed from the actual conversations, but I can still almost hear him talking."

"You miss him, don't you?"

"I—"

"He misses you, Cawti."

"Let's not start on that, all right?"

"If you wish."

"It's complicated, Kiera. It's difficult. I don't know any of the answers. Yes, I miss him. But we couldn't live together."

"He's changed, you know."

"Are you trying to get us back together, Kiera?"

"I don't know. I think at least he should know about—"

"Let's not talk about it."

"All right. Maybe I should summarize even more."

"No, you're doing fine."

"I have to say, though, that I don't have a very good memory for conversations, so a lot of this I'm reconstructing and making up. But you get the gist of it."

"I do indeed. You must have had a few words for him when he got back to the house. I know I would have."

"Oh, yes."

Chapter Seven

"WELL," I SAID slowly. "Congratulations, Vlad."

He looked at me and waited for the punch line.

I said, "You've now not only got the Jhereg after you but also the Empire, and, as soon as they tie you to the documents we stole, the House of the Orca will want you, too—and me, by the way. That leaves only fourteen more Houses to go and you'll have the set. Then you can start on the Easterners and the Serioli. Good work."

"It's a talent," he said. "I can't take credit for it."

I studied him while considering his story. He was looking—I don't know, *smug* wasn't quite right, but maybe something like, *amused with a veneer of self-satisfaction.* Sometimes I forget just how devious he is, and how good he is at improvising, and his skill at calculating odds and pulling off improbable gambits. Sometimes he thinks he's better at these things than he actually is, and it is likely to get him killed one of these days—especially now, when, between the gold and the black Phoenix Sx he wears, he is entirely cut off from those who would be most willing and able to help him.

"All right," I said. "Either Fyres was murdered or the Empire is afraid Fyres was murdered, and, in either case, the Empire doesn't want it known."

"Someone in the Empire," Vlad amended.

"No," I said. "The Empire."

"You mean the Empress—"

"I wouldn't say the Empress knows, but it doesn't matter either way."

"I don't understand."

"If it isn't the Empress, it's someone almost as important, and it's with the cooperation of the highest level of government."

"What makes you so sure? An hour ago you didn't even believe—"

"Your story was very convincing," I said. "And you told me things you probably didn't know you were telling me." I frowned. "The way Loftis talked to Domm, and the way Domm and Timmer talked to each other, tell me—"

"That Timmer doesn't—or, perhaps, *didn't*—know about it."

"That's not the point, Vlad. They were acting under orders, and they have support that not only goes high, it goes broad—widespread. At the Imperial level, too many people are involved for there to be just one person pulling the strings from behind a closet."

"Hmmm. I see your point. But with that many involved, how can it stay secret?"

"There's secret, and then there's secret, Vlad. If, in a year or two, the Empress starts to hear whispers about so-and-so having pulled a scam in the Fyres's investigation, there won't be much she can do about it, depending on who so-and-so is."

"In other words, it can leak, as long as it doesn't break."

"Something like that." I shrugged. "I'm just speculating, based on what I know about the Court, but it's a pretty good guess. You know," I added, "you're in over your head, Vlad. I'd call for help."

Vlad laughed without humor. "Call for help? From whom? Sethra Lavode? She's taken on the whole Empire before. You think she'd do it now? Without knowing why, or what's involved? And just what exactly are Iceflame and the power of Dzur Mountain going to do against a snotty little intrigue? Or maybe you mean Morrolan. He could solve the whole thing by inviting our hostess to move into Castle Black, but I don't think she'll go for it, and he doesn't have any connections in the House of the Orca. Aliera would love to go charging into this, Kiera, but subtlety isn't her strong suit—she'd just kill everyone who was acting dirty, and we'd have the same mess with a bunch of bodies to complicate things. Norathar would be the one who could solve it—if this was the Dragon Reign. But, last I heard, Zerika is still on the throne—at least technically."

I didn't quite know how to answer that, so I didn't. He said, "And remember, I don't really care what the Empire is doing or to whom, as long I can do what I promised Hid— Hwid—the old woman I'd do and she can help Savn. Do you care?"

That was tough. I *did* care—but . . . "No," I said. "You're right. But it may be that we have to deal with the whole thing in order to solve our little problem. I don't know."

"Neither do I," said Vlad.

"What do we know, then?"

"We know the Empire is covering up something—very possibly murder. We know that not all of the investigators know about it, and we know that not all of the ones who do

are happy about it, but that the orders include killing anyone who knows what's going on. We know that there is a
big tangle about who owns what parts of Fyres's property,
and that finding out who owns this blue cottage and its en-
virons is not going to be easy. And we know that something, somewhere, is very wrong."

"Wrong how?" I said.

"The timing—it's funny and I'm not laughing."

"Go on," I said, though I was starting to realize that I
knew—that I'd been subconsciously aware of something
being strange about how things had been happening.

"What's the hurry? When someone as rich as Fyres dies,
it's sort of expected to take fifty or a hundred or two hundred years to sort out who owns what. But they're not only
putting a coat of paint over this investigation, they're doing
it in an awful hurry. And not just the Empire—everyone associated with it."

"What do you mean by everyone?"

"I mean," he said carefully, "that Fyres had been dead
for maybe a week when our hostess was told to vacate, and
she was given six months in which to do it. Now, that
doesn't make any sense at all, unless there are two things
going on: one, the land is valuable somehow; and, two,
someone, somewhere, is panicking."

I nodded. Yeah, that was it. I said, "Almost. I agree
about the panic, but the land doesn't have to be particularly
valuable."

"Oh? Then why—"

"Someone wants to take it, get as much cash as he can
for it, and be gone before it comes out that it wasn't his
land to sell in the first place."

"Ah," said Vlad. "Yes, that makes sense." He thought for
a moment. "Unfortunately, it doesn't help—it doesn't point

to anyone in particular, and it doesn't even eliminate anyone."

"True," I said.

"Which still leaves us with the problem of finding out,
which, in turn, brings up the next question: What now?"

I was able to answer that one, anyway. "Now," I said,
"we sleep on it. It's late, and my brain is tired. We'll talk
again in the morning."

"Okay. Meet here?"

"Yes."

"I'll cook breakfast."

"I'll bring something to cook."

"It's a pleasure working with you, Kiera."

I spent the night trying to make sense of everything I'd
learned; I'd have bet Juinan's Pearl against a pound of tea
that Vlad did the same. And I'd have won, judging by the
look on his face when I got there the next morning.

"Not much sleep?" I suggested sweetly.

He scowled and went back to making klava. I put the
groceries on the counter next to him and said, "Goose eggs,
sneershrimp, endive, cynth, orange and black fungus, and
various sweet and hot peppers. Also a pound of flatbread.
Make breakfast."

"Onions?"

"She has them growing in back."

"Garlic?"

"Hanging in a basket about six centimeters from your
right hand. Observant, aren't we?"

"You can talk to Loiosh," he said.

Loiosh, curled up with Rocza near the cold hearth,
twitched and probably said something to Vlad. Hwdf'rjaanci
emerged from the back, toweling her hair dry. "You've
made the klava," she said.

"Yeah," said Vlad. "I hope it isn't too strong."

"Don't make jokes," she said.

Savn was still wrapped up in his furs, but he was awake and staring at the ceiling. I noticed that Vlad was looking at him, too. The old woman said, "I'm going to go in today."

I heard Vlad's sharp intake of breath—or maybe it was mine. "Dreamwalk?" I said.

"No, I'm just going to heal the physical damage. There isn't much of it, and I've looked carefully—it won't hurt him, and it might start the healing process."

Vlad nodded, turned back to the kitchen, and began to prepare breakfast. Hwdf'rjaanci sat on the floor near Savn's head. I chopped things and sampled them. He didn't make any comments about my doing so, which meant either he was unique in my experience with cooks, or he was distracted, or he was uncomfortable because no one had done that since he and Cawti had broken up. I felt a little bad for him, but not bad enough to stop sampling things. The peppers were exquisite.

He said, "There are few sounds more beautiful than that made by a mess of onions landing on a cast-iron skillet with a layer of hot oil. The trick is getting them to just the right degree of done before you start adding other things, and then to not let them go too much further before you add the eggs—the eggs have to be last because they don't take as long—"

"What's on your mind, Vlad?"

He shrugged. "The same thing that's on yours, of course—are we going to be able to solve our hostess's problem without taking on, in effect, the whole Empire? And, if we do have to take on the Empire, how can we win? It's bound to be tricky."

"Tricky," I said. I shook my head. "You're nothing if not confident."

He shrugged. "It shouldn't be any problem. I'll just work my way through these special Guardsmen, find out who their boss is, kill him, take his position, use that to get close to the Empress, kill her, take the Orb, and rule Dragaera myself, exploiting the Empire ruthlessly in order to enrich myself and punish those who have offended me throughout my life, in preparation for conquering the East and eventually making myself ruler of the entire world." He paused from whipping the eggs, looked at me, and nodded somberly. "*Then* I'd meet some girls, I'll bet." He covered the pan. "Want to set the table for four?"

"Three," said our hostess, who was still seated next to the boy but was now staring down at him while holding both of his shoulders. "Savn will be needing his rest."

I looked at her, then at Savn, then at Vlad, who was looking at me. I opened my mouth to speak and then felt the casting of a spell. Vlad apparently felt it, too, or more accurately Loiosh did; in any case we both turned to watch, then looked again at each other. Vlad's eyes were a bit wide, but he shrugged.

"Don't let the food burn," I said.

"I shan't," said Vlad, and turned his attention back to the skillet. I set the table. The feeling of sorcery went away about two minutes after it had started, and then the old woman joined us at the table and we ate. She didn't seem quite comfortable with Loiosh and Rocza joining us and eating scraps from Vlad's plate, even though she should have been used to it by now. But she didn't say anything. Buddy sat next to the table and spoke most eloquently with his eyes but got nothing for his trouble, poor beast. The food was good and there was no conversation for quite some time, until I noticed that Vlad was watching me.

I said, "What is it?"

"Don't you care for it?"

"Are you fishing for compliments?"

"No."

I shrugged. "I like it quite a bit."

"All right," he said.

I don't know anyone like Vlad: it's like his mind never shuts off. Even Morrolan relaxes from time to time, but I've never seen Vlad when he wasn't thinking. I very much wanted to know what he was thinking about just then, but there was no polite way to ask.

Vlad broke down before I did. He said, "Well, Mother?"

She said, "Yes?"

He cleared his throat. "How did—that is, is Savn all right?"

"You mean his injury?"

"Yes."

"Yes, I healed it. It isn't difficult if you know what you're doing. I'm not really a physicker, but I am a sorceress"—she looked at me as she said it, as if expecting me to argue—"and this is the sort of problem I'm most familiar with."

"So it went well?" asked Vlad. Vlad needing reassurance was something outside of my experience.

"Quite well."

"Uh, good," he said.

"What now?" I asked her.

"Now? Well, repairing the physical damage ought to help him, so now we see if there's any change in his behavior—better or worse. If not, then I'll go back to trying to understand the inside of his head well enough to risk a dreamwalk. If there is a change, well, then we'll just have to see what the change is and do our best from there."

"Oh," said Vlad. He glanced at Savn, who was sleeping peacefully, and fell silent.

We finished eating, and Vlad and I cleaned up. I took my

time, because I wasn't in a hurry to go back to talking about how we were going to approach the problem. Vlad also seemed to be moving a bit slowly, I suspect for the same reason. I drew the water, he set it to heating, then we took our time sorting things that went into the compost from things to be burned and things to feed to Buddy. When the water was hot, I started in on the dishes. Vlad cleaned the table and the stove.

As we were finishing up, I said, "How's the arm?"

"Fine."

"Let's take a look at it."

"When did you become a physicker?"

"One learns a bit of everything in my line of work—or in yours."

"Yeah."

He took his shirt off. His chest was still full of hairs; I tried not to react. I unwrapped the bandage. Some people look at their wounds, others look away. Vlad looked, but he seemed a bit queasy. The lower wrappings of the bandage were bloody, but not horribly so, and the wound itself showed no signs of infection.

I said, "If you want to take the Phoenix Stone off, I can have that healed up in—"

"No, thanks," said Vlad.

"You're probably right," I said.

I washed it and rewrapped it. Hwdf'rjaanci watched but made no effort to help—maybe blood made her queasy; maybe she considered herself too much of a specialist to be bothered with simple wounds.

I said, "Okay, if you've changed your mind about ruling the world, and you don't want to ask anyone for help, what's our next step?"

"I went through the notes again last night, after you left," said Vlad.

"And?"

"And nothing. If we had all the files as well as the Imperial record, and maybe some of the records of a few Jhereg, and we combined those with what we've got, and we had a hundred accountants working full-time, we could probably find the answer—and maybe even find it soon enough to do some good. But we don't, so we're going to have to start from the other end."

"And the other end is?"

"The investigation. We have a piece of something—all I can think of to do is follow it and see where it leads."

I nodded. "Yeah. I was afraid it was going to come to that."

"Meanwhile," he said, "I'm going to see just how much money it will take to buy the land."

I nodded. "Yes. The amount should tell us if you're right about there being something valuable about this piece of property. If it comes down to nothing more than finding a sum of money, there are ways to do that."

I noticed Hwdf'rjaanci looking at us. Vlad said, "That, of course, is my end of things. What do you want to do?"

"I want to find out just who Loftis is working for, what his orders are, what he knows, what he guesses, and what he plans to do about it," I said.

"Good thinking," said Vlad. "How do you plan to go about it?"

"I don't know. I thought maybe I'd ask him."

"I can't see why that wouldn't work."

"Yeah."

"Then let's do it," said Vlad.

I finished bandaging him, and he put his shirt on, then his cloak, then his sword belt. He petted Buddy, recommended the cottage to him, collected Loiosh, and left with a sweeping bow.

"They're disgusting," said Hwdf'rjaanci.

"Who?"

"Easterners," she said.

I said, "Ah. I'll tell him you said so, Mother."

"Oh don't," she said, looking suddenly distressed. "It would hurt his feelings."

I collected my things and stepped out of the door. Unlike Vlad, I had no reason not to teleport, so I did, arriving at a place I knew where I could change my garb a little, which I did. I arrived outside of City Hall at just about the tenth hour, which was when things ought to begin moving there. I took a position across the street, became inconspicuous, and waited.

I'd been there for more than an hour when Vlad showed up and went in, and then nothing happened for quite some time, and I was beginning to think I'd missed Loftis—that he'd gotten in early—when I saw him on the other side of the street, just approaching; from Vlad's description, it had to be Loftis. I crossed over and walked past him, and even that brief a glance was enough to confirm that Vlad was right—this wasn't someone to mess around with casually. He was frowning as he walked, like he had something on his mind; it wasn't hard to guess what it was.

I found an inn that let rooms by the hour and rented one—this is a good way to find a place where you won't be disturbed and won't be talked about, even if you don't use the room for the reasons they expect you to. They had put in a real door, to ensure the guests had privacy, and I liked that, too. Instead of a tag, it was Loftis's papers and possessions that I spread out on the bed; then I commenced to study them. He had not, in fact, been polite enough to be carrying a note that spelled out what he'd been asked to do, the reasons behind it, and the name of his superior officer, but we make do with what we have, and the pouch of an Imperial investigator can hardly fail to be revealing.

His name was, indeed, Loftis, a Dragonlord of the e'Drien line, same as Morrolan; and he was the Viscount of Clovenrocks Wood, which was in a far northeastern province, if I could trust a memory that wasn't my own. He had three Signets. I knew he'd have at least one, I was counting on it—but three indicated he was, indeed, high up in the counsels of the great and powerful who ran the Empire. And the oldest of the Signets—which included authorization to make arrests—was two hundred years old, which meant he'd have to have been in the Imperial Service at least two hundred and fifty years, which is a long time to only be a lieutenant—unless, of course, he was in one of those branches of the service where traditional ranks were meaningless, which would explain the irony Vlad had detected when he and Domm had called each other by their ranks.

I knew about four such services, all of them more or less independent. Well, there was a fifth, but that hadn't existed in some years except for one person—and whoever Loftis was, he wasn't Sethra Lavode. I considered the four services I knew about, and speculated uncomfortably about the possibility of there being one I hadn't heard of.

One of them was the Imperial Surveillance Corps. They were responsible to the Prime Minister, when there was one, or to the Minister of the Houses when there wasn't. The Minister of the Houses was presently an Issola named Indus, and I'd play cards with her only as long as she never got near the deck. She was tricky, but she was loyal—she'd do something like this if she was ordered to, and it might well fall within her province, but the order would have to come from Zerika. If anyone but the Empress tried to use Indus . . . well, anyone who knew enough about her to ask would know better than to try. So either it wasn't Indus, or the order came from the Empress, and I was convinced the order hadn't come from the Empress.

The same argument applied to "Third Floor Relic," which was named for the room where they supposedly met with Her Majesty. There were only about twenty or thirty of them at any one time, and, while they were very good at what they did, it took the Empress's orders to get them to do it. Also, it seemed unlikely that they'd be involved in something this widespread—narrow and specific objectives were more their style.

The other two units I knew about were both part of the military. One of them, the one that was publicly acknowledged to exist, was Division Six of the Imperial Army General Staff Consultants. They did most of their work on foreign soil, but could certainly be used in the Empire if the situation warranted. They were big, unwieldy, often confused, sometimes brilliant, and responsible to the Warlord. The Warlord wouldn't allow them to be used this way if the Empress didn't approve, but they were big enough that it just might be possible for someone in the hierarchy to have been corrupted. If it *was* Division Six, though, they'd be unlikely to be able to keep it secret very long—at least, not secret from those who knew where to look.

And then there was the Special Tasks Group, which was small, very well trained, easily capable of covering up mistakes by the other groups (and was often used for exactly that), and, in fact, perfect for jobs like this. But *they* reported to Lord Khaavren—he would never allow them to be used this way without orders from the Empress, and if the Empress did give such an order, he'd have another one of his temper tantrums and resign again.

I chewed it over as I put the contents of Loftis's pouch back together. Then I sat on the bed (the only piece of fur-

niture in the room) and continued thinking it over. There
were good reasons why it couldn't be any of those groups,
but it seemed very unlikely that there was another team involved that I hadn't heard of—I keep very well abreast of
what's happening around the Palace, on both sides of the
walls, as they say.

I tried to remember everything Vlad had told me about
his dealings with the group, including every nuance of expression he'd picked up. Of course, it isn't easy when
you're twice removed from the conversation. And I didn't
have long to figure it out, either. I checked the time. No, I
didn't have long at all.

I went over all the information again and shook my head.
If I had to guess, I'd say Surveillance, just because it involved the Empire and the House of the Orca and, above
all, because under normal circumstances they're the ones
who would conduct such an investigation—being checked
up on, no doubt, by the Third Floor group. But it still didn't
make sense. Could it be Division Six? While they were the
most likely in that they'd think they could get away with it,
they just didn't have the reputation for switching so easily
from pulling cover-up jobs to rough stuff—they were
mostly a bunch of clerks with a big budget, some half-
competent thieves, and a lot of people who knew how to
spread money around. No, Surveillance was more likely,
only I had trouble squaring that with what I knew about
Lady Indus—if a request like that fell into her lap, she'd—

Now, what did that remind me of?

*Or we could just dump the whole thing on Papa-cat's
lap.*

That had been a threat. A threat to tell the man in charge
what they were doing—which meant, first, that, although
they were acting under orders, they weren't acting under

orders of their own chief. And, second, that the man in charge was, in fact, a man, which neatly eliminated Indus.

Papa-cat.

Cat.

Tiassa.

Lord Khaavren.

As Vlad would say, "Ah ha."

There was the sound of heavy boots outside the room, and the door went crashing down. I was looking at a man and a woman, both of whom had swords drawn and pointed at me. I tossed the purse to the man and said, "In the first place, Loftis, tell Timmer to go back to City Hall, it's you I want to talk to. And in the second place, you'll be paying for that door out of your own pocket; I don't think Papa-cat will authorize it when he hears what it's for—*if* he hears what it's for."

They stared at me.

I said, "Well? What are you waiting for? Lose your associate, come in here, and sit down. Oh, Ensign, on your way out, set up a sound field around this room—I assume you're equipped for that, aren't you? And take care of anyone who might be coming up to look into the noise of the door breaking. Tell the host it's all right and your friend will pay for the damages. Which he will," I added.

She looked at Loftis. He gave her a bit of a half-smile, as if to say, "Whatever this is, it's bound to be good," then nodded. She gave me one quick glance, and I could see her committing me to memory, then she was gone. Loftis came in and leaned against the far wall, still holding his sword.

I said, "Put that thing away."

He said, "Sure. As soon as you explain why I shouldn't arrest you."

I rolled my eyes. "You think I'm a thief?"

He shook his head. "I *know* you're a thief—and quite an

accomplished one, since you got this off me just passing in the street. But I don't know what *else* you are."

I shrugged. "I'm a thief, Lieutenant. I'm a thief who happens to know your name, your rank, your associate's name and rank, and that you work for Lord Khaavren's Special Tasks Group; and I'm so stupid that I took your purse but didn't bother with a spell to prevent you from tracing the Signets, didn't *ditch* the Signets, but instead just sat here waiting for you to arrive so I could hand the purse back to you. That's right, Lieutenant, I'm a thief."

He shrugged. "When someone starts reeling off what he knows like that, it always makes me wonder if I'm supposed to be so impressed that I'll start reeling things off, too. What do you say?"

He wasn't stupid. "That you're not stupid. But you're still pointing a sword at me, and I find that irritating."

"Learn to live with it. Who are you and what do you want? If you really went through all of that just to get me here, you're either very foolish or you have some explanation that—"

"Do you remember a certain affair three or four years ago, that started out with Division Six looking into the activities of a wizard working for, uh, a foreign kingdom, and ending up with a Jenoine at Dzur Mountain."

He stared at me, licked his lips, and said, "I've heard about it."

"Do you remember what you—your group—was assigned to do after Division Six had bungled it?"

He watched me very closely. "Yes," he said.

"That's what I'm here to do, only this time it's you who are making a mess of things."

He was silent for a moment. "Possible," he said.

"Then let's talk. I'm not armed—"

He laughed. "Sure you're not. And Temping had no reserves at the Battle of Plowman's Bridge."

I raised my eyebrows at him. He said, "Eighth Cycle, two hundred and fifth year of the Tiassa Reign, the Whetstone Rising. The Warlord was—"

"I am not, in fact, armed," I cut him off. "At least, not with a conventional weapon."

He raised his eyebrows back at me.

I said, "What I've got for armament is a letter, being held quite safely, that is ready to go to Her Majesty if I fail to appear. The object, in fact, doesn't have anything to do with you, it's to make sure certain influential parties are disassociated from this affair, and appear clean when it blows up. What it will do to your career is, in fact, just a side effect, but that won't change how it hits you when Lord Khaavren learns what you've been up to. You know him better than I do, my dear lieutenant—what will he do? And it won't help to try to keep the letter from reaching the Imperial Palace the way you, or your people, did in the Berdoign business, because the letter is already in the Palace. I think that's better than a conventional weapon, under the circumstances, don't you?"

"You are very well informed," he said. I could see him wondering if I was lying, then deciding he couldn't take the chance. He smiled, bowed his head slightly, and sheathed his sword. "Let's talk, then," he said. "I'm listening."

"Good. We'll start with the basics. You've been given an assignment that you dislike—"

He snorted. " 'Dislike' would cover it," he said, "if stretched very thin."

"Nevertheless," I continued, "you're doing what you were instructed to do. Whatever else you are, you're a soldier."

He shrugged.

I said, "I represent, as I said, certain interests very close to, but not quite the same as, those who required you to carry out this mission. I would prefer that our efforts were combined, to a limited extent, because my job, to put it simply, is to clean up after your efforts to clean up. I have a certain hold on you, but not, I know, a strong one—"

"You got that right," he said, smiling.

"—in that you'd prefer Lord Khaavren didn't learn what you're up to."

"Don't think you can push that too far, lady," he said.

"I know how far I can push it."

"Maybe. And what do I call you, by the way?"

"Margaret," I said. "I fancy Eastern names."

"Heh. You and Her Majesty."

He'd thrown that out, I assumed, to see if I was up on current gossip; I gave him a slight smile to show that I was. He said, "Very well, then, Margaret. For whom do you work?"

"For whom do *you* work?"

"But you know that—or, at least, you laid out a theory which I haven't disputed."

"No, I've told you that I know the organization you work for, not where the orders came from to slide through the Fyres's investigation."

"So do you know who gave those orders?"

"Why don't you tell me, Loftis?"

He smiled. "So we've found a piece of information you lack."

"Maybe," I said, returning his smile. "And maybe I'm just trying to find out if you're planning to be straight with me."

"Trade?" he suggested.

"No," I said. "You'd lie. I'd lie. Besides, in point of fact, I know, anyway."

"Oh?"

"There's only one possibility."

He looked inscrutable. "If you say so."

I shrugged.

He said, "All right, then. What do you want?"

"As I told you before, cooperation."

"What sort of cooperation? Be specific. You don't want to share information, because we'd both lie, and because you don't seem to need any, and because there's really nothing I need to know. So what *do* you want, exactly?"

"Wrong on several counts," I said.

"Oh?"

"As I told you, I'm here to keep this business from getting out of hand. I'll blow the whistle on you if I have to, but I, and those who've given me this job, would prefer I didn't. Now, what we have—"

"What cleanup are you talking about, Margaret?"

"Oh, come on, Loftis. Your security's been broken all over town. Didn't you just have someone show up out of nowhere, interrogate your interrogators, lead your shadows all over the region, pump them some more, and then almost kill them in a public inn? Is that your idea of secrecy?"

He studied me carefully, and I wondered if I'd gone too far. He grunted and said, "My compliments on your sources, Margaret."

"Well?"

"Okay, you've made your point. What do you want?"

"Let's start with the basics," I said. "I have to know what I'm working with."

"Heh," he said. "There's something you don't know?"

I smiled. "How many on your team?"

"Six, with another three on standby."

"How many know what you're up to?"

"Domm and I."

"And Timmer," I added, "as of last night."

He frowned. "Are you sure?"

I shrugged. "She may not know precisely, but she knows something's up, and, if she thinks about it, she'll probably figure out most of it. She isn't stupid."

He nodded. "Okay. What else do you want to know?"

"What actually happened to Fyres."

Loftis shrugged. "He was murdered."

I shook my head. "I know that. But who killed him?"

"An assassin. A good one. Hundred to one it was a Jhereg, and another hundred to one that we wouldn't catch him even if we were trying to."

"Yeah," I said. "Okay. Who had it done?"

"I don't know," said Loftis. "That isn't what we were trying to find out."

"Sure, but you probably have an idea."

"An idea? Hell, yeah. His wife hated him, his son loathed him, one daughter wants to be rich and the other one wants to be left alone. Is that good enough for a start?"

"No," I said.

He looked at me, then turned away. "Yeah, it wasn't them. Or, at least, it wasn't just them."

"Well, then?"

"The House of the Orca, I think. And the Jhereg. And someone, somewhere, high up in the Empire—like, maybe, whoever it was who hired you?" He'd slipped his right hand down behind his leg, where he was, no doubt, concealing something, and I hadn't even seen him do it.

"No," I said. "But good guess."

He shrugged. "What else do you want to know?"

I wanted to know how Loftis had been conned, or pressured, into doing this in the first place, but this was the wrong time to ask. I said, "That'll do for now. I'll be in touch."

"Okay. Pleasure meeting you, Margaret."

"And you, Lieutenant."

I got up and walked out of the room, my back itching as I passed him, but he made no move. On the way out of the inn, I flipped the host a couple of imperials and apologized about the door. I walked around some corners to make sure I wasn't being followed, then I teleported back to the blue cottage and went in.

Vlad was waiting for me. He said, "Well?"

One disadvantage of teleports is that they sometimes get you there too quickly—I hadn't had time to sort out my thoughts yet. I said, "Is there anything to eat?"

"No. I could cook something."

I nodded. "That would be good. I'm a bit tired."

"Oh?" said Vlad.

"I'll get to it."

He shrugged. Savn was near the hearth, sitting up and looking at nothing. Hwdf'rjaanci sat hear him, with Buddy at her feet. Buddy watched me as he always did, but wasn't unfriendly. Loiosh sat on Vlad's shoulder. I felt like I'd been through a pitched battle, and it was somehow amazing that no one in the house shared my exhaustion.

Vlad said, "Do you want to hear my news first, or after yours?"

I said, "Let's look at your arm."

Vlad shrugged, started to speak, and then apparently realized that I wasn't ready to think about anything quite yet. He wordlessly took off his shirt. I undid the bandage and inspected the wound, which seemed about the same as it had four hours earlier.

Only four hours!

I washed it and walked over to the linen chest to find something clean to wrap it in.

"It's fine," I said.

"I suppose so," said Vlad.

"You've been stabbed," said Savn.

Chapter Eight

EVEN BUDDY—TAIL thumping and floppy ears vainly trying to prick forward—was staring at him. He, in turn, was staring at Vlad's arm—an intense stare, a creepy stare; he was standing up, his whole body rigid. Savn's voice had the uneven rasp of long disuse, or of young adulthood, take your pick. He said, "You were stabbed with a knife."

"That's right, Savn," said Vlad, and I could hear him working to keep his voice even. He didn't move a muscle. Hwdf'rjaanci wasn't moving, either; for that matter, neither was I.

"Was it really cold when it went in? Did it hurt? How deep did it go?"

Vlad made some odd sort of sound from his throat. Savn's questions came slowly, as if there was a great deal of consideration behind them; but the tone was of casual curiosity, which in turn was at odds with his posture—it was very unsettling for me, and I could see that it was even more so for Vlad.

"Not all knives have points, you know," said Savn. "Some of them you can't stab with, only *cut*." As he said that word, he made a quick cutting gesture with his right hand; and that was creepy, too, because while he did it the rest of his body didn't move, and his face didn't change expression; it was only the arm movement and the emphasis in his voice.

"Only cut," he said again.

Then he didn't say anything else. We waited, not moving, for several minutes, but he'd said what he had to say. Vlad said, "Savn?" and got no response. Savn sat down again, but that also showed something—he hadn't been told to. Vlad came over and knelt down facing him. "Savn? Are you . . . are you all right?"

The boy just sat the way he'd been sitting all along. Vlad turned and said, "What happened, Mother?"

"I don't know," she said. "But I think it's a good sign. I know it's a good sign. I don't know how good, but we're getting somewhere."

"You think that came from healing the injury?"

"Maybe. Or maybe it was time. Or the right stimulus. Or some combination. Have you been cut in the last year?"

"Not even threatened," said Vlad.

"Then that may be it."

"What do we do now? Should I cut myself some more?" I wasn't certain he was joking.

"I'm not sure," she said. "Talk about knives, maybe."

I was watching Savn the whole time, and at the word "knives" there was a perceptible twitch around the left side of his mouth. Vlad saw it, too. He said, "Savn, do you want to talk about knives?"

The boy's expression didn't change, but he said, "You have to take care of the good ones. A good knife is expensive. The good ones stay sharp longer, too. Sometimes you have to cut people to heal them, and you should use a really good one, and a really sharp one for that. You can hurt someone more with a dull knife than with a sharp knife."

"Are you afraid of knives?" said Vlad.

Savn didn't seem to hear him. He said, "You should always clean it when you're done—wash it and dry it. You have to dry it, especially. It won't rust—the good ones are made so they don't rust. But if you leave something on it, it can corrode, and that ruins it, and good knives are expensive. Good knives stay sharp. They get sharper and sharper the more they're used, until they get so sharp they can cut you right in half just by looking at you."

"Knives don't get sharper on their own," said Vlad.

"And they can stab you, too. If the point is sharp, it can stab all the way through you, and all the way through everybody, and stab the sky until it falls, and stab all the way through everything."

Then he fell silent once more. After a couple of minutes, Vlad turned around and said, "He isn't responding to what I say, Mother."

"No," she said. "But you got him started. That means, on some level, he is responding to you."

Vlad turned back and looked at him some more. I tried to read the expression on Vlad's face, then decided I didn't want to.

He got up and came over to where Hwdf'rjaanci and I stood watching. He whispered to her, "Should I try again, or let him rest?"

She frowned. "Let him rest, I think. If he starts up again on his own, we'll take it from there."

"Doing what?" I said.

"I don't know. I'm encouraged, but I don't know."

"All right," said Vlad. "I'm going to make some klava."

By the time it was done, Savn had gone to sleep—perhaps talking for the first time after a year's silence had tired him out. We drank our klava standing on the far side of the room, near the stove and the oven. Hwdf'rjaanci eventually went over and sat down next to the boy, watching him while he slept. Vlad took a deep breath and said, "All right, let's hear it."

"Huh? Hear what?"

He laughed. "What you came in with an hour ago, and were so excited about that you had to take some time before you could talk about it. Remember?"

"Oh." I felt myself smiling. "Oh, that."

"Yeah. Let's hear it."

I nodded and gave him the short version, which took about ten minutes. He said, "Let's have it all."

"Do you really need it?"

"I won't know until I hear it."

I was going to argue, but then I realized that if he'd given me the short version of his sortie, I wouldn't have made the connection to Lord Khaavren, and my talk with Loftis would have gone rather differently. So I filled in most of the details, helped now and then by Vlad's questions. He seemed especially interested in exactly when everything had happened and in precisely how I'd fooled Loftis—that, in particular, he wanted me to go over several times, until I felt like I was being questioned under the Orb. I pleaded poor memory for the parts of it I didn't want to talk about and eventually he relented, but when I was done, he looked at me oddly.

"What is it?" I said.

"Eh? Oh, nothing, Kiera. I'm just impressed—I didn't know you had that in you."

"The deception or remembering the details?"

"Both, actually."

I shrugged. "And how was your day?"

"Much shorter, much simpler, much easier to report, and probably more mystifying."

"Oh?"

"In a word: they're closed."

"Huh?"

"Gone. Finished. Doors locked, signs gone."

"Who is?"

"All of them: Northport Securities, Brugan Exchange, Westman—all of them."

"The whole building?"

"About three-quarters of the building, near as I can tell—but all of the companies that were part of Fyres's little empire are gone."

"Verra! What did you do?"

"I went to City Hall—remember, you saw me there?"

"Yes, but for what?"

"Well, the building was still open; I thought I'd find out who owned it."

"Good thinking. And who owns the building?"

"A company called Dion and Sons Management."

"And?"

He shrugged. "And they're located right in the same building, and they're out of business, too."

"Oh."

"Yeah. So much for bright ideas."

"Well, what now, Vlad?"

"I don't know. How can they sell the land if the company that claims ownership doesn't exist? If they can't, we could just forget the whole thing right now; all we're really trying to accomplish is to keep the old woman on her land. But I'm afraid that, if we do that, someone will show up—"

"Is that it?"

"What do you mean and why are you smiling?"

"I just have a feeling that you're hooked on this thing

now—you have to find out what's going on for its own sake."

He smiled. "You think so? Well, you may be right, I *am* curious, but you show me some proof that our hostess here is going to be able to keep her lovely blue cottage and I'll be gone so fast you'll only feel the breeze."

"Heh."

He shrugged. "What about you?"

"Me?"

"Yeah. Aren't you curious?"

"Oh, heavens yes. That's a big part of why I signed onto this. But I'm willing to admit it, and you—"

"Yeah, well, ask me again tomorrow and I might give you a different answer. Meanwhile—"

"Yes. Meanwhile, what next?"

"Well, any interest in starting at the top and trying to find out who in the Empire is behind all this?"

"No."

"Me, neither." He thought for a minute. "Well, I'm not sure if I've gotten anywhere with the daughters, so we can't count on that for anything, but we've got one foot in the door with our dear friend from the Tasks Group—thanks to you. And we've got another foot in the door with the Jhereg—thanks to you. So how about if we try for a third foot—anatomically interesting, if nothing else—and triangulate?"

"What did you have in mind?"

"Finding this bank that closed down."

I thought it over. "Not bad. Just keep worrying away at different sides of the problem and see what gives?"

He spread his hands. "That's all I can think of."

"It makes sense. Do you want me to do it?"

He nodded. "I think you'll be more effective dealing

with bankers than I will. I'm going to hang tight right here, and see if I can do Savn any good."

He said it conversationally, but I could tell there was a lot of tension behind the words. I spoke lightly, saying, "Yes, that makes sense. I'll see what I can find."

"After lunch," he suggested.

Lunch, on this occasion, involved a loaf of bread which was hollowed out and filled with some kind of reddish sauce that had large chunks of this and that in it, featuring pieces of chicken with the skin but without the bones. Savn sat at the table with us, eating mechanically and appearing, once more, oblivious to everything around him. This dampened the conversation a bit. It seemed odd that Savn happily used the knife in front of him to eat with and didn't seem at all put out or unduly fascinated by it, but the ways of the mind are strange, I guess.

I suggested to Vlad that if the Jhereg really wanted to find him, all they had to do was keep track of garlic consumption throughout the Empire. He suggested that I not spread the idea around, because he'd as soon let them find him as quit eating garlic.

Then we got onto business. I said, "Mother, you said the bank closed?"

She nodded.

"Which bank?"

She glanced at me, then at Vlad, opened her mouth, closed it, shrugged, and said, "Northport Private Services Bank. Are you going to rob it?"

"If it's closed," I said, "I doubt there's any money in it—or anything else for that matter."

"Probably," said Vlad. Then he frowned. "Unless . . ."

"Unless what?"

"I'm remembering something."

I waited.

He said, "That gossip sheet, *Rutter's Rag,* said something about the banks."

"Yes?"

"It made a point of how quickly everyone got out of there." He turned to Hwdf'rjaanci. "Do you know anything about that, Mother?"

She said, "I know it closed down fast. My friend Henbrook—it was her bank, too, and I don't know *what* she's going to do—anyway, she was in town that day, and she said they were open just like usual at thirteen o'clock, and at fourteen there were these wagons there—the big wagons, with armed guards and everything—and by noon it was shut up tight."

Vlad nodded. "Two hours. They took two hours to clear the place out."

Hwdf'rjaanci agreed. "They had a hundred men, and wagons lined up all down the street. And the other banks, too, went the same way, at the same time, near as I can tell."

"In which case," said Vlad, "they can't have done a very good job of it."

"What do you mean?"

"I mean clearing things out. They were in a hurry to be gone before their customers got to them, and—"

"Then why not seal things inside?"

He shrugged. "Too much sorcery floating around. Get people mad enough, and at least one of them will be able to tear down the building."

"Okay," I said. "I'll buy that. But do you really think it likely that there's anything still in there?"

"Oh, I doubt there's any money in it, but you never know what might be left behind."

"You mean, papers and things?"

He nodded.

"If they went under, wouldn't they be careful to clean up anything worth looking at?"

"How much time would it take to clean up every last scrap of paper, Kiera? Could they do it in two hours?"

"Probably not. But all the important ones—"

"Maybe. But maybe not. I don't know how banks operate, but they're bound to generate immense amounts of paperwork, and—"

"And you're willing to wade through immense amounts of paper, just to see if there might be something useful?"

"Right now, any edge we can get amounts to a lot. Yeah, I don't mind taking an evening to go through their wastebaskets—or, rather, papers that missed the wastebaskets—and see if there's something that points us anywhere interesting."

I thought it over for a minute. "You're right," I said. "I'll look around and get what I can; it should be easy enough." I turned to Hwdf'rjaanci. "Where is it?"

"In town," she said. "Stonework Road, near the Potter's Field Road." She gave me more precise directions.

"Okay," I said. "I'll look around it today. Since you're so used to going to City Hall, can you—"

"Find out who owns it? Sure."

"But just get the name and address."

"Right. I should have cooked some vegetables to go with this."

"I wouldn't have had room for them," I said.

"That's true. You don't eat much, do you?"

"I'm trying to keep my slender girlish figure."

"Ah. That's what it is."

We finished, and, since I was doing the dangerous work, I allowed him to volunteer to clean up. Not that there was that much to clean up after Loiosh, Rocza, and Buddy got through with the plates.

"All right," I said, " 'Once more upon the path, and may the wind cry our tale.' "

"Villsni?"

"Kliburr." I headed out the door.

Vlad said, "I don't know how you do it, Kiera."

"Eh? You're the one with all the quotations. I was just imitating you."

"No, not that—teleporting right after a meal. I just don't know how you manage."

I managed fine, bringing myself, first, home to Adri-lankha to acquire some tools, and then to the same teleport spot I'd used before, it being one of very few I knew in Northport. Then I set out to find the bank, which was easy from the directions I'd been given. I was looking forward to this. I'd never broken into a bank before, and certainly never in the middle of the day; the fact that the bank was now out of business only took a little of the fun away.

And it was, indeed, out of business—there was a large sign on it that spelled out "Permanently Closed," along with the water and hand symbol for those who couldn't read, and there were large boards over all the windows, and bars across the doors. I walked around it once. It was an attractive building, two stories high with a set of six pillars in front, and all done in very fine stonework. It took up about a hundred and forty meters across the front and went back about a hundred and ninety meters, and there were no alleys behind it—just a big cleared area that had become an impromptu produce market since it closed. The cleared area was, no doubt, to make sure that the guards had a good view.

On the other hand, now that it was closed, there seemed to be no security worth mentioning—certainly no one on duty there, and only the most basic and easily defeated alarm spells, proving that there was no money left in it. *Anyone* could have broken into the bank at this stage, and anyone would have done so just the way I was going to— which showed that no one thought there was anything at all of interest there. I shrugged. I'd know soon enough.

One of the devices I'd gotten from home was in the form of a tube that fit snugly into my hand. I palmed it and leaned against the building. I placed the tube against the wall, and in a few seconds I was seeing the inside of the building, and in a few more seconds I was seeing it clearly enough to teleport; no one was looking at me, so I did.

There was a minor spell inside to detect sorcery, so I disabled it before doing a light spell, then I started looking around.

There really isn't any point in going into the details. It was big, and it was empty, and there was a lot of small offices, two vaults, and a basement, and I looked at them all, and it took me about four and a half hours, and at the end of it I had a bag full of scraps of paper. The good news, or the bad news, was that I'd found right away a very large bin full of papers that they'd never gotten around to throwing into the stove—good news because it meant there was a lot of material, bad news because if any of it was important it would have been taken or destroyed. But I wasn't the one who had to go through them all.

I kept them sorted just a bit, in case Vlad would want to know which ones were found where. I knew that most of them, probably all of them, would be worthless, but Vlad would be stuck with going over them, so I had no problem doing the collecting. When I was done, I teleported directly back to the cottage. Buddy, who was outside, started barking when I appeared, but settled down quickly.

"Hey," I told him. "Don't worry. I got the goods."

He wagged his tail.

Vlad came to the door, probably in response to Buddy, and held it open for me. He said, "Well?"

I held up the sack full of papers. "Enjoy."

"No problems?"

"None. How about the boy?"

"He started talking about knives again—this time without any prompting at all. I can't decide if that's good or bad. Maybe it's both. And he's sleeping an awful lot."

I sat down. The boy was asleep. Hwdf'rjaanci was sitting by him, quietly singing what sounded like a lullaby. Vlad accepted the papers. He seemed a bit startled by how heavy the bag was; he weighed it in his hands and whistled appreciatively.

"What did you find out?" I asked him.

"The banker was—or is—Lady Vonnith, House of the Orca, naturally. She owned the bank completely, according to the paperwork at City Hall, which may or may not be reliable. She's also the 'pointer'—whatever that means—for three other banks, one of which has gone under and the other two of which are still solvent, but both of which have issued a 'Hold of Purchase'; again, whatever that is. She lives not too far from Endra." He gave me the address.

"Okay."

"What's a pointer?"

"I don't know where the term came from," I said. "But it means she's in charge of the business, she runs it, even if she doesn't own it. At a guess, she gets a whomping big cut of the profits, or she's a part owner, or, most likely, she's the full owner under a different name."

"Why do that?"

I smiled. "Because if one of her banks files surrender of debts, which just happened, she can keep running the others without the debts of one being assessed against the income of the others, which the Empire is supposed to do."

"Oh. Is that legal?"

"If she isn't caught."

"I see. What is a Hold of Purchase?"

"It means the bank has the right to keep your money."

"Huh?"

"It was a law passed in the twelfth Teckla Reign. It prevents everyone from pulling his money out all at once and driving the bank under. There are all sorts of laws about when it can be invoked, and for how long, and what percentage of their cash they have to release, and to whom, and I don't really understand it myself. But it may mean they're in trouble, or, more likely, it means that with banks going under they're afraid of a general panic and they're taking steps to prevent one."

"They," he repeated. "The owners of the bank, or the Empire?"

"The owners request it, the Empire grants it—or doesn't."

"I see. That's interesting. Who in the Empire would they go to to get such an order?"

"The Minister of the Treasury's office."

"Who's the Minister of the Treasury?"

"His name is Shortisle."

"Shortisle," said Vlad. "Hmmm."

"What?"

"That name came up in Fyres's notes, somewhere. Something about it struck me as odd, but I didn't pay much attention, and now I can't remember what it was. I guess they met for dinner or something."

"Hardly surprising," I said. "The Minister of the Treasury and a major entrepreneur? Sure."

"Yes, but . . . never mind. I'll think about it. House?"

"Shortisle? Orca."

He nodded, and fell into a reverie of contemplation.

"Is there anything else?"

"Huh? Yeah. Go home. I'll go over your booty tonight, which should leave me with, oh, at least half an hour to sleep. Tomorrow you make contact with the banker and see what you can learn."

"All right," I said. "Should I check with you first, to see what you've found out?"

"Yeah. But don't hurry—I want a chance to at least close my eyes and snore once before you show up."

"Okay. Sleep well."

He looked at the bag full of dusty scrap paper in his hand and favored me with a thin smile. Loiosh stretched his wings and hissed, as if he were laughing at us both.

When I returned in the morning, the table near the stove was filled with the papers I'd discovered, all neatly sorted into four stacks, and, if I remembered the quantity correctly, reduced by about three-quarters. Vlad had the bleary-eyed look of someone who had just woken up, and Savn was still asleep by the hearth, Loiosh, Rocza, and Buddy curled up with him. Buddy thumped his tail once, gave a dog yawn, gave a whiny sigh, and put his head down on his paws. There were pieces of charcoal on the floor, more testimony to Vlad's state; the water was boiling, and I could see the klava tin next to it, and Vlad was staring at them like he'd forgotten what they were for.

I said, "What did you learn?"

He said, "Huh?"

"Make the klava."

"Yeah. Right."

"The water goes into the inverted cone sitting on the—"

"I know how to make Verra-be-damned klava."

"Right."

He completed the operation, not spilling any water,

which impressed me, then he scowled at the floor and went looking for a broom. I said, "I take it it will be a while before I get my answers."

"Huh? Yeah. Just let me drink a cup of this poison."

"Poison? I thought you liked klava."

"She's out of honey," he said, practically snarling.

"Back in a minute," I said.

By the time the klava was done, I was back with a crock of honey, and Vlad said, "You must be sure to permit me to be cut into pieces for you sometime."

"Been reading Paarfi again?"

"I don't know how to read. In an hour, maybe I'll know how to read."

He put honey into the mugs, pressed the klava, and poured a little bit more than two mugs' worth into two mugs. He cursed. I said, "I'll clean it up."

"I'll also be immolated for you whenever you wish."

"Noted," I said.

Half an hour later he was himself again, more or less. I said, "Okay, what did you learn?"

"I learned," he said slowly, "that either it takes a trained expert to learn things from pieces of scrap paper, or it takes an amateur a long, long time to look for a greenstalk in the grass."

"In other words, you learned nothing?"

"Oh, I wouldn't say *nothing*."

He was smiling. He'd gotten something. I nodded and waited. He said, "Most of it was numbers. There were a lot of numbers. I didn't pay much attention to them, until I realized they probably meant money; then they caused me a certain distress. But that still wasn't helpful. I haven't thrown them away, because you never know, but I did set them aside."

I kept waiting.

"A few of those scraps of paper had names, sometimes with cryptic notes. Those I paid more attention to. I sorted them into three groups. One pile has mostly numbers but maybe a name, or a word that might be a code word, or something like that. Another has messages—things like, 'Lunch, Firstday, Swallowtail, Lady Preft,' or 'Modify collateral policy on mortgage holdings—meeting three o'clock.' The third pile—"

He stood up, walked over to the table, and picked up a few pieces of paper. "The third pile contains the results of going through the other two—these are scraps I came up with after looking at and rejecting a lot more. There isn't much, but there may be something."

He brought them over and handed them to me. "Okay, Kiera," he said. "Let's see if you're as devious as I am. Take them one at a time, in order, and try to put it together."

"Okay," I said. "I like games."

There were four slips of paper—two of them obviously torn off from larger sheets, the other two on very plain paper. The one on top, one of the torn fragments, was written in a very elegant, precise hand, an easy one to read. It read, *5D for BT, 5&10, 8:00, Skyday, Cklshl.*

I said, "Well, 5D, if we were talking about money, is probably five dots: five thousand imperials. But that's a Jhereg term—I wouldn't have expected a banker to use it."

"Yep. That's exactly what caught my eye. Keep going."

I shrugged. "Skyday is easy, and so is 8:00. But I don't know what BT means, 5&10, or what cee kay ell ess aech ell spells."

He said, "Start with the last. There's a small inn, not far from the bank, that's marked by a sign of a seashell, and it's called the Cockleshell. Our hostess told me about it.

She says it isn't the sort of place one might normally find a banker."

"Hmmm. This *is* getting interesting. A payoff of some sort?"

Vlad nodded. "Look at the time again."

I did so. "Right," I said. "Whether it's eight in the morning or eight at night, it isn't at a time when banks are open."

"Exactly. Now, what do you make of the 5&10?"

"Five- and ten-imperial notes, or pieces?"

He nodded. "That's my guess. Coins, probably. Clumsy to carry, but safer to negotiate."

"Then it *is* a payoff. And BT is the person being paid off—out of bank funds. Any idea who that is?"

"Try the next note."

It was just like the first—same hand, same amount, different day and time, only no place was mentioned, and the "5&10" was missing. It had been crumbled up, like someone had thrown it at a wastepaper basket and missed. I said, "Well? They did it at the bank?"

"Maybe. Or maybe we've found an early one and a late one, and there was no need to name the place or the denominations because by now she knew it. And another thing: look at the blotting on both of them."

"It's sloppy."

"Right. They were just notes by—I presume—Lady Vonnith to herself. If they were ever turned into official copies, those were filed, processed, and taken—or, more likely, destroyed. But she scribbled these while doing calculations or talking to someone, and then apparently tossed them at the wastepaper basket and missed."

"Yes," I said. "And this one is fairly recent—like, perhaps, the day they closed down."

"Right."

I nodded. "I recognize the hand, by the way."

"You recognize it?"

"Only in the sense that I remember where these came from, and there was a lot of paper there, most of it, like this, crumbled up into balls and lying on the floor, and a bunch of them that, just guessing, had fallen behind a desk or a filing cabinet and weren't worth retrieving. And it was, indeed, the biggest office in the place, so I'd guess you're right about whose notes these are."

He nodded. "Okay. After I'd gotten that far, I went through all the notes again, looking for any reference at all to BT."

"I take it you found something?"

"Yep. Read the next one."

"Different hand," I said. "Probably a man. Was it found in the same place?"

"Yes."

"Then it was written *to* her, not by her. Hmmm. Not as legible, but I think I can make it out. 'There are questions about dispersals to BT—I think we should tighten it up before it mirrors. Should we use the disc. fund?' And I can't read the signature at all—I imagine it's the scrawl someone uses informally."

"Yes, I suspect you're right. So what do you make of that one?"

"That's a curious little phrase, 'before it mirrors.' "

"Yeah, that's what I thought. Why not say, 'before it reflects?' And what would that mean, anyway? Do you have a guess?"

"Do you?"

"Yeah. Let's hear yours, though."

" 'Before it mirrors.' Hmmm."

"Give up?"

"Not yet; you're enjoying this too much." I pondered for

a while and came up with nothing. "All right, I give up. What did you see that I didn't?"

Vlad smiled with one side of his face. "The next note."

"Heh. Okay." I looked at the fourth and last of the notes Vlad had found. This was the longest, and, as far as I could tell, the most innocuous. It said, *Lady—Lord Sustorr was in again—he now wants to secure his loan with his share of Northport Coal. I told him he had to talk to you, but it seems reasonable. I'm going to start running numbers on it. Some big shot from the Ministry of the Treasury was in today looking for you. He didn't leave his name, but says he'll be back tomorrow—it may be an Imperial Audit, but I don't think we have anything to worry about. I spoke with Nurtria about the complaint we received, and he promises to be more polite in the future. Lady Aise was in about the Club meeting. She left the flyer that's attached to this note. Firrna is still sick; we may have to replace him if this goes on—remind me to talk to you about it.* It was signed with the same illegible scrawl as the last one. I read it three times, then looked up at Vlad.

"Well?" he said. "Do you see it?"

"It's pretty thin," I said. "It fits, but it's pretty thin."

"It can't be that thin," said Vlad, "or you wouldn't have picked up on it."

I shrugged. "We think alike. That doesn't mean we're right."

"It explains the mirror line. What you see in a mirror is yourself, and if he was looking for what he must have been looking for—" Vlad punctuated the sentence with a shrug.

"No, I admit that. But still . . ."

"Yeah. It's something to go on when I talk to Her Ladyship the banker."

I stared at the letter again.

My, my, my.

Chapter Nine

VLAD HAD SAID something about missing the people who once did his legwork for him, but I have my own ways of finding out what I need to know. Breaking into Fyres's house, when I had the house plans and all of the information ahead of time, was nice, and it had left me free to only look for certain things. This time, when I wasn't even going to break in, I had more leisure—I'd even had the leisure to return home and study up on the House of the Orca, so I wouldn't make any mistakes that I could avoid, although there could easily be pitfalls I wouldn't know about. But if you're trying to pull off a scam, the more information you have the better, so I went about collecting the information—my way.

I stood in a small wooded area, about two hundred meters from Lady Vonnith's front door, and studied her. That is, I studied her grounds and her house, which told me a great deal more about her than a similar study had told Vlad about Endra or Reega. But then, I have the advantage of age, and of spending a great deal of time learning about people only by seeing their houses (and especially trying to judge the inside by what I see of the outside), so maybe it isn't a fair comparison.

Vonnith's home was much older than Fyres's place, and, without doubt, had been built for an Orca. The gentle curves of roof and front were the trademark of the way they had liked their homes in the late Fifteenth and early Sixteenth Cycles—perhaps because it reminded them of their ships, but more likely because it reminded them of the sea. The late Fifteenth and early Sixteenth Cycles, incidentally, were also one of the periods when the richest of them made a point of living as far inland as duty and fortune would permit, which was a further indication, as we were several leagues from the shore and there wasn't even a river in sight.

There was a high, ivy-covered stone wall running along one side of the grounds. It was recent enough that it had to be Vonnith who had it put in. It certainly wasn't for security, or it would have gone around all the grounds, and it wasn't attractive enough to have been put in for aesthetic reasons, so it was probably done to hide whatever was on the other side of it, which a quick glance told me was more of the same gentle, grass-covered hill Vonnith's house was built on. Conclusion: she wanted to mark her boundaries. Second conclusion: she spent a great deal of time in that room on the second floor whose window looked out that way, with additional evidence provided by a not-unattractive stone monument midway between house and wall.

The monument was of a person, probably an ancestor, most likely the person who had had the house built, yet it seemed new enough that Vonnith had had it put up herself. This was starting to look like she had increased the family fortunes, in which case there should be signs of additions and improvements on the house. And, looking for them, there they were—a bit on the far side that, however well it blended in, had to have been added, and, yes, all the dormers, and even some stonework running up alongside the doors.

She seemed to have quite a fixation on stonework— maybe it had something to do with being an Orca and knowing that stone sinks, or maybe it had to do with being rich and wanting to do something that lasted. At a guess, the latter seemed most likely.

Well, her bank hadn't lasted.

I wondered how she'd taken that. Was she one of those who would shrug it off and make excuses for it, even to herself? Would it destroy her? Would she mourn for a while, or would it inspire her to try again? Fyres was the last sort, I knew—every time his schemes had fallen apart, he'd started over again. I had to admire that.

There were four guards out in the open, and after a few minutes I found another four concealed—one of them close enough to make me uncomfortable, even though I was doing nothing illegal. I continued watching, noticing the glass on the windows, just like Fyres's place, and the inlay work on the stones around the front door, the carriage posts for guests' conveyances, and the glint that came off the door clapper. Yes. She, too, had her ostentatious side, although it was nothing like Vlad had described Endra's house.

Come to that, though, I hadn't seen what the inside looked like. Still, all this time, I was only barely aware that my subconscious was putting together a layout of the house. It wasn't that I expected to need one, it's just how my mind works. I am, quite frankly, very good at it, and maybe that's where the real pleasure comes in—just the joy of doing something you do well. There are worse reasons for doing things; maybe there aren't any better ones.

I was doing something I was good at now, too: I was wearing makeup, to which I was unaccustomed, but I was being a good enough Orca to fool an Orca. Or so I hoped.

I walked up to the front door and pulled the clapper. You know it's a well-built house when you pull the clapper and you don't even hear the faintest echoes of it from outside—that is, either it's a well-built house or else the clapper's broken.

Evidently the clapper was working. The man who opened the door was at once recognizable as an Issola, and a fine specimen he was—old, perhaps a shade tall, well groomed, graceful in movements, plainly delighted to see me even though he had no idea who I was or what I was doing there. He said, "Welcome to the home of my lady Side-Captain Vonnith, Countess of Licotta and Baroness of T'rae. My name is Hub. What may we do to please you?"

I said, "Good morning, Hub. I am Third-Chart-Master Areik, from Adrilankha, with a message for the Side-Captain. If you wish, Sir Hub, I will wait outside; please tell her I'm from her friend in the Ministry of the Treasury and there may be some small difficulty with the arrangements."

He said, "There is no need for you to wait outside, Third-Chart-Master; please follow me." I did so, and he left me in a parlor while he went to deliver the message.

Vonnith had gone for the big, roomy look: I had the impression, even in the entryway, of lots of space. I was prepared for it because I'd been able to see the dimensions and the height of the ceilings from the outside, but it was different actually feeling it. It occurred to me for the first time that there was something strange about an Orca wanting to live in a big, spacious, airy house—and a house, looking

around, that had no hint or pieces of shipboard life anywhere. One explanation was that, if they're used to life on a
ship, that's the last thing they want to be reminded of when
they're ashore. But I suspect the real explanation is that,
just as most Jhereg have nothing to do with criminal activity, most Orca live out their whole lives on land, channeling
their mercantile instincts into other pursuits—running
banks, for example.

Hub returned. "The Side-Captain awaits you in West
Room."

There were no hallways on this floor—it just flowed
from one room to another, which meant all of them were
big and open. From the parlor, where I'd been waiting, we
passed into a dining room with a very long lacquered table,
and from there we entered a spacious room with dark pan-
eling and traces of something tangy-sweet—maybe in-
cense, maybe something else. The chairs in this room were
all stuffed and comfortable-looking, and set in clumps of
three or four, as if to turn the one large room into several
smaller ones without the benefit of walls. There was very
little that seemed worth stealing, except some of the contents of the buffet, and I dislike stealing things that break
easily.

I bowed to the woman before me and said, "Side-Captain
Vonnith?"

She nodded and pointed to a chair. I sat. She looked at
Hub and nodded, and he poured me a glass of wine. She already had one. I said, "Thank you." We both drank some. It
was the sort of wine that Vlad calls *brandy,* and it was quite
good. She nodded to Hub again. He bowed and left the
room.

She said, "I wasn't aware that I had a friend in the Ministry of the Treasury. In fact, I don't believe I know anyone
at all who works there."

I drank some more wine to give me time to think. She had invited me in, and she had given me wine, and now she was denying knowing what I was talking about. So, okay, she was playing a game, but was I supposed to play along with it, or convince her it was unnecessary?

"I understand," I said. "But if you did . . ."

"Yes? If I did?"

Okay, sometimes luck will out.

"You would probably be interested in knowing that the fire is getting hotter."

"I beg your pardon?"

"Questions are being asked."

"And are the answers forthcoming?"

"No." And I added, "Not yet."

Her lips tightened. "Some," she said, "might interpret that as a threat."

"No, no," I said. "Not a threat. But you know Lord Shortisle."

"Do I?" she said. "What makes you think so?"

"I mean, you know how he works."

"I thought I did," she said. "But now you say he's not threatening me, and yet—"

Well, well. All the way to the top. I said, "He's not. What I mean is, he's getting pressure from, well, you can guess where the pressure's coming from."

She frowned. "Actually, I can't. The Phoenix is off cavorting with her lover, as I understand it, so it can't be her, and there isn't anyone else who is in a position to threaten us, or has the desire to."

Now, that was extremely interesting. I said, "Because Her Majesty is gone doesn't mean she's out of touch."

For the first time, she looked worried. "It is her? Something has slipped?"

"Yes," I said.

"What?"

"I don't know; I'm just a messenger."

"How bad is it?"

"Not bad—yet. It's just a whisper. But Lord Sh—That is, certain parties thought you should be informed."

"Yes, yes. What does he say I should do?"

"Do you know Lord Loftis, who is running the—"

"Of course I do."

"That's where the pressure is coming down."

"Has he slipped?"

"Not badly, but enough so there's some danger. You should be prepared to move."

"Huh? What do you mean, move?"

"I mean run."

"Oh. Do you think it might come to that?"

"We hope not."

She nodded. "All right. Why didn't—uh—why wasn't I reached directly? Why send you?"

Hmmm. Good question. "Why do you think?"

For a moment I thought she wasn't going to be able to come up with anything, but her eyes got big. "The Empress? Using the Orb? She wouldn't! She's a *Phoenix*!"

I shrugged. "She hasn't yet, and she may not, but it would be the obvious next step, wouldn't it?"

"Impossible. Shortisle is getting paranoid."

"Maybe," I said. "Probably."

"Certainly. No one has done that since the seventh Jhereg Reign, and you know what happened then!"

"So is there any harm in being careful?"

"No, I suppose not." She shook her head. "We should have been more careful from the beginning—we should have arranged for methods of making contact, and signals." *That's right, you should have.* "But then, no one planned anything—it just happened, one thing led to another."

"Yes," I said. She looked like she was about to start asking questions, so I finished the wine and stood up. "There's a great deal to do, but nothing that should be impossible." That was general enough that I didn't think I could get into trouble with it.

"Of course," she said. "Tell him I'll await his word, but that I'll be ready to, as you put it, *move*."

"Very good. I—or someone—will be in touch. For the future, whoever it is will say he's from the Adrilankha Eleemosynary Society."

"Adrilankha Eleemosynary Society," she said. "All right. Good luck."

"Yes," I said. "And you be careful."

I didn't realize how tense I was until I walked out the door. And even then I couldn't completely relax, because they might be watching me. I didn't think I gave myself away, but I couldn't be sure; Vonnith was the sort who could play the game on me that I thought I was playing on her.

I got up to the road and teleported to the Imperial Palace's Orca Wing just in case they decided to trace the teleport. It crossed my mind to visit the Ministry of the Treasury while I was there, but on reflection there was too much chance of my being recognized by the Jhereg who have business there from time to time, so I just waited for about ten or fifteen minutes, then teleported back to the cottage.

Vlad was talking to Hwdf'rjaanci, probably about Savn's condition, while Savn slept. When I came in, Vlad said, "Well?"

"I don't know," I told him. "I think it went well, but—

"What did you learn?"

Buddy insinuated his nose into my person. I petted him and pushed him away. Loiosh, who was on Vlad's left

shoulder, twitched his head in what was probably laughter.
"It goes all the way to the top," I said.

"You mean Big Shot Treasury is Shortisle himself?"

"Not necessarily, but Shortisle is involved somewhere
along the line."

Vlad whistled softly. "Let's have the details," he said.

I gave him the conversation as well as I could remember
it, and a few notes on architecture as well, after which he
said, "Yeah, Shortisle's in it, all right. I suspect the Empress is not going to be happy about this, and I suspect that,
if any of a number of people find out what we're doing, we
could be in some very serious trouble."

"Right on both counts," I told him.

"Could Shortisle have enough pull to enlist the Tasks
Group?"

"No chance," I said. "There has to be someone else."

"Okay." I could see him accept that. "The Tiassa? Lord
Khaavren?"

"I know about him. I don't believe it. And you're the one
who heard the way Loftis talked about him, and I threatened Loftis with telling him."

"The Empress?"

"Even less likely. I'd even risk 'impossible.' "

"Then who, dammit? Who else can order the Tasks
Group to do something like this?"

"No one."

"Oh, good. Well, that's helpful." He frowned. "I remember I was at Dzur Mountain once—have you ever been
there?"

I shrugged.

"Yeah. Well, I was there once, talking to Sethra Lavode,
the Enchantress—"

"I know who she is."

"Right. She was telling me about the Dragon-Jhereg war."

"Yes."

"It was pretty ugly as I understand it. Were you involved in that?"

"Sure," I said. "On the side of the Dragons."

He gave me a polite smile. "The Dragons had the real power, but the Jhereg had one advantage—they always went for the top. While the Dragonlords were busily killing every Jhereg they came across—whether he worked for the Organization or not—the Jhereg were carefully wiping out all the military leaders in the House of the Dragon. It was a nasty little war, and, by the end, Sethra Lavode had to get involved. Do you know about that?"

"Go on."

"All she did was announce that she was in charge, and then, as she told me, she did nothing—she just sat in Dzur Mountain and waited for the Jhereg to try to assassinate her, and wiped them out as they did, which was pretty stupid on the part of the Jhereg, really. No one is going to assassinate the Enchantress of Dzur Mountain, unless maybe Mario reappears. But that's not the point. She also mentioned a time in Eighth Cycle when she was Warlord, and she had six hundred troops to defend this little hill against—"

"What's your point, Vlad?"

"That they're occupying the strong position—they don't have to do anything. We've been nipping at them here, and scouting them there, and we've learned a lot, but mostly what we've learned is that they're way tougher than we are, and they're in a secured position. All they have to do is dig in, and we can't touch them. If we tell the Empire what's going on, they'll go to ground and it'll take a hundred years to sort everything out. If we keep nibbling away at them, it'll take even longer."

"I see your point. So what do we do?"

"We need to get Sethra Lavode to leave Dzur Mountain—figuratively speaking."

I nodded slowly. "Yes, I see what you're getting at. How do you propose to do it?"

"They're scared as it is," he said. "That is, Loftis has been given the job of covering over Fyres's murder, and Vonnith is obviously up to something, and so is Shortisle. So I propose we give them something to chase—like me. Then we turn the chase around and nail them."

"Uh-huh. And, if they do chase you, how are you going to stay alive long enough to, as you put it, turn the chase around?"

He rubbed the spot above his lip where his facial hair was just starting to grow back. "I haven't worked that part out yet," he said.

"Yeah. Well, be sure and let me know when you do."

"Well, so what's *your* bright idea?"

"Let's go back to the beginning, Vlad. What do we know about Fyres?"

Vlad shrugged. "Not much. We have something to start with, but—"

"Yeah. I'd like to find out more."

"Kiera, that could take years. We have some of his private notes, okay. But between empty companies, and fake ships, and loans without backing, and reams of paper— most of which we *don't* have—we're never going to be able to track down what was really going on."

"Maybe," I said. "But remember Stony?"

"Your Jhereg friend? Sure."

"I'm thinking that if the Jhereg has been involved in this, then someone, somewhere, knows what's going on."

"And why would you think that?"

"Sheer number of Jhereg, Vlad. There are so many of us involved in financing this kind that at least one of them was bound to have been smart enough not to jump in, but to investigate the guy. All we have to do is find out who that is and get the information already collected."

He looked skeptical. "Do you think you can do that? That is, find just the right guy and get the information without giving the game away?"

"I can do it," I told him.

He shrugged. "Okay. Go to it."

"It may take a few days."

"All right."

"And there's something else I want to do, but we're going to have to think about whether it's a good idea."

"I'm not sure I like the sound of that."

"You're wise, Vlad. I'm not sure it's something we ought to do, but I'm thinking about it."

"Let's hear it, Kiera."

"You like honey in your klava, don't you?"

"Ah. So that's how it is?"

"You're very quick."

"Only because I've been stung. Let's hear what you have in mind."

I gave him the general outline, omitting details he didn't need and wouldn't have been happy knowing. He listened very intently, then he said, "Yes, indeed. And we don't even have gloves, much less whatever you're supposed to use to protect your face. The question is, how big is the swarm, and how nasty do they get when they're roused?"

"Yeah, that's the question. And can you think of a better way to find out?"

He sighed and shook his head. "Unfortunately, Kiera, I can't."

"So I should go ahead?"

He nodded briefly, like he didn't enjoy the prospect. Well, neither did I, come to that. I said, "What are you going to do while I'm off gathering sweets?"

A peculiar sort of smile came to his lips. "I'll think of something," he said.

All we had to do was keep our heads down and keep learning things, and eventually, maybe, we'd start to get an idea about what was going on; then, just maybe, we'd be able to figure out what to do about it. That, at least, was what I was thinking as I stepped out of the little cottage and repaired home to make myself annoying in a couple of different ways to several different people.

The next two days were no more fun than I'd thought they would be—most of those I spoke to I didn't like, and they didn't like me, and they couldn't or wouldn't tell me anything useful, anyway—but in the end I came up with some hard information. I noted it down carefully, and, psychic communication being impossible while Vlad wore the Phoenix Stones, I had to hold on to what I'd learned until I would see him next: tomorrow or the day after, depending on how things went tonight. When I was done asking irritating questions of irritating people, which was in the afternoon of the second day, I picked up the tools I was going to need and prepared to do what I was good at.

Vlad and I, back in the old days, used to compare our respective crafts, and one of the things common to both was the need for preparation, and, in conjunction, how dangerous it was to try to do anything in a hurry. The trouble was, things were happening too fast, and I had the feeling they were going to happen even faster.

Well, I didn't like it, but there wasn't much I could do about it. After getting what I needed from home, I spent the

rest of the afternoon going from place to place in Adrilankha, trying to get the information I needed to have a
chance to pull this off.

I wished I had a familiar to grumble at while I did so.
Vlad's told me about several times Loiosh has saved his
life, or suggested the solution to a problem, or provided the
necessary help to complete a witchcraft spell, but I have the
feeling that the most important thing Loiosh does for Vlad
is give him someone to grumble at. You feel stupid grum-
bling to yourself, so I didn't.

The day was waning when I had finally acquired everything I needed. I took about four hours to study the situation, curse about everything I didn't know, and come up
with a tentative way in, a provisional agenda, and a possible way out, with maybe a couple of alternatives for the
last, all of which I knew would likely be rendered useless if
something went wrong. For the first time in more years
than I could remember I actually thought about how humil-
iating it would be to get caught, because for the first time in
more years than I could remember it seemed like a real possibility.

I cursed yet again and made my way to the Imperial
Palace, Orca Wing.

The phrase "breaking into the Imperial Palace" has been
used among people I know for a long time as an expression
of the unthinkable: "Argue philosophy with an Athyra?
Might as well break into the Imperial Palace," or, "Bet the
round stones? Sure. And then we'll break into the Imperial
Palace." That sort of thing. It's a fascinating little phrase,
because it only makes sense if it goes back to the early days
of the Empire, when all that existed was the old nucleus
that became the Imperial Wing; breaking into the Imperial
Palace is as easy in the execution as it is meaningless as a

concept: most of the doors you can just walk into; *where* in the Imperial Palace do you want to break into?

And, of course, to do what?

In any case, I "broke into the Imperial Palace" by walking into the Orca Wing. I wore a nice, full coat of Jhereg grey with natty black fringe, a hood in case it got cold, and one that was sufficiently voluminous to hide my tools. I nodded to the tired-looking Orca watchman as I went by.

So let's see. One, two, third corridor to the left, up the stairs, down the hall to the statue. A long way. There was no bloody statue of Sealord Cren; how old was that information, anyway? Well, it had to be either this passage or this one, and . . . yes, there were the marks where the statue used to be. Good. Now another stairway, and two more turnings, and it had been quite some time since I'd seen anyone. The Orca were forced to work long, irregular hours when at sea; they made up for it ashore by working no more than they had to.

There were supposed to be a couple more watchmen to circumvent right before I reached my destination, and I became worried when I didn't see them. But I waited in the corridor outside the doorway into the Ministry until at last I heard one walk by; the footsteps were measured and casual and went away after a while. Nine and a half minutes later I heard a different set. Eleven minutes later the first set returned. I spent another half hour there, just to make sure of the timing, then moved.

The door into the Ministry had only the most cursory lock, and the alarm was trivial. Once past it, I had to get into Shortisle's office, and I spent most of the seven minutes I'd given myself in checking for alarms; then I retreated once more to wait for another cycle of the watch. The next time I spent only five minutes more checking for alarms, about a minute disabling them, and maybe twenty seconds opening the door, slipping through, shutting it, and locking it again. Then I put the alarms back up in case the guards checked them. I put some cloth under the door so that no one would see light peeking out, then looked around.

There was a door in his office that had a nice little sign on it reading, "Records."

If Shortisle was engaged in anything shady—or, in fact, even if he wasn't—he wouldn't make it easy to get to the financial records of the Empire, so I intended to take this carefully and slowly, and make sure I'd found everything before I moved.

I studied the door, the floor, and the ceiling first, looking for anything obvious, and found nothing. Next I looked as closely as I could through and into the keyhole, but I didn't see anything that looked like an alarm.

The next step was to feel for the presence of sorcery in the area, and, yes indeed, it was all over the place; there was nothing subtle about it. Was it double-trapped? That is, would looking at it closely set off an alarm? Well, there are the tendrils of spells that hang in the real world like abandoned cobwebs; and one knows the feel of these strands if one has ever walked through a dark and gloomy place—so, too, were these bits of amorphia all around me in that place that was dark to the outer eye, but now filled with light to the inner. I can brush past cobwebs without making them fall, but what if the web is not abandoned, after all? Then the spider will know I am there; and if there is anyone watching the spider, then I cannot brush her or her threads aside without all the world being aware of me.

Ah, little spider, you have a bite, do you? And someone watching over you? Well, let him watch, little spider, and you—find me if you can, for I know cobwebs better even than you, and I will send up my own spider that will look like you, and act like you, and gobble you up, and then sit fat and happy in your place while the watcher watches, oblivious.

I took a few minutes to catch my breath before I proceeded. One becomes exhausted when using sorcery in proportion to the intricacy of the spell, not the amount of energy used; a fact that I think Vlad still doesn't understand since he still compares it to witchcraft—an art I've never begun to understand.

When I felt better, I used the same device I'd used at the bank to look into the room in preparation for teleporting. It was a fairly small room, but full to overflowing with cabinets, maybe forty-five or fifty of them, all of which were, no doubt, full to overflowing with the recent financial records of the Empire—whatever I was looking for was probably in there. I checked the room over carefully, fixed it in my mind, prepared to teleport, and stopped cold.

Something wasn't right.

I put the tube back against the wall, held it tight, relaxed, and looked again. The room was entirely dark, and I hadn't wanted to risk light until I could be sure they had nothing to detect it, so I'd used a spell that affected my sight rather than the room; this is tricky because it is very easy to miss things that are near other things—objects tend to blur and merge in the magical vision—but it seemed that there was something odd next to one of the cabinets against the wall.

I checked again, and there was no trace of sorcery except for those spells I had already found and circumvented, which meant, if this was an alarm, it wasn't a magical one. Of course, there was no reason to believe it was an alarm— it was just something that wasn't a filing cabinet or a pen, or an inkwell, or anything else I could readily identify. I almost talked myself into going in, but you don't get to be my age without developing some instincts and learning to trust them, so I put a little more effort into seeing it.

If the ceiling was as high as the ceiling of this room, then the filing cabinets were about eight meters tall, in which case the object sitting on the floor was about two meters tall (scale can be a problem when seeing this way—try it yourself) and resembled, more than anything else, a small gong, with some sort of round plate attached to a thin frame by a pair of wires, and even what might be a diminutive beater positioned in front of it, attached to the frame. I couldn't see how thick any of it was for sure, which didn't help any. I doubted it was actually a gong but I couldn't figure out what it was, or what it was doing there.

If it was magical, I'd lost all of my skills, and if it wasn't magical, what was it? Could one use witchcraft to create an alarm? My guess was no, but I couldn't reach Vlad to ask him, and I didn't want to ask Cawti because she'd ask questions. No, I didn't think witchcraft could do something like that. And I really doubted that Shortisle would think to hire a witch, anyway.

It was probably something completely harmless that had nothing to do with anything, and when I looked at it I'd laugh. Except that I still had this feeling.

Well, if it *was* an alarm, it had to be connected to a device to notify someone, or a device to trigger a trap, or a device to make a noise, or *something*. And if the connection wasn't magical, it had to be physical. Well, was there a string or a wire running from it to somewhere else?

I looked, and focused, and . . .

Yes, there was.

A wire or a string ran from it up to the ceiling and disappeared above the room.

Maybe it *was* an alarm.

If so, how did it work? What was it supposed to detect,

and how would it respond? How could it send a magical impulse through the string if there was no magic around the device? And if it wasn't supposed to send a magical impulse, what could it send? I had the sudden image of someone creating an artifact that did nothing at all, but knowing that if there was a strange device in the room, no competent thief would break in before figuring out what it did. An effective deterrent to be sure, but I suspected there was more to this object than that.

Well, what would have happened if I'd teleported into the room? Nothing. I'd have been there, maybe right by the device, maybe not, but it couldn't sense me, anyway, so . . .

Slow down, Kiera.

What happens when someone teleports into a room?

The same thing, more or less, that happens when someone opens a door and *walks* into the room: air gets pushed around—just a little when the door is opened, more when you materialize from a teleport. And if that gonglike thing is thin, then just a little air movement would be enough to make it tap against the beater, and if that was a metal wire, it could carry the sound, or the vibration, through the Palace to a place where it could be amplified, and someone, somewhere, would know that the integrity of the room had been violated.

I'd have whistled to myself if I weren't being especially conscious of sound. It was a very clever device; just the sort of thing the Orca would come up with, and I was only surprised that no one had thought of it, or a variation on it, years and years ago: simple, elegant, and almost impossible to detect.

Almost impossible.

Thing is, I'm not just a good thief, I'm the best thief in the Empire. I reached the fingers of magic into the room and felt the thin metal plate. Careful now, Kiera. Don't get cocky with all those thoughts about how good you are: you're good because you're careful, and you're careful because you're patient. Take it slowly, and . . .

It was immobilized.

I sighed, took a breath, and teleported into the room. Nothing went off, nothing moved. I did yet another check for magic, then made a light and began looking through the Imperial financial records. These were, you understand, only the most recent and active sets: the rest were saved by some method known only to the sorcerers of the House of the Lyorn and the archivists of the House of the Orca, but it was the recent and active records I needed.

I imagine the organization of the packets in the cabinets, and, indeed, the arrangement of the cabinets, all of them marked with numbers or symbols or a combination, made sense to those who worked here, and I would even guess that somewhere was a key to the whole thing that would explain how to interpret everything else, but I had no clue how to make sense of any of it. Fortunately, I didn't need to. I opened a packet at random, saw nothing that meant anything to me, closed it, and put it back. Then I went to another cabinet and did the same. Then another, until I had opened at least one packet in each of them, and riffled through probably two hundred collections of notes, invoices, receipts, and other accounting arcana.

That done, I slipped out of the room, stopping long enough to erase any psychic traces of myself that I might have left. Then I locked the door behind me and very, very carefully released the spell that was holding the little wind-alarm. It didn't go off. As the last step, I got a metaphorical spider back and had it cough up the one it had euphemistically eaten.

I looked around the rest of the area until I found what

had to be Shortisle's desk, judging from the size, the location, and his name appearing on plaques, markers, and papers all around it. Unlike the records, here there was a chance I could learn something if, indeed, Shortisle was the guilty party, and if he left evidence of his crimes lying around. Phrased that way, I didn't think much of my chances, but it wouldn't hurt to explore a little.

The alarms built into his desk were all sorcerous, and not terribly effective, which meant that he had nothing to hide—or he wasn't hiding it in his desk, at any rate. I dismantled the alarms, picked the locks, and looked through the contents. There were, in fact, no notes saying, "Today I accepted a large bribe from Vonnith in exchange for allowing her to close her bank and run with whatever money she could scrape together."

Oh, well.

The most irritating thing was that he had two small, hidden compartments in the desk, both of which required a great deal of time and effort to open, and both of which turned out to be entirely empty—not even a psiprint of his mistress. I took this as a personal affront.

When I finished with the desk, I realized just how exhausted I was. That's the most dangerous part: when you're all done, and you're tired, and everything has gone well, it becomes too easy to let your guard down and make some little mistake that will bring the watch running or allow you to be found after the fact. I made myself go slowly and carefully in removing all traces of my presence, both psychic and mundane, then I made sure of the timing of the watch (judging by the footsteps, they weren't the same pair who'd been there before) before I opened the last door between me and escape.

Even after I was past that, I was careful to avoid crowded places, and took little-known paths through the Palace, walking for almost two more hours until I could emerge from the Yendi Wing (just for the pleasure of giving the inhabitants something to wonder about) and teleported straight back home, where I poured myself a glass of the same kind of wine Vonnith had given me, drank it down at a single draught, and climbed into my bed, after which I slept soundly for several very pleasant hours that were only marred by a few dreams in which spiders were banging on gongs.

When at last I roused myself late the next morning, I took care of morning things, broke my fast with warmed nutbread, maizepie, and Eastern-style coffee (which Vlad claims is too bitter for him), and teleported back to Northport. I found a large and busy inn very close to City Hall, so I went in, found a table in the middle of the room, and began to drink klava, with the intention of continuing until something either happened or failed to happen.

I was, in effect, making myself a target. With any luck, I'd have stirred up Shortisle, or someone in his office, and it seemed likely that, with a little work, whoever it was would be able to figure out that the visitor had been Kiera the Thief (although, to be sure, no one would be able to prove it), and I expected to be able to learn something from who showed up and what he did when he got here—I'd be surprised if I had to sit here for more than two days.

This was a part of the plan Vlad knew nothing about, because he would have wanted to be involved. I have a great deal of confidence in my ability to get myself out of anything I get myself into, but if you add a hot-tempered assassin whose blade is often faster than his head, it might be that I'd save myself a few moments of worry and, in exchange, lose a lot of useful information.

Vlad, however, would not have liked the idea of my doing it.

By noon I was tired of klava, so I switched to a "seaman's ale," as they call it in Northport, or "storm brew," as it is called in Adrilankha, which is a very dark ale with traces of ginger; it was heavy, so I could pretend it was lunch. I felt very exposed at the table, and I hoped I wouldn't have to wait there too long. I finished the seaman's ale and ordered another, and considered asking for a bowl of whatever it was I could smell from the kitchen. People walked by the open window and often looked in, because that's what one does when walking by an inn, and I kept wondering if any of these were people who were spotting me. I rubbed my eyes. At one point, I thought I saw Devera go by, but if so she didn't recognize me, and it wasn't very likely, anyway. I drank some more seaman's ale. It was good. Two Jhereg came in, walked right up to my table, and sat down. They were Funnel-head and Mockman, both of whom had been in Stony's office when I'd visited him. This was something I hadn't expected at all.

Funnel-head said, "Stony wants to see you."

"All right," I said. "Now?"

"If you please."

I left the ale unfinished, which was a shame, and stood up. They flanked me as we stepped out of the inn. They each had a sword, and Funnel-head, on my right, had a long dagger concealed under his left arm, and no doubt they each had a few other things that would help them not at all if I decided not to accompany them, but they didn't know that.

Funnel-head said, "Shall we teleport?"

"I'd rather walk," I said, because I don't let strangers teleport me.

"It's a couple of miles," he said.

"It's a nice day."

"All right."

We exchanged no more words until we got there. We walked right up past where Dor was very careful not to be, then Funnel-head clapped outside Stony's door and said, "She's here, boss."

There was a muffled response, and Funnel-head opened the door and indicated I was to go in. I did so, stopping only long enough to hand him his dagger. "You dropped this," I said. He stared at it, then gave me a glare into which I smiled as I closed the door.

I sat down. "What is it, Stony? Why the summons?"

Stony, apparently, couldn't decide if he should be amused or annoyed by my interaction with his flunky; eventually he settled on ignoring it.

"I'm worried about you," he said.

"Worried about me?"

"About you, and for you."

I waited.

"Yeah," he said. "You've been looking into Fyres's death, and some people are getting itchy."

"People?" I said.

He shook his head. "You know I can't name names, Kiera."

"Then what are you saying?"

He shrugged. "I'm saying you should drop this, whatever it is, or else be very careful, that's all."

"What about you?"

"I'm not involved," he said. "I just heard that you lightened some files in some Orca's office at the Palace, and some Orca with connections to the Organization want you to go swimming. I thought you should know about it."

"You're not asking me to back off?"

He shook his head. "No. As I say, this isn't my game. I just thought you ought to be aware of it, you know?"

"Yes," I said. "Okay, thanks. Anything else?"

"No," he said.

"All right. See you around."

"Yeah. See you."

I got up and left. No one tried to stop me. I was glad Stony hadn't asked about Vlad again, because I hate lying to friends.

I hastened back to the Awful Blue Cottage to tell Vlad what I'd learned. It was late afternoon when I got there. Buddy ran out of the house, and I had to spend a moment getting reacquainted with him and allaying his suspicions before venturing inside.

Hwdf'rjaanci was seated at the table next to Vlad. Savn was sitting up in the chair facing the hearth, and he turned and looked at me as I came in, which caught me up short. I said, "Hello, Savn." He didn't say anything, but returned to staring at the fire.

"Good evening," I said. I gestured toward the boy. "I see some improvement."

"Some," agreed Vlad.

Hwdf'rjaanci nodded a greeting to me and asked if I wanted some tea, which I didn't.

I was pleased, and even a bit surprised, to note that Vlad didn't have any fresh wounds. He was drinking klava, and by the lack of sleep in his eyes I suspect he was on at least his second cup. Loiosh, on the other hand, was sound asleep next to Rocza, which was unusual for a jhereg in the middle of the day. "I have some information," I said.

"Me, too," said Vlad.

"Should I go first, or do you want to?"

"You might as well," said Vlad.

I sat down next to him. Hwdf'rjaanci got up and sat over by Savn—I had the impression she didn't want to know about any of this. I decided I couldn't really blame her.

"Did you do it?" he said.

"You mean enrage the bees? Yeah."

"Tell me about it."

"All right." This time I just gave him the brief version of my activities, especially the break-in, because the long version would have required telling him things I'd rather he didn't know, then I gave him all the details on the rest of it. I sort of brushed over the part about making myself a target, but I saw him press his lips together, so I quickly went on to discuss the conversation with Stony, and, before he could ask about that, I started in on the results of my inquiries the first couple of days.

I said, "I found a couple of them, Vlad. Three, really, but one had refused him a loan just because he didn't like Fyres's smell, so that didn't help us any. But there were two of them who actually did the checking."

"How many that didn't?"

"A lot. He was very good at making people trust him."

Vlad nodded. "Okay. Those who did check up on him—what did they find out?"

"That he was very good at making people trust him."

Vlad's smile came and went. "Yeah. What else?"

"Vlad, he didn't have *anything*. He had a great deal on paper, but all of his enterprises, worth maybe sixty million imperials—"

Vlad looked shocked. "That's right," I said. "Sixty million imperials. Sixty million imperials' worth of loans, that went for office space, marketing, buying up other companies that, in point of fact, he didn't know how to run so they went into surrender of debts inside of ten or twenty years—all of this was based on a contract, and a contract never fulfilled, by the way, for five men-o'-war for the Imperial Navy."

"House of the Orca, of course," said Vlad.

"Sure, Imperial Navy."

"I wonder," said Vlad.

"Yes?"

"I wonder why legitimate banks were loaning him money at all. I mean, I can see the Jhereg, but—"

"Are you sure they were? We know about Vonnith, but do we know there were any others?"

"Yes," he said. "I'll tell you about it."

"Okay. I don't know the answer, though. But it makes sense. It explains why the loans were at bank rates, not Jhereg rates."

"They were?"

"Yes. All of them."

"Interesting. Maybe the Jhereg loans went through the banks." He spread his palms. "Or the other way around, for all we know."

I nodded.

He said, "But all right. The Jhereg is in it deep, then?"

"Lots of us, Vlad. All the way up to the Council."

"Did either of your friends try to spread the word about the guy?"

"One of them tried to let a few friends know, but no one would listen. The other, apparently, doesn't have any friends, and figured he could eliminate a great deal of competition. He was right, by the way—some very heavy people will be going down over this."

Hwdf'rjaanci got up and went outside, I suppose because she could still hear us. Buddy looked at her, thumped his tail once, but decided he wanted to stay and listen.

Vlad considered my remark and said, "That ties Fyres into the Jhereg without any question, but . . . how did he land that contract with the Imperial Navy, after having proved what he was twice before?"

"Ah," I said. "Very good. That *is* the question, isn't it? Because that brings the Empire into this. The answer is, I don't know. Somewhere along the line, he talked someone into something."

"Yep," said Vlad. He was quiet for quite a while then— maybe a minute. Then he said, "And that someone screwed up and then tried to cover himself. And I think . . . yeah, it all fits, I'm afraid."

"What does?"

"Here's what I think happened—no, on second thought, I'll tell you what I've been up to for the last couple of days, and see if you can put it together."

"All right," I said. "Go to it."

Chapter Ten

LET ME THINK now. When did you leave? A lot has happened since then. It was early afternoon, right? Okay, I'll just take it as it happened.

After you left, I made an effort to get Savn talking again, and he went off on knives some more. I decided that it probably wasn't healthy to keep him fixated like that, and the old woman told me the same thing a few minutes later, so that was about it. I couldn't think of anything else to do with him, and eventually I realized that half the reason I wanted to was to avoid having to do something I was a bit afraid of. Let me explain.

I kept thinking about that banker, and what you'd said about the Jhereg connections, and what I couldn't get away from was the idea that, if the Jhereg was connected to Fyres, and Fyres was connected to the Empire, then the Jhereg was connected to the Empire. If that was true, what was the connection, and how did it work, and like that? Now Side-Captain Vonnith—what's a side-captain, by the

way?—must have been tied into Fyres because she'd
jumped ship, so to speak, within a week of Fyres's death,
and you'd proven that she was connected to the Empire, so
I couldn't help wondering if she was connected to the
Jhereg, too.

The trouble was, I couldn't go waltzing into Stony's office and ask about it, because he'd kill me on the spot and
because you'd be annoyed with me, which meant I'd have
to work through either Vonnith or Loftis. From what you
said, I had the impression that Vonnith would bolt if she
got any more jumpy, and that might be inconvenient, so
that left Loftis.

Loftis.

I have to tell you, Kiera: I wasn't all that excited about
going up against him straight, and I wasn't very happy
about trying to put anything past him again. You've met
him, too, and you know what I'm talking about—I think we
were both lucky the first time we ran into him.

The only thing I could think of was to keep him off balance long enough for me to learn what I needed to learn,
and, with him alerted, I didn't think much of my chances of
shoving another barrel of lies at him. To the left, however,
telling him the truth wouldn't get me anywhere. So that left
giving him some of the truth, and either feeding it to him a
bit at a time—trading information, in other words—or hit-
ting him with enough of the truth to make him stumble, and
hoping to get something while he was recovering his balance, if you follow my metaphor. As for which of those I'd
do, I didn't know—I was just going to approach him, talk
to him, keep my ideas in mind, and see how it went.

That, at any rate, was the plan—if you can so dignify
vague intentions with the word. After arriving at this magnificent conclusion, I had to make some food, and then
clean up, and then try to talk to Savn about something other

than knives, which produced no response at all. Unfortunately, after all of that, there was still time to visit Loftis, and I couldn't find any more reasons for putting it off, and Loiosh was making fun of me, so I got myself dressed up as myself—that is, an Easterner, although not a Jhereg—and headed into town.

I liked your method of finding a quiet place to talk, so I used it myself. When I'd located a suitable establishment, I paid for two rooms, across the hall from each other. The host probably wondered exactly what sort of bizarre activity I was going to engage in, but she didn't ask and I didn't volunteer the information. I found a kid to act as messenger and gave him a note to pass on to Loftis. The note said where I was, including the room number, and I signed it Margaret—I hope you don't mind. Then I went into the room across the hall from the one I'd given him, and amused myself by talking to Loiosh, who was, by the way, waiting outside the building—I didn't want to introduce that complication into things at this point, and I admit I was worried, because Loftis was potentially in touch with the Jhereg, and the Jhereg was looking for an Easterner with a pair of jhereg, so why take chances? The two-room bit, by the way, proved unnecessary. The idea was that if he decided to show up with a couple of additional blades, it would give me an edge to be behind him, but he had no such plans.

It took him about an hour and a half to get there, but eventually I heard him—that is, I heard one set of footsteps, and someone clapped outside the door. I moved the curtain back, and he turned quickly, and he saw me. Then he looked at me again, more closely, and I could see him start to put things together—Kaldor to the Easterner, the Easterner to Margaret, Margaret to the Empire, the Empire to Kaldor—and I took a certain pleasure in shocking him. I said, "I don't like this place for conversations. Let's walk. You lead." Then, in spite of my words, I stepped in front of him and led the way out of the place. He followed.

"Anything?"

"All clear, boss."

"Stay out of sight. I don't know where we're going, so—"

"I've done this before, boss. Honest."

When we reached the street, I indicated that he should take us somewhere, and he set off in a direction where there would be less traffic. I didn't want to give him too much time to think, so I said, "Margaret sends her regrets, but she was detained by the need to look into the Jhereg end of this— I assume you know about that?"

"Who are you?"

"Padraic," I said.

"And you're working with Margaret, is that it?"

I shrugged. "Things are happening faster than we'd thought they would, especially on the Jhereg side."

"What is the Jhereg side?"

"Don't play stupid, we don't have time for it. Vonnith is ready to bolt, and Shortisle is getting jumpy."

"Getting jumpy?"

"All right, getting even more jumpy. How soon can you close up shop?"

"We can finish tomorrow, if you don't care about everyone figuring out that we didn't run a real investigation. Now, I want to know—"

"I don't care what you want to know," I said. "What did Timmer say? Has she put it together?"

He fumed for a moment, then said, "If she has, she isn't saying anything."

"Huh," I said. "That's probably wise."

"How is it," he said grimly, "that you, that an Easterner, came to be involved in the security of the Empire?"

"Perhaps," I said, giving him a smile that was almost a leer, "Her Majesty doesn't have the same feelings about Easterners that you do." He scowled. He's heard the rumors about Her Majesty's lover, too, but perhaps hadn't believed them. But then, I'm not sure if I believe them, either. Before he could come up with an answer, I said, "Are you aware how high this goes?"

"Yeah," he said.

I wished I knew. "All right, then. No, don't make it obvious, but hurry it up. Get your work done as fast as you can and get out."

He held up his hand in a signal to stop, and he began looking around. I did, too, and didn't see anything. The area we were walking through was almost empty of traffic and anything else—there were a couple of closed shops, a couple of houses with boards across the door, and a scattering of places that looked lived in. I said, "What is it?"

"Nothing special."

I looked around again, but still saw nothing except a desolate neighborhood, of which I'd seen plenty in South Adrilankha. I said, "Where are we?"

"I just wanted you to see this."

"What?"

"This area."

"What about it?"

"Look."

I'd been looking, but now I looked closer, and realized that the paint was new on most of the buildings and houses, and, furthermore, the houses, though small, looked like they'd been built for one family, and they were still in good condition. In fact, very good condition for how few people were here. I gave him a puzzled look.

He nodded. "When I got to town, just a couple of weeks

ago, that place was open, and that place was open, and there were people living there, there, and there."

"Where are they now?"

"Gone," he said. "Maybe on the street, maybe moved to another town, maybe out in the woods hunting and living in tents. I don't know."

"Two weeks?" I said.

"Yeah."

"Fyres?"

"Yeah. The bank closings, and the closing of the three shipbuilders—"

"Three shipbuilders?"

"Yeah. He had a stake in about six or seven, and in three cases it was enough to shut them down. This area was developed about three hundred years ago by Sorenet and Family, Shipwrights, and pretty much everyone who lived around here worked for them. Some Orca, some Chreotha, mostly Teckla just in from your favorite village a generation ago. Now Sorenet is gone, and so is everyone who worked there."

"I've never seen a neighborhood die so quickly," I said.

"Nor have I."

We started walking again. "You've surprised me in another way," I said. "I hadn't been convinced that Fyres was ever involved in anything real at all."

He shrugged. "I wasn't, either. I still don't know how involved he was, or why, or what the mechanics are. That's the sort of thing we'd be finding out, if we were really doing what we're supposed to be doing."

This neighborhood seemed about the same as where we'd stopped. It was making me nervous. Loiosh, who was staying out of sight behind me, reported that nothing terrible was about to happen. I said, "Do you really think you can keep the Tiassa from finding out what you're up to?"

"Probably," he said. "He won't check on us—he trusts

us." There was enough bitterness in that remark to ruin a hundred gallons of ale.

I said, "It isn't like you had a choice."

"I could have resigned."

"And done what? And what would you have told the Tiassa when he asked you why? And on top of it, you'd have known someone else was doing it, and probably bungling it—frankly, I don't trust your man Domm."

"The lieutenant's all right," he said quickly. "He has a bit of Waitman in him, but that just means he'll lose a few times before the Stand at Spinning Lake, which is nothing to be ashamed of. Waitman got an Imperial title for that, which isn't bad for someone with that sort of disposition."

"Maybe," I said. "And please don't explain. The point is, they knew just how to put the screws in."

"Sure," he said. "And who to put them to."

In case you've missed it, Kiera, I was now the one who was off balance; while showing me around the neighborhood, he'd had a chance to do some thinking, and now it was me who wanted some time to sort things out.

We had apparently sold Loftis on our story far more completely than I'd expected to, and that puzzled me. But more than that, I just couldn't reconcile everything he was saying with the idea that he was the sort of guy who'd go in for this kind of action. There was a piece of this—a *big* piece of this—that didn't make sense, and I was no longer at all sure how to proceed. I had this awful urge to just flat out ask him everything I needed to know, like, for example, who *was* behind this, and how exactly had the pressure been brought; but someone like Loftis is going to figure out more from the questions you ask than you will from the answers he gives, and if he figured out too much, he'd stop answering the questions at all. A damned tricky business, that made me long for the days when all I had to do was kill someone and not worry about it.

I needed a distraction.

I said, "There's another thing that's puzzling me."

"There's a lot that's puzzling me."

"Some of the smaller companies in Fyres's little Empire—"

"Not so little, Padraic."

"Yeah. Some of them hold land."

"Sure."

"And they're selling the land."

He nodded.

"And they're going under."

"Right."

"So they're not able to sell it."

"I guess. What's your point? If it's the legalities of it—"

"No, no. We have more advocates than the Orb has facets. I'm trying to figure out what sort of business sense that makes, or what kind of other sense it makes that overrides business sense."

"You think they have any choice?"

"Maybe."

He shook his head. "If you're going somewhere, I can't see it. As far as I can tell, they're bailing out as they go, and if that means they lose some property, they'll let the property courts and the advocates worry about it later. I don't think there's any plan involved."

This was all news to me. I said, "I'm not convinced."

"You have a devious mind."

"It goes with the job."

"Do you have any evidence? Any reason to think so?"

"Just a feeling. That's why I wanted to find out if you'd had any ideas about it."

"No."

"Okay," I said.

We were heading back in the general direction from which we'd come. He said, "So, all right, what is it you wanted? You had me make contact with you for some reason, and so far all we've done is chat, along with a warning so general there's no point in giving it, and a question you could have had a messenger ask. What are you after?"

Damn. I had certainly given him too much time to think. I said, "There's someone who knows too much about what you're doing, and I can't find him."

"What do you mean?"

"I mean that something's slipped, and I'm pretty sure it's at the top, or near the top at any rate. I'm running into opposition, and I can't pin it down."

He shook his head. "I haven't run into it yet. The only suspicious action I've seen so far has been you and your friend Margaret."

Damn again. That wasn't the sort of thing I wanted him thinking about.

"Look," I said, "I'm going to have to trust you."

"Trust all you want," he said. "I haven't shut you down, but I'm not under your orders."

He was ahead of me again.

"And now I want a few answers."

And gaining.

"Your friend Margaret claimed to have a certain hold on me."

"The letters. Yes. They're real."

"I told her then they wouldn't go very far, and this is as far as they go. Exactly who do you work for, and what is your job?"

"I know *your* job, friend Loftis; but if you want to put everything out in front, then let's hear you say who *you* work for." As I said that, I was desperately trying to remember the names of the different groups you'd mentioned, and figure out which one I could most reasonably claim to be part of.

"Heh. I am a lieutenant in the Imperial Army, Corps of the Phoenix Guards, Special Tasks Group."

"And you know bloody well that wasn't my question."

"Are all Easterners psychically invisible, or just you? And is that why you were hired, or is it just a bonus?"

"It helps," I said.

"Exactly what are you after?"

"I've told you that."

"Yes, you have, haven't you? You've told me just about everything my heart could desire, haven't you?"

I shook my head. "Play all the games you want, Loftis, but I don't have time to muck around, not if I'm going to do what I was sent here to do."

"Shall we get something to eat?" he said.

Add another damn or two. He was pulling all of my tricks, and he was better at them than I was—which I suppose only made sense. I said, "I've been told that Undauntra always wanted her troops to fight hungry, whereas Sethra Lavode always wanted hers to fight with a full meal in them."

"I've heard that, too," he said. "But it isn't true. About Sethra, that is."

"I'll take your word for it. I'm also told that when a Jhereg boss hires an assassin, the deal is usually made during a meal."

"I can believe that."

"And I happen to know that there is a curious custom in parts of the East of making a big ceremony out of the last meal someone eats before he's executed. He's given pretty much anything he wants, and it's prepared and served quite carefully, and then they kill him. Isn't that odd?"

"I suppose, but I think it's rather nice, actually."

I shook my head. "If I were about to be executed, I either

wouldn't be able to eat, or I'd lose the meal on the way to the Executioner's Star, or the gallows, or the Pilgrim's Block, or wherever they were to lead me."

"I see your point," he said. "But I think I'd like the meal, anyway."

"Well, perhaps I would, too."

"There's got to be someplace around here."

We stopped at the first place we came to, which meant nothing since he'd been leading the way. It was marked by a sign that was so faded I couldn't make it out, and reached from the street by walking down three steps below a hostel. It had probably been on the street level a few hundred years earlier—it seemed old enough, at any rate.

"What do you think, Loiosh?"

"I don't like it, boss. There's no one hanging around outside, but he had plenty of time to set something up before we got here."

"Good point."

"If you want to make a break, I can keep him busy."

"No. I'm going to run with it."

"Boss—"

"Stay alert."

The ceiling was low, the stone walls were damp, and the place was dark enough to be irritating—I suspected that, except for sinking, it hadn't changed much in quite some time. There was a big table with two long benches, about half of which were occupied by tradesmen, and a few isolated tables scattered about the room. We sat at one of those. It was toward the back, and Loftis could watch the front door while I watched the curtained-off doorway that presumably led to a private room of some sort. I could have made an issue about this—in fact, I was almost tempted to since I didn't have Loiosh with me—but I still had some faint hopes of convincing him that the story we'd given was true.

"What do you recommend?" I asked.

"I don't know; I've never been here before."

After too long, we realized that no one was going to bring us anything, so we went up to the bar and acquired a bottle of wine, a loaf of bread, two bowls of fish stew, glasses, spoons, a wooden platter to carry them all on. I did the paying, he did the carrying. We brought the stuff back to the table, sat down, poured, and sampled.

"The stew is too salty," suggested Loftis.

"The bread's all right."

"Better than the stew," he agreed.

"Or the wine," I added.

"I was thinking about bringing you in," he said.

"Do you have better wine than this?"

"A little better. Not enough to get excited about. The trouble is, we can't find your friend."

"You just haven't looked hard enough."

"Oh?"

"I know some excellent Eastern wines."

"Make a list of them for me. And while you're filling it out, maybe you can write down an address where I can find dear Margaret."

"I'll be sure to do that. But I don't feel too bad for you. You can't have been looking for more than half an hour. What do you expect? Searches and wines take time to mature."

"Wines do, certainly. But searches can be helped. And I'd take it as a personal favor."

"How about if I just pay for the next bottle of wine, instead?"

"That's a thought. You don't seem worried, Padraic. Is that your real name, by the way?"

"I don't remember anymore."

"Too much wine can do that to one's memory." He poured

me some more. "You probably should be worried, though. Because, when I say that I might have to bring you in—"

"Please," I said. "Don't ruin the surprise. Or the meal, for that matter."

"You know, I can't even eat this stew. I wonder if they have anything else."

"I wouldn't risk it if they did. We got what they recommended; what do you suppose the inferior stuff is like?"

"Good point. Who did you say you're working for?"

"An unnamed Imperial group, devoted to the interests of the State."

"Excellent. I believe you, too. Only, I will require some form of identification, or a contact in the Imperial Palace, or a Signet."

I poured him some wine. "That could be problematical," I said.

"Yes. What exactly are you trying to do?"

"There's an old lady whose land is being taken away from her. We're trying to find out who owns the land so we can buy it for her, but the company is out of business. She's being evicted, you see—"

He held up his hand. "Say no more," he said. "Just give me her name, and I'll see that it's taken care of."

The worst of it was that he might be able to, and perhaps he even would; but I couldn't count on it, and I certainly couldn't give him any help in tracking you down, Kiera; especially after all the work I'd just gone through to destroy all the work you'd done in setting this up. I said, "I can't seem to remember, just at the moment. It must be the wine."

"Probably."

"Boss, there are a couple of blades I don't recognize outside the door."

"Outside the door? What are they doing?"

"If I didn't know better, I'd say they were getting ready to go charging in."

"Oh."

Loftis sighed and pushed the food away. "Execrable," he said. "What am I going to do with you?"

Under the table, I let a dagger fall into my left hand, and made sure my sword was loose in its sheath. "You could paint me blue and trade me for bagpipes."

"Yes, that would be an option. But I'm afraid, as much as I've enjoyed sharing a meal with you, I'm going to have to insist on your accompanying me back to a place where I'm better equipped to get answers to questions."

"Damn," I said. "I just remembered. My niece is getting married this evening, and I have to pick out some new clothes, so I'm afraid I won't be able to make it today."

"Oh, I'm sure your niece will understand. Just what was her name, and where might I find her?" He smiled, then the smile went away and he looked at me very hard. "There are really only a couple of questions I need answered, but I *do* need them answered. Do you understand?"

I matched his stare.

He said, "Who do you work for, and what are you trying to accomplish? If you give me those answers, maybe we can work something out. If you don't, I'm going to have to start squeezing you."

"It isn't going to happen," I said.

"Boss, they're coming in!"

I rose to my feet, and I had my weapon halfway out when two men came through the curtain I was facing. I stepped to the side so Loftis couldn't get an easy shot at me and flipped my dagger at one of them; when he flinched, I lunged for the other one, knocking his weapon out of line and nailing him in the throat. I risked a quick glance toward the door, and then saw the other two, who were looking a little startled to see me noticing them and smiling; Loftis was now on his feet, too, and he had a weapon out, but he was looking at the pair who'd come through the door. He was facing away from me, so I couldn't see his expression, nor did I have time for a close look, because there was still the one I'd thrown my knife at. But Loftis did take the time to look at me, and there was no particular expression in that look. He said, "He didn't break the stick," which was just damned informative, but I didn't have the time to ask for an explanation.

As I turned back to the one I'd distracted, he made a break to get past me; that was fine, they could all run away as far as I was concerned.

Only he didn't run away.

He got past me, then he buried his sword in Loftis's skull, then he kept running out the door. The other two followed behind; they were gone before I realized it.

"Boss?"

"Don't worry, Loiosh. They weren't after me."

"They weren't?"

"Right. On the other hand, I suppose that means you can go ahead and worry."

Everyone in the room was staring at Loftis, and there was no sound, until the Dragonlord dropped his weapon, which made an appalling clamor as it hit the floor.

He turned very slowly and looked at me; there was an expression of surprise on his face. He opened his mouth, then closed it. I could see the muscles of his neck straining, and realized that it was hard work for him to keep his head straight with the weight of a sword attached to it.

Loftis sank to his knees, then he fell forward onto his face, looking absurd and pitiful with the sword still sticking out of the back of his head.

Chapter Eleven

I GOT OUT of there in a hurry, before anyone in the place could think to stop me.

Loiosh said, *"Should I follow them? Oh, never mind; they've just teleported. I can show you where they teleported from if you want."*

"I have no intention of tracing anyone's teleport, Loiosh; I just want to get out of here. Keep watching."

"Okay, boss."

I crossed the street and turned right at the first corner I came to, then right again, then left, then left again, and then right, then I went straight for a while, then I stopped and looked around, having gotten myself lost enough to have a chance of confusing anyone else."

"Well?"

"All clear, boss."

"Okay, back home, then."

"I'll keep watching."

We made it back to the cottage, both of us looking

around fairly often. Buddy seemed happy to see me, Rocza seemed happy to see Loiosh, the old woman didn't seem happy about anything, and Savn didn't seem to care one way or another. I sat down at the table, closed my eyes, and took my first deep breath in what seemed like a year or so.

The old woman looked at me and didn't ask any questions, wherefore I gave her no answers. I really wished you were here, Kiera, because I felt the need to confess and to have some help sorting out what had just happened. It had all made sense—Loftis figuring it out, sitting me down where he could give me one chance to come clean, and then having his people arrest me—up to the point where they'd killed him.

They'd killed *him.*

Had he been surprised by who came through the door? Or that anyone showed up? Or only by what they did?

He didn't break the stick.

That was a good one; I'd love to have found out what it meant, but there was no one around to ask. If I'd understood it, no doubt it would turn out to be the code phrase that made everything clear, and indicated exactly what I should do next. More probably, it went back to his childhood and had something to do with being hurt—at least, that's the sort of thing that went through my head when I decided I was about to become damaged, or maybe dead.

I regretted him. He was an honest son of a bitch, in spite of what he was doing, and he'd struck me as good at his job, although the only trace of evidence for that was that he'd hit you the same way, Kiera, so maybe he was really just a fool who knew how to impress people like us.

I wished his last meal had been better, though.

I said, "How's the boy, Mother?"

"No change," she said.

I said, "Savn?" He didn't seem to hear me. He was staring into the hearth as if it was the only thing in the world. At least there weren't any knives in it. I said, "Do you have any great ideas?"

She glared at me, then stood up, which took her quite a while. She came over and sat beside me, saying in a low voice, "I don't think I'm going to attempt the dreamwalk; at least, not for a while. He is responding, in a way, so that's some improvement. I want to know how far we'll get. I want to know if we can get him talking about something other than knives."

"How are you going to do that?"

"I've been talking to him. You could try it too."

"Just talking to him?"

"Yes."

"Even though he doesn't respond?"

"Yes."

"All right," I said.

She nodded, and I went over and sat down next to him. "So how are you, boy?" I said. He didn't respond. "I hope you're feeling well physically, at least." I felt like an idiot. The old woman got up and went outside, taking Buddy with her.

"It's been about a year now, Savn." I said. "Look, I hope you know that I'm sorry about what happened. You were never supposed to get involved in it."

He stared at the hearth and didn't move.

"You saved my life, you know. Twice. First, when I was injured, and then again. That isn't something I forget. And all those things you said to me, they were hard to hear, but it was probably good for me." I laughed a little. "Most things that are good for you hurt, maybe. To the left, though, most things that hurt aren't good for you. There's a nice riddle, if you want one. Do you like riddles? Do you like puzzles? I'm working on a puzzle now, Savn, and it has me pretty thoroughly stumped. I'd like to talk it over with you. You're a pretty sharp kid, you know.

"Why was Loftis killed? That's a puzzler, isn't it? He was working for someone in the Empire who was trying to hide the fact that Fyres was murdered, because if Fyres was murdered, they'd have to look into who killed him, and they'd probably never find out, but they *would* find out who wanted him dead, and that was a lot of people with a lot of connections to some of the people who keep our Empire chugging along. So maybe someone didn't want the information hidden. I can imagine that, Savn. But that's no reason to kill Loftis—it would be much easier, and probably cheaper, just to let someone, say the Warlord, or Lord Khaavren, or even Her Majesty, know what was going on. Killing Loftis doesn't make any sense.

"And it couldn't be to help hide what he was doing, because now they're going to have to investigate *that,* and that will almost certainly lead them to find out everything. But if that was the goal, it was going about it the hard way, and the dangerous way, and people don't do that when there's a safe way and an easy way to do things—except maybe Dzurlords, and they don't get into the sort of subtle thinking that goes along with it. I just can't make it fit, Savn. What do you think?"

Evidently he thought the hearth was fascinating.

"There's got to be a piece of this I'm not seeing—a piece of information I don't have. I wish I had more sources, like I used to. It used to be I could just snap my fingers and people would go scurrying to discover everything I needed to know. Now all I've got is what I can learn myself (with the help of Loiosh and Rocza, and a few minstrels). Should I go find a minstrel and talk to him, Savn? You were there the last time I did that, and I got some useful information, too. Remember her? She was quite something, wasn't she?

I remember thinking you were getting a crush on her, and I couldn't blame you. I was, too, if truth be known, but she's Dragaeran, and I'm an Easterner, and there you have it. Besides, I imagine she doesn't think much of me now, with what I've done to you. I suspect she blames me, and she's right to. I blame me, too."

I sat next to him and stared at the hearth. It was getting a bit chilly; maybe I should get a fire started. Back where Savn had come from, they were harvesting flax about now. They probably missed him.

"All right," I told him. "I'll go find a minstrel, and I'll see what the word is about Fyres, and about the investigation, and about the banks. Maybe I'll learn something. At least it'll keep me busy."

I stood up. "I'll talk to you later, all right?" He didn't object, so I headed out the door. The old woman was sitting on a wicker chair in front of the house, Buddy curled up beside her. I had the uncomfortable feeling she'd heard everything I said. I wondered if her whole reason for having me talk to him was so she could listen in, but I dismissed the thought; if there was one person in the whole mess who wasn't devious, it was her. But this affair was enough to make anyone paranoid, so I acquitted myself of paranoia and wrapped my cloak a little tighter around myself, because it was getting cold. Why is it you notice the weather more when you're out of town? I don't remember paying much attention to the weather when I lived in Adrilankha, even though I spent a lot of time walking around outside.

Minstrels, I've found, are rather like boot hooks—you keep running into them every time you go into your closet to find something else, but the minute you realize you need one they vanish without a trace. After walking all the way into Northport, I must have spent three hours going from one inn to another, and nowhere was there anyone singing for his supper, or telling stories in exchange for a room, or even sitting passed-out in the corner with a reed-pipe on his lap.

But diligence is sometimes rewarded. Seven times I asked locals where I might find some music. One didn't know, three didn't bother talking to me, and two were rude enough that I felt obligated to give them some minor damage as a lesson in courtesy. The seventh, however, was a pleasant young Teckla woman with flowing skirts and amazing black eyes who directed me to a public house about half a mile away, with feathers on its sign. I found it with no trouble (which surprised me just a little, as I'd become pessimistic about the whole adventure by that point) and I made my way into the small, smoke-filled little inn, in amongst a large crowd of mostly Teckla, with a couple of Orca and Chreotha surrounded by the entourage the minor nobility invariably attracts in such places, and, at the far end, a middle-aged Teckla playing a fretted gordstring as softly as such a twangy instrument can be played, and actually fairly well.

One part of a bench in the middle of the room was open, and I took it. Loiosh was with me, which may have accounted for some of the looks I got, but more likely they just weren't used to Easterners in there. The singer's voice was high and probably would have been unpleasant, but he picked songs that fit it—I suppose that's part of being a minstrel, just like part of being an assassin is knowing which jobs to take and which ones to leave alone. Eventually someone came by and brought me some wine, which I drank quickly because it wasn't very good, and some time later the minstrel stopped playing.

He stayed where he was and drank, and after a while I approached him. He looked at me, looked at Loiosh, and seemed uncomfortable, which was only natural. I said quietly, "My name is Vlad," and watched his face very closely for any sign of recognition.

"Yes?" he said. No, he didn't seem to recognize the name, which was good news. The first time a minstrel recognizes my name is the last time I can pull this stunt.

"Can we talk for a few minutes?"

"About what?"

I showed him the ring, then quickly put it away. The ring, by the way, represented one of the last things I arranged before I left Adrilankha; its design is a recognition symbol for the Minstrels' Guild, so when I showed it to him, he just said, "I see" and "Yes."

"I'm going to walk outside and cross the street. Meet me in twenty minutes, all right?"

"All right. Yes. How much—?"

"Ten imperials, or maybe more if you can help me."

"All right."

I nodded and left the place, walking around for a little while and eventually circling back. Loiosh flew around to look for signs of someone setting something up, but I didn't expect anything like that, and there wasn't.

After twenty minutes, he left the inn and crossed the street, and I stepped up next to him. "Let's walk together," I said, handing him ten coins. I'd said that to someone earlier that day, too.

We strolled together through the dark and quiet streets. This part of the city was far from the docks, and very narrow, and looked nothing at all like anywhere in Adrilankha, which I rather liked. I said, "What have you heard about Fyres?"

"The Orca?"

"Yes."

"Well, I mean, you know that he's dead."

"Yes. How did he die?"

"An accident on his yacht."

"Are you certain?"

We walked a little further. He said, "I've heard rumors, whispers. You know."

"No," I said. "I don't. Tell me."

"Who are you?"

"A friend of the Guild."

"Is there going—? That is, am I—?"

"In danger? No, as long we aren't seen together, and probably not even if we are."

"Probably not?"

"That's why we aren't talking inside, and why we're staying to areas without much light. Now, you were saying?"

"There's been talk that he was murdered."

"By whom?"

"People."

"What sort of people?"

"Just people."

"Why do they think so?"

"I don't know. But I'll tell you something: every time someone famous dies, however he dies, people say he was murdered."

"You think that's all it is?"

"Yeah. Am I wrong?"

"I don't know. I'm trying to find out. I'm asking you questions to find out. And I'm paying you. You have no reason to suspect—uh—foul play?"

"Not really, no."

"All right. What about all these bank closings?"

"It's the Empire."

"The Empire closed the banks?"

"No, but they allowed it."

"What do you mean?"

"I mean they aren't supposed to do that—let banks just close, anytime they want to; they're supposed to protect people."

"Why didn't they?"

"Because the bankers paid them."

"Are you sure about that?"

"Yeah."

"How do you know?"

"I know."

"How?"

He didn't answer. I said, "How much did you lose?"

"Almost eight hundred imperials."

"I see. Is that how you know?"

He didn't answer. I sighed. I wasn't getting a whole lot that I could use. I said, "What about the Jhereg?"

"What about them?"

"Are they involved?"

"With the banks? I don't know. I hadn't thought of that."

Oh, good. I was supposed to be tracking down rumors, and instead I was starting them. What I wanted to say was, "Can you tell me anything useful?" but that wasn't likely to produce results. I said, "What can you tell me about the people being kicked off their land?"

"Just what everyone knows," he said. "It's happening a lot, and no one knows why."

"What do you mean, no one knows why?"

He shrugged. "Well, it doesn't make any sense, does it? You get a notice of eviction, and then you go see if you can buy the place, and the owners have gone out of business."

"That's been happening a lot?"

"Sure. All over the place. I'm one of the lucky ones: we're still on Lord Sevaana's land, and he's still all right, as far as anyone knows. But I have friends and relatives who don't know what's going on, or what to do about it, or anything."

I don't know why I'd assumed the old woman's case was unique, but apparently I was wrong. That was certainly interesting. Who could stand to gain by forcing people to leave their land so it could be sold and then not selling it? And why force them to move before offering *them* the chance to buy it themselves? And how could Fyres's death have set all this off? And who wanted Loftis dead, and why? And—

No, wait a minute.

"Has anyone actually been made to move off his land yet?"

"Huh? Not this soon. No one could move that quickly, even if they made us."

"Yeah, I suppose you're right." But still . . .

"Is there anything else?" said the minstrel.

"Huh? What? On, no. Here. Vanish." I gave him another ten imperials. He vanished.

"What is it, boss?"

"The inkling of the germ of a thread that might lead to the beginning of an idea."

"Sure, boss. Whatever you say."

"I think I might have a piece of something, anyway. Let me think for a minute."

He was polite enough not to make any of the obvious rejoinders, so I thought as I strolled. It isn't all that easy to just think, keeping your mind concentrated on the subject, unless you're talking to someone or writing things down, which is one reason I like to talk to Loiosh as I'm putting things together, but what I had right then wouldn't fit itself into words because it wasn't precise enough—it was just the vague, unformed notion that I'd, well, not exactly *missed* something, but that I'd been putting the wrong slant on things.

After a while I said, *"The trouble is, Loiosh, that the way Kiera and I got involved in this was through whatever oddity is involved in this business of putting what's-her-name's land on the market and then making it hard to track down, followed by impossible to track down. Just because that's where we started doesn't make that an important piece of whatever it is that's going on."*

"You knew that already, boss."

"Sure. But knowing it is one thing; being aware of it as you work and taking it into account whenever you look at new information—"

"What are you saying?"

"Heh. That I've been looking at this thing skewed by what I knew about it. I have to look at it straight on. And I have a theory."

"Oh, good. Only that was missing. All right, then, where to now?"

"I don't know." And, in my mind, Loiosh spoke the words as I did. *"You're funny, Loiosh,"* I told him. *"Do you have any great ideas?"*

"Yeah. Let's get out of here."

I looked around, but didn't see anything.

"No," he said. *"This city. This area. It isn't good, boss. They're still looking for you, and when you're in a city like this, you're too easy to find. I don't like it."*

Neither did I, come to that. *"Soon,"* I told him. *"As soon as we get this settled."*

"You can't do Savn any good with a Morganti knife between your shoulder blades."

"True."

"If I'd known we were going to be here this long, and that we'd be going around stirring up—"

"Okay, okay. I get the point." I'd thought about it, of course. Loiosh was right: a city, even one as small as Northport, was not a good place for me to hide when the whole Organization was looking for me. And, if what I'd just figured out was true, then I'd pretty much done what I'd agreed to do—the old woman would be able to stay on her land, and everything was fine.

"Where would we go instead?"

"The East."

"We've been there, remember?"

"It's big, there are lots of places. And no one would find us."

"Good point." There really wasn't any reason to stay here, if I could be certain that what I'd just figured out was true, and I could probably find that out.

Except that someone had cut Loftis down right in front of me, and there were neighborhoods full of people who had to leave because they no longer had any work, and I didn't understand why any of it was happening.

I said, *"The old woman is doing so well with Savn, it would be a shame to take him away so soon."*

"Boss—"

"Let's just take a few more days, all right?"

"You're the boss."

I wondered what you were finding out, Kiera; what would we learn about Fyres from the Jhereg? And, come to that, how heavily were the Jhereg involved? And if he'd gotten the Jhereg into it, why did he need the banks?

Did he need the banks at all?

There was only one banker we knew for certain was involved with Fyres, and that was Vonnith, and we knew she was bribing Imperial officials, which almost made her a Jhereg, too. Did I know of any legitimate banks that had made loans to Fyres? Did I even have any reason to suspect there were any?

How could I find out? Walking around pretending to be someone else has its uses, and we'd gotten some information that way, but there's a time for just being who you are. Had we reached it yet? Who was I, anyway?

Hmmm.

"Could work, boss."

"It's worth a shot."

"And even if it doesn't work, I'll enjoy it."

"Yeah, you probably will."

"And you won't?"

It wasn't easy finding a tailor's shop that was open at this hour—in fact, there were none. But after disturbing the tailor, it was easy enough to get what I wanted just by setting an appropriately large number of coins in front of him. My reserves of cash had been getting a bit low lately, and I wasn't excited about going to any of the places I'd need to in order to retrieve more of my wealth—for one thing, I'd have to remove the gold Phoenix Stone in order to teleport—but I could do it if I had to.

However, I was able to put in the order and he promised that he'd have what I needed early in the morning. That done, I wandered for a while, thinking over the plan and refining it in conversation with Loiosh.

I discovered that my feet were taking me back toward the cottage, and I decided to let them have their way, now that I had a plan for tomorrow. I walked, and I thought, and Loiosh flew above me, or sometimes sat on my shoulder, but kept watching so that I had the freedom to let ideas roll around in my head and turn into conclusions. I thought about stopping and performing a quick spell to make my feet hurt less, but I'd have to remove one of the Phoenix Stones or the other, and Loiosh gave me the benefit of his opinion on the wisdom of that, so by the time I reached the cottage I'd come to the conclusion that I was very tired of walking. I explained this to Buddy when he came out to greet me. He wagged his tail and sneezed in sympathy. Good dog.

Savn was sitting next to the hearth this time, not facing it. The old woman was next to him, talking to him softly. As I came in I waited to see if he would acknowledge my presence, but it was as if I didn't exist, as if nothing existed, even the old woman who was talking to him.

I walked over. "Hello, Savn," I said.

He didn't look at me, but he said, "Do you have a knife?"

I said, "Do you know my name?"

"You have a knife, don't you?"

"You know who I am, don't you Savn?"

"I . . . I lost Paener's knife, you know. I let it—"

"It's all right, Savn. No one is angry about that. Do you know who I am?"

"It was a good knife. It was very sharp."

"Let's talk about something else, Savn."

"I used it to cut—to cut things."

The old woman said, "Savn, your sister is all right."

He didn't seem to hear her any more than he'd heard me, but his hands started opening and closing. We sat there, but he didn't say anything else.

I looked at the old woman, who shrugged and stood up. She pulled me over to a corner and spoke in a low voice, saying, "I'm beginning to understand what's going on with him."

"His sister?"

She nodded. "She's the key. He thinks he killed her, or something. I'm not sure. He isn't really rational, you know.

He doesn't know when he's dreaming and when he's really experiencing things."

"I could bring him back and show her to him."

She shook her head. "Not yet. He'd just think it was a dream."

"Then what do we do?"

"Just what we've been doing. We keep talking to him, even though he only wants to talk about knives and cutting, and we try to get him to talk about other things."

"Will that work?"

She shrugged. "If I'm right about what's going on in his head, then it should help, eventually. But I don't know what you mean by work. There's no way to know how much he'll recover, or what he'll be like. But we might be able to get him to the point where he responds to us, and then maybe we can teach him to look after himself."

"That would be good," I said.

"How about my problem?"

"You mean, about the cottage?"

"Yes."

"I'm not sure. I think I've figured out some of it. If my theories are right, you don't have anything to worry about. But you ought to worry about the possibility that my theories are wrong."

"All right," she said. "What if you're wrong?"

"Don't worry about it," I said.

Chapter Twelve

I WAS UP early, and, after almost enough klava, I stopped by the tailor's to retrieve the items that I'd ordered. The tailor had, evidently, been thinking, which can be unhealthy, but it had only frightened him, which is a natural survival reaction. I reassured him with words and coins, got the items, and left him reasonably content. Then I went by a weaponsmith and picked up a few things. Then I found an inn that was serving breakfast, stepped into the privy, and, amid odors that I will not bother describing, I spent some time getting dressed and set—it took me a while to remember how to conceal knives about my person without them showing, which surprised me a little. I covered everything, including the cloak, with my regular, nondescript brown cloak, which was far too hot for inside the privy, but would be only slightly too warm for the walk out to Vonnith's place.

I left the tavern a bit more bulky than I went in and made my plodding way out of Northport toward the home of our dear friend, Side-Captain Vonnith, and what *is* a side-captain, anyway?

There's no need to tell you about the trip out there—you did it yourself. And my compliments, Kiera, on the accuracy of the report, which gave me an excellent idea of what to expect, and when to expect it. About half a mile away, then, I took off the extra cloak, and appeared before some nameless birds and small animals as me, the old me, Vlad Taltos, Jhereg, assassin, and friend to old ladies. I continued after stashing the brown cloak in a thicket at the side of the road, and Loiosh grudgingly agreed to wait outside after making a few remarks about who got to have all the fun. I guess his idea of fun is different than mine.

Or maybe not.

Vonnith's guards got to me as I was walking up to the front door. Two of them, flanking me as neat as you please. They made no hostile moves, so I kept walking. They said, "My lord, may we be of some service to you?"

"If you wish," I said. "You may tell the Side-Captain that a friend is here to see her."

"A friend, my lord?"

"That's right. Don't I look friendly?" I smiled at them, but they didn't answer. We reached the door. I said, "If you wish, you may tell her that I represent the Adrilankha Eleemosynary Society."

"The—?"

"Adrilankha Eleemosynary Society."

"Uh, wait just a moment," he said. He was quiet for a time, I assume making psychic contact with someone, then he looked over at his companion and nodded once. The companion hadn't opened his mouth the entire time, but he was standing the right distance away from me, so I assume he knew his business. In any case, they both inclined their heads to me slightly and went back to their stations. I shrugged, gave a last adjustment to my brand-new clothing, and pulled the clapper.

Hub appeared, looking just as you'd described him, and gave me a greeting that made me miss Teldra. Have you met Teldra? Never mind. He showed me in and brought me to the same room she met you in, and there was Vonnith, just where she was supposed to be.

She stood up and gave me a slight bow—I don't think she knew how polite she was supposed to be to me—and started to speak. I sat down and said, "Give me the names of all the banks Fyres was involved in. I don't need yours, we know about those. Which other ones?"

She frowned. "Why do you need to know that? And who are you, anyway?"

"I'm not going to tell you my real name; you should know that. And I don't have the energy to invent a good one. You know who I work for—"

"You're a Jhereg!"

"Yes. And an Easterner. What's your point? We need to know what other banks Fyres was involved with, and we need to know before they go under."

"But how can you not know? How can—?" She seemed very puzzled, but I had no interest in letting her work things out; I'd made that mistake yesterday.

"Maybe we do know," I said, and let her put it together herself—wrong, of course. It's disgustingly easy to let people lie to themselves, and they do it so much better than you can. But as she was coming to the conclusion that this was all a test, and deciding how she ought to react to that, she wasn't considering the possibility that I wasn't involved with anyone except an old hedge-wizard and a notorious thief.

She said, "I don't know them all. I know the big ones, of course."

"Size isn't important; I mean the ones with heavy enough investments that they're at risk, or at any rate they've been seriously hurt."

"Oh," she said, and somehow that made things all right—perhaps she decided that she wasn't really being tested, we just didn't know who was heavily committed to Fyres. Or maybe she came up with some other explanation, I don't know. But I got what I was after. She said, "Well, the Bank of the Empire, of course."

Cracks and shards! "Yes. Go on."

"And the Turmoli Trust, and Havinger's."

"Quite."

"Should I include the House treasuries?"

House treasuries?

"Yes."

"Well, the only ones I know about are the Dragon and the Jhegaala. And the Orca, naturally."

"Naturally," I echoed, trying to keep my eyes from bulging too obviously. The Orca Treasury! The *Dragon* Treasury!

"I think those are the only Houses, or at least the only ones with potentially dangerous investments."

"Not the Jhereg?" I said.

"No," she said. "As far as I know, you—they are only in for small change. I think that was the deal to convince the Dragons to invest."

"That would make sense," I said. *Besides, what does the Jhereg Treasury matter if all the Jhereg in Northport and half the Jhereg in Adrilankha had already gotten involved?* But then, maybe they hadn't—I still didn't know what you were going to uncover in Adrilankha, I was just guessing based on what your friend Stony had said.

She kept talking, and I kept listening, but the details aren't important. She named about twenty or thirty banks, trusts, and moneylenders who were either going under or were in danger of going under, and, as I said, the Bank of the Empire, which embodies the Imperial Treasury, was at the very top of the list.

What happens if the Empire has to file surrender of debts, Kiera? Who can it surrender its debts *to?* It occurs to me that there are probably scholars of the House of the Orca who sit around and discuss things like this, or write long books about it, but nothing like it had ever crossed my mind before. When she finally ran down, I said, "Good. That's what we needed."

"But you knew all that."

"Maybe," I said. "That isn't your concern, is it?"

"I suppose not," she said, and looked at me with maybe just the hint of suspicion.

As if it were just an afterthought to the conversation, I said, "Loftis was killed yesterday."

"So I heard," she said coolly. "Poor fellow. Do the authorities know who did it?"

"Nope," I said.

She studied her fingernails. "I heard he was eating lunch with an Easterner at the time."

She heard that? Well, maybe that explained why she was so ready to believe I was who I claimed to be. That was almost funny. "It's possible," I said.

"It seemed like a professional job."

I looked at her and alarm bells went off inside my head. She knew as much about professionalism in assassination as I knew about professionalism in finance. And, in fact, it *hadn't* been a professional job; at least, not the way the Jhereg would have done it. Too many people involved, and too much left to chance, including a target who had the opportunity to draw his blade and a witness left alive. Whoever killed Loftis, it wasn't the Jhereg.

So who was it?

I tried to remember enough about the assassins to guess their House, but I couldn't really. They weren't Dzurlords, and they weren't Dragonlords. Orca? Maybe. Probably.

But, above all, why was she pretending it was a Jhereg job? Did she think I was pretending it was a Jhereg job, and she was just going along with it, even though she knew better? I looked at her, and my instincts answered *yes*.

"What is it?" she said. I'd been looking at her, even though I hadn't been aware of it, and apparently this was making her nervous. Good.

"What do you know?" I said.

"What do you mean?"

"You know something."

"About what?"

"You tell me."

"I don't—"

"I know we didn't do Loftis, and you know we didn't do Loftis. You've been scared, and you're getting ready to jump. You know something you shouldn't know, and that's scaring you, and well it should. What is it?"

"I don't know what you're talking about."

"Don't you?"

She tried to scowl at me. I stared back at her. I was Vlad again, a Jhereg assassin, if only for a moment, and she was an Orca—rich and fat, at least metaphorically. I'd become an assassin in the first place just for the pleasure of killing people like her. So I glared and waited, and eventually she cracked. It wasn't obvious, but I could see her resistance break down, and she knew I could see.

I said, "Well? Who killed him?"

She shook her head.

I said, "Don't be stupid. You know who I represent.

Whoever you're scared of, you should be more scared of me. Now, which one of them was it?"

I threw in the "which one of them was it" phrase because it makes it sound like you know what you're talking about even when you don't, and this time it paid off. She said, "Reega."

"Good," I said. "Congratulations, you've just saved your life. How deep into her are you?"

"Heh," she said. "I'm not into her, she's into me."

"Same thing, isn't it? If she goes down, you follow her."

She nodded.

"Very well, Side-Captain. You know that we're all a little shy these days about throwing money at someone to keep an operation from going under—especially that bloodline. But it is possible something can be worked out."

"Something *has* been worked out," she snapped. "And if you people would just leave us alone—"

"You mean the land swindle? I know about that. What makes you think it's going to work?"

"What do you mean?"

"It isn't like it's a secret, Side-Captain."

"Who knows?"

"Everyone."

"Everyone?"

"Except maybe the victims."

"Well, it doesn't matter, does it? As long as the v—as long as the tenants don't find out, it doesn't matter who else does."

"Sure. But how long will it be until they realize what's going on? And then what?"

"We'll be gone by then."

"Do you really think you can move that quickly?"

"We can be done this week."

I pretended to consider. "It might work," I said.

"It will work. The Empire won't prosecute, and I don't even know what law they'd prosecute under if they wanted to. Right now we've got twelve thousand tenants who will go into debt for life to buy land at three times its value. If that isn't worth a little short-term Jhereg investment—"

"The Jhereg," I said, "doesn't have much to invest. You know why as well as I do."

She shrugged. "But I also know that you can come up with the funds, if you want to."

"Yes," I agreed. "We can."

"Boss! Trouble!"

"Just a moment," I said. *"What is it, Loiosh?"*

"Someone's just teleported in. Male, Jhereg colors, two bodyguards."

"Oh, nuts."

I stood up. "You must excuse me; there's a problem back home. I'll talk to my bosses."

Hub came into the room and whispered in Vonnith's ear. She nodded to him, then looked at me. "No need," she said. "I think your boss is here already."

I started heading toward where the back door had to be. *"Boss, two more just appeared in back."*

I looked at her, and realized she was in psychic communication—no doubt with whoever the Jhereg was. She focused on me and said, "Who are you?"

"Now don't you feel stupid," I told her.

The back was out and the front was out. *"Anyone watching the side windows, Loiosh?"*

"Two."

Damn.

"Who *are* you?"

"Did you tell him that there was one of his people here?" I asked. "And did you mention it was an Easterner?"

"Who are you?" she said, as I saw the affirmative in her

eyes. She had no idea why he'd reacted as he had, but now I was trapped. If I teleported, they'd just trace it, and I'd have to remove the black Phoenix Stone. I looked around. Here was as good as anywhere, I decided. So the question was, stand, or attempt to break out? I drew my blade.

"Are they Jhereg at the side window?"

"No, Orca."

So that was the best path. I came to this conclusion about ten seconds too late, however, as three of them walked into the room. The one in the middle I knew from your description had to be Stony.

"Vlad Taltos," he said. "A pleasure to meet you."

"You, too, dead man."

He smiled.

His two "associates" spread out on either side of me. Vonnith said, "Not here!"

I said, "This is pretty sloppy work, you know, dead man."

"I know," said Stony. "Inelegant. But it's the best we can do, under the circumstances." He was armed as well, with a short, heavy sword, but he didn't look like someone who'd be all that good with it, whereas the two who were flanking me seemed to know their business.

"Boss?"

"I'm going to be busy in here in a minute, Loiosh. If anyone else shows up to join the party, let me know, and if any escape routes show up, let me know that, too."

"Sure, boss," he said in the tone that indicated he had his own plan and to the Falls with mine, so I wasn't startled when there was the sound of breaking glass, although everyone else was.

I took two steps that lasted about ten years each, and I was very much aware that my back was to a pair of blades, but Stony was taking twenty years to stop looking at

Loiosh, so he wasn't ready for me and I took him, neat and clean, right through the heart. Then I turned around, drew a knife, and threw it at the one Loiosh wasn't busy with. To my amazement it actually hit him point-first, sticking in a spot on the left side of his lower chest, where it would certainly give him something to think about, and gave me time to step away from Stony, who was still on his feet and therefore dangerous. I prepared another knife very carefully.

"*Up!*"

Loiosh flew straight up to the ceiling and I threw, and, wouldn't you know it, the one I'd had time to aim hit him sort of edge-on in the stomach and did no damage to speak of, but that was all right, because Loiosh had scratched his face up pretty good and had bit him as well, so he probably had enough to keep him occupied.

I turned back to Stony, who picked that moment to fall over.

"*Good work, Loiosh.*"

"*Let's go, boss.*"

Side-Captain Vonnith stared at us with her mouth hanging open. I said, "Sorry about your window," and we headed for the front door, walking right in front of Hub, who looked like he wanted to say something polite but just couldn't manage. Lady Teldra would have.

"*Why don't we teleport?*"

"*Because if Stony had any sense, he let someone know what was going down, and they'll be looking for me with everything they've got, just in case. If I take off the Phoenix Stone, I'll last just long enough to wish I hadn't.*"

"*Oh.*"

"*Are you all right, Loiosh?*"

"*Pretty much, boss. I cut myself on the glass a bit, but it isn't too bad.*"

"Then why do you sound that way?"

"Well, okay, so I'm bleeding a bit."

"Come here."

I looked him over, and found a nasty gash just where his left wing joined his body, and another on the left side of his neck. Both of them were bleeding. He licked himself a bit and said, *"It's not as bad as it looks."*

He folded himself up and I tucked him under my cloak, trusting him to hold on, and I stepped out of the doorway, blade first.

There were two Jhereg in front of me, and a pair of Vonnith's personal guardsmen next to them, and they all looked ready to scuffle. They stood, almost motionless, waiting for me to move. Back in the old days I'd have had a handful of nasty little things to throw at them to keep them busy, but these days I only had a few throwing knives, and I'd already lost half of them. It didn't look good, especially with Loiosh clinging helplessly to the inside of my cloak; I was morally certain that if this came to a true melee, one of them would end up skewering my familiar by accident, and I would hate that.

I looked at how everyone was positioned, then I pointed to the two Orca, one at a time, with my blade. "You two," I said. "Five hundred gold each if you nail these two for me.

No, they weren't going to go for it, but the Jhereg couldn't know that. They each stepped back and took a look at the Orca, and that was just long enough for me to nail one in the throat. He went down and I faced the other one for a second, then said, "Okay, so maybe you don't want to attack them. I still think you're best off out of there. This isn't your fight, you know. And you won't get any of the reward in any case. Ask the Side-Captain if you don't believe me. I'll wait."

I'm afraid I lied to them, Kiera; while they were checking in, I took a step and a lunge, cutting the other Jhereg's wrist, then shoulder, then face. He went back and I went forward and he tried to counter and I parried, riposted, and got him lightly in the chest. He backed up some more and raised his blade to charge me; I gave him a very nice cut on his forearm, and his blade fell to the ground.

"Get out of here," I suggested. He turned and ran up toward the road without another word.

There's no question that the two Orca could have taken me then, but I had to hope they were a little intimidated by now, and that they weren't even sure this was their fight in the first place—aside from which, I really expected to see a good number of Jhereg showing up any minute, so I didn't have time for anything fancy. I looked at them; they shrugged and lowered their weapons.

"See you," I said, and made tracks, aware of the weight of Loiosh clinging to my cloak, and to the increasing wetness against my side.

It was a long, long way to the main road, Kiera, but nothing untoward happened before I reached it. I headed back toward Northport, ducking into the woods as soon as there was enough woods to duck into.

"I think we might make it, Loiosh," I said.

Then, *"Loiosh?"*

I stopped where I was, and if every assassin in the Empire had shown up just then, I don't think I would have noticed. He was gripping the inside of my cloak, and the first thing I noticed was that his chest was still rising and falling, and there was still blood seeping from the two wounds. I took the cloak off and spread it on the ground, then I gently spread his wings so I could look at the injuries. They didn't seem very deep, but the one near his wing was jagged and ugly. I spent a great deal of time looking for slivers of glass, but I didn't find any, which was good.

I didn't know what to do, so I cut the Jhereg cloak into strips and bandaged him up as best I could, binding his left wing tight to his body. Then I looked at the other wound and scowled mightily. I'd made jokes before, especially with Kragar and Melestev, about how they should be prepared to put a tourniquet around my throat if anyone cut it, but now that I was faced with the absurd problem of trying to put a bandage around Loiosh's snakelike neck, there wasn't anything funny about it. In the end, I just used a great deal of cloth and kept the wrapping loose enough so it wouldn't stop his breathing, and then I pressed my hand against it and held it there.

"Loiosh?"

No response.

I picked him up and made my way through the woods, doing my best to keep track of where I was, but I've never been a good woodsman.

Some animals, I'm told, will fall into a deep sleep in order to heal themselves. I didn't know if jhereg did that. Isn't that funny? Loiosh and I had been together since I was a kid, and there were so many things I didn't know about him. I wondered what that said about me, and whether it was something I wanted to hear. No doubt Savn—the old Savn, before he went away—would have had a great deal to say about it. He was a sharp kid, was Savn. I hoped that Savn wasn't gone forever. I hoped Loiosh wasn't gone forever. Cawti, the old Cawti, the woman I'd married, was probably gone forever. How much of all of this was my fault?

These were my thoughts, Kiera, as I tried to make my way to Northport, moving as fast as I could with the bundle of my familiar in front of me and thicket all around me. Good thing it was still daylight or I'd have killed myself; too bad it was daylight, because the Jhereg would have an easier time finding me. Where were they now? Had they arrived in force, and were they combing the woods, or had they not yet learned that I had escaped? They must, by now, have realized that Stony was dead, and at least they'd be sending someone to investigate.

There was a flapping above me, and I looked up, and there was Rocza. She landed on my shoulder and looked at me. Okay. I can take a hint.

I stopped, spread out the cloak, and removed the bandages from Loiosh's wounds. Rocza waited patiently while I did so, then gave me a look of stern disapproval and began methodically licking the wounds clean. I don't know if there's something about jhereg saliva, or if she was using her poison and there's something about *that,* but the bleeding had stopped by the time she was done. I reached out to pick up Loiosh, but Rocza hissed at me and I stopped. She picked him up in her talons, flapped once, and took to the air, though it seemed with a bit of trouble.

"Okay," I said. "Have it your way."

She flew in a careful circle, just over my head.

"I hope," I said aloud, "that you can lead me back home. And that you want to, for that matter."

I don't know if she understood me, or if she thought of it on her own, but she began flying, and she did such a good job of letting me stay in sight that it can't have been accidental. From time to time she would carefully lay Loiosh down in a tree limb, rest for a moment, and then fly around as if to scope out the area—maybe that's what she was doing, in which case Loiosh had certainly taught her well, because we didn't run into anyone. Once, when she had deposited Loiosh, another jhereg came and sat near him. Rocza returned and spread her wings and hissed with great enthusiasm, and the other jhereg flew off. I applauded silently.

Eventually the woods gave way to grassland, and I felt rather naked and exposed walking through it, except that by then it was growing dark, so I delayed a little while to give the darkness more time to settle in and get comfortable. Rocza didn't like that, and hissed at me, but then she probably decided she needed the rest, too, so she set Loiosh down in the grass and licked him some more, and when the light had faded enough we started off again.

It took a long time, but eventually we found the road through the woods, and then we found the hideous blue cottage, and we were home. Buddy came out, looked at us, barked once, then followed us in. Rocza flew into the house, went straight to the table, and gently laid Loiosh on it. It was only when I noticed how pleasantly warm the place was that I realized I'd been cold.

The old woman stood up.

"It's a long story," I said, "and I don't think you want to hear it. But Loiosh has been hurt, and—wait a minute."

Rocza flew over to where Savn was staring off into space, landed on his shoulder, and hissed at him. Savn very slowly turned to face her. The old woman and I looked at each other, then turned back to them.

Rocza hissed again, then flew over to the table. Savn followed her with his eyes. She flew back to his shoulder, hissed, then flew back to Loiosh.

Savn rose unsteadily to his feet and walked over to the table, and looked down at Loiosh.

"I'll need some water," he said to no one in particular. "And a small needle, as sharp as you can find, and some stout thread, a candle, and clean cloth."

He worked on Loiosh far into the night.

INTERLUDE

"You're looking puzzled again, Cawti."

"Yes. Your conversation with Loftis."

"What about it?"

"How did you convince him that you were involved with the Empire?"

"Just what I said. I fed him a few details about things his group had been involved in."

"But *what* details? What activities of theirs did you know about?"

"You and Vlad."

"Huh?"

"I mean, he wanted to know that, too. He positively interrogated me about it."

"And you said?"

"That I didn't care to discuss it."

"Oh."

"Sorry."

"I understand. How is Loiosh?"

"You want me to get ahead of the story?"

"Yes."

"Loiosh is fine, as far as I know."

"Okay."

"Should I go on?"

"Please do."

"All right."

Chapter Thirteen

I SAT FOR a long time after Vlad had finished speaking, digesting his words slowly and carefully, the way one might digest a seventeen-course Lyorn High Feast on Kieron's Eve—a day I've never celebrated for personal reasons, though I've had the feast. I kept looking back and forth between Loiosh and Savn, who had perhaps gone a long way toward healing each other, although Loiosh showed no signs of injury save that he wasn't moving much, and Savn showed no signs of healing save that he'd moved a little bit.

"Well?" said Vlad when he'd judged I'd been silent long enough.

"Well what?"

"Have you put it together?"

"Oh. Sorry, I was thinking about"—I gestured toward Savn—"other things."

He nodded. "Do you want to try, or should I explain it?"

"Some of it, at least, is pretty obvious."

"You mean, the land deal?"

"Yes. It was just a subtheme to the concerto: a few of them need to come up with a lot of cash in a hurry, so they buy out Fyres's companies cheap, since they're going under, anyway, then threaten people like our good Hwdf'rjaanci with eviction to make them worried, then vanish so they don't know what's happening so they'll panic, and then, in a day or two, our heroes will come back with offers to sell them the land at outrageous prices, in cash."

He nodded. "With nice offers of loans at Jhereg-style interest rates to go with them."

"So our hostess isn't really in danger of losing her cottage, and, if she's careful, she can probably avoid being overcharged too much. In fact, if we can come up with some cash for her, she can even avoid the interest rates."

"I think we can do that," said Vlad.

"Between us," I said, "I have no doubt that we can."

"What about the rest of it?" he said. "Can you put it together?"

"Maybe. Do you know it all?"

"Almost," he said. "There's still a piece or two missing, but I have some theories; and there's also a lot of background stuff that you can probably explain."

"What's missing?"

"Loftis."

"You mean, why did Reega have him killed?"

"Yes. If it was Reega."

"You think Vonnith was lying?"

"Not lying. But we don't know yet if it was Reega's choice, or if she just arranged it."

"Why would she arrange it?"

"Because she was in a position to. She had a lot to gain, and she was in touch with Loftis."

"How do you know that?" I said.

"Because of the way she reacted when I told her the Empire was covering up something."

"Oh, right. I'd forgotten. Yeah, she might have just arranged it. But, if so, who did she arrange it for? And why?"

"Good questions. That's what I'm still missing." He shook his head. "I wish I knew what 'he didn't break the stick' means."

"I think I know," I said.

"Huh?"

"It goes back to the Fifth and Sixth Cycles, and even into the Seventh, before flashstones."

"Yes?"

"Some elite corps were given sorcery. Nothing fancy, just a couple of location spells, and usually one or two offensive weapons to be used over a distance. They weren't all that effective, by the way."

"Go on."

"Whoever was the brigade's sorcerer would bind the spells into a stick so that any idiot could release the spell. They used wood because binding them into stone took longer and was more difficult, although also more reliable." I shrugged. "You point the stick at someone, and you release the spell, which doesn't take a lot of skill, and you get a nasty scrape on your palm, and whoever you pointed the stick at has a much nastier burn. You can kill with it, and at a pretty good distance, if your hand is steady and your eye is good and, mostly, if the spell was put on right in the first place. Which it usually wasn't," I added, "according to the histories."

"But what does—"

"Right. The thing is, the sticks were smoothed a bit to take the spell, but otherwise they were just sticks. Once you got into battle, you might be looking around and see one on

the ground, but you'd have no way of knowing if it was
discharged or not—that is, unless you were fairly skilled,
the only way to find out if it had been used already was to
discharge it. You can imagine that it might be embarrassing
to pick one up on the field and assume it had a charge when
it didn't, or even the reverse."

"Yeah, I can see that."

"So the custom was to break it in half as soon as you'd
discharged it."

"And you think that's what he was talking about?"

" 'Breaking the stick' became a handy way of referring
to leaving a signal, especially a warning."

"How long since it's been used?"

"A long time."

"Then—"

"He was a military historian, Vlad. Remember how he
kept making references to obscure—"

"Got it."

I shrugged. "Maybe it meant something else, but . . ."

"Well, that's all very interesting." He closed his eyes for
a moment, and I could practically hear the tides of his
thoughts break against the shore of facts as he put things together in new ways; I waited and wondered. "Hmmm. Yes,
Kiera, it's *all* very interesting."

"What do you mean?"

"I mean, I think I have the rest of it. And then some."

"And then some?"

"Yeah, I got more than I wanted. But never mind that, it
doesn't matter. Can you put it together?"

"Maybe," I said. "Well, let's see what we have. We have
Fyres murdered, and someone desperate to hide that fact.
We have companies he was into falling like Teckla at the
Wall of Baritt's Tomb. We have someone, or someones, in

the Empire desperate to hide the fact that Fyres was murdered. Am I doing all right so far?"

"Yep. Keep going."

"Okay. We have Jhereg involvement with Fyres, and Imperial involvement with the banks, and—wait a minute."

"Yes?"

"Fyres owed the Jhereg. Fyres owed the banks. The banks and the Jhereg were depending on Fyres. The Empire was protecting the banks, and the banks were supporting the Empire. Have I got it?"

"Right. Conclusion?"

"The Empire is working with the Jhereg."

"Exactly," said Vlad. "Supporting the Jhereg, borrowing from the Jhereg, and, probably, using the Jhereg."

"Just as you were saying."

"Yeah, I guess it all seemed to be heading that way. But push it a little further, Kiera: what would the empire do if word of the Jhereg's influence in the Empire was about to emerge into the public?"

I shrugged. "Everything it could to hide that fact."

"Everything?"

I nodded. "Yes. Or, if it's what you want, everything including covering up the Fyres murder, and even—yes, and even murdering their own investigator if they thought he was no longer reliable."

"Yep. That's what 'he didn't break the stick' meant. It bothered me that someone like Loftis would be that careless. It either meant we were wrong about him or there was something we didn't know, and now we've figured it out."

"Yes," I said. "He was set up by his own side."

Vlad nodded. "He wasn't given the warning he was supposed to get if there was any danger. They'd probably picked that spot out, and there was supposed to be some indication either that it was all right or that it wasn't. And so he thought he was safe, and that's why they could take him out so easily."

"Right. Domm?"

"His name popped into my head," said Vlad.

I nodded. "Domm would be a safe guess. Reega set it up, and Domm made sure Loftis wouldn't be ready to defend himself, and they used you—"

I stopped, and looked at Vlad. He said, "What?" Then, "Oh."

"They were *too* ready, and you were too convenient."

"I didn't give the game away," said Vlad. "I didn't slip up. They already knew about me when I walked in, which means they already knew about you."

I nodded. "And that explains something else: namely, why it's been so easy to fool these people. We haven't fooled anyone, except maybe Vonnith. They've been playing with us, and letting us think we were playing with them."

"Not Vonnith, either," said Vlad. "She was onto me from the moment I first showed up."

"Stony?"

"Yes. I figured that it was just bad timing, him being there right then. But she must have gotten hold of him when I got there, and then all she had to do was delay me until he was ready to move."

I nodded.

He said, "Well, aren't we a couple of idiots?"

I nodded again. "Stony," I said. "That son of a bitch."

"What now, then?"

"Now, Vlad? What is there to do? We've solved Hwdf'rjaanci's problem, which was all we intended, and we've figured out what's going on, and we've also figured out that they had our number from the beginning. We're done."

He stared at me. "You mean, let them get away with it?"

I grinned. "I will if you will."

"For a minute there," he said, "you had me worried." Then he frowned. "When do you think they caught onto us?"

"Early," I said. "Remember Stony asking if I'd seen you?"

"Sure. I just figured it was a sign of how bad they want me, and they know we know each other."

"That's what I thought, too. And, right then, that's probably all it was. But then they put it together. Fyres's place is broken into, right?"

"Right."

"Okay. You didn't tell me why you wanted me to do that. If you had, maybe I'd have been messier, or done something atypical, but, as it was, it was a usual Kiera job, and anyone who knows my work, which certainly includes Stony, would—" I held up my hand as he started to speak. "No, I'm not blaming you: you had no reason to think I'd be involved after doing what you wanted; neither did I, really, I just got interested. But think about it. What's the next thing that happens after I break into Fyres's old place and steal his private papers?"

"You start asking Stony questions about him."

"Right."

"And we didn't know that Stony was involved enough to be hearing everything that happened regarding Fyres, the banks, the investigations, and everything else."

"That's it," I said. "Stony knows, right then and there, that I'm looking into Fyres's death, though he probably doesn't know why. But he knows Kiera the Thief is sniffing around the death of this rich guy who's made so much trouble."

"And then what does he do?"

I said, "He starts asking himself where the next logical place to look is, if someone is interested in Fyres's death. And it is?"

"The Imperial investigation."

"Exactly. So there he is, alerting Loftis and his merry band that Kiera the Thief might appear out of nowhere, or maybe someone working for Kiera. And who shows up there, right on schedule, but to everyone's amazement?"

Vlad nodded. "I do," he said, with more than a touch of bitterness in his voice. "In my great disguise that fooled them so completely."

"Yes. Loftis is looking for people to show up asking questions, and he's looking carefully for anyone in disguise, and there you are. We had no way of knowing that Loftis and Stony were in touch—and maybe they weren't, directly. But, one way or another, Stony hears that Loftis had a visit from an Easterner trying to disguise himself as a Chreotha. 'Tell me about this Easterner,' he probably says. "And what kind of questions did he ask?' "

Vlad nodded. "Yes. And, all of a sudden, you and I are tied together, looking into Fyres's death."

"Right. Now the Jhereg is hot for you. Somehow or other, Reega learns of it."

"Not somehow or other," said Vlad. "Because they went to her, the same way they went to Vonnith, and probably Endra as well. After all, they followed me. I let them. I thought I was being clever. Vonnith is so far into the Jhereg that she had no choice, and they probably offered her a good piece of change to help them. But Reega had her own ideas."

"You're right," I said. "That's probably how it worked. If we'd gone back to Reega, rather than to Vonnith, the same thing would have happened, most likely. But first,

Reega either decided or, more likely, was told to get rid of Loftis."

"Yes. And Loftis was told to try to pump me. So Loftis tries to pump me, and he brings me to this place where the arrest is planned, and then, bang, no more Loftis. All without the Jhereg's knowledge, because the Jhereg wouldn't have let me out of there alive. Do I have it?"

"That's how I read it," I said.

"Kiera, we have been thoroughly taken."

"Yes."

"You don't like it any more than I do, do you?"

"Rather less, in fact, I would imagine."

"So, what are we going to do about it?"

"At the moment," I said, "I cannot say. But, no doubt, something will occur. Let us consider the matter."

"Right," said Vlad, who was looking at me a little funny.

I said, "What about the information from Vonnith? Can we trust it, if she knew you weren't who you claimed to be?"

"I think so," said Vlad. "She knew her job; she was supposed to keep me there long enough for them to kill me. Why bother to think up lies when the guy who's hearing the truth is about to become deceased?"

"Good point."

"So, what now?"

I said, "Lieutenant Domm?"

"Eh?" said Vlad. And, "Oh. You think he's the one who wanted Loftis out of the way? There was no love lost between them, but they were in the same corps."

"Were they?" I said.

"Eh?"

"Think back to that conversation you overheard—"

"You don't mean that was staged, do you? I don't believe—"

"Neither do I. No, at that point they didn't know who you were, and they weren't looking for witchcraft. I mean after that."

"My talk with Domm at the Riversend?"

"Yes. They probably hadn't had time to figure out who you were yet, so you might have even had them fooled. But maybe not. Think over that conversation. You made Domm slip and let what's-her-name, Timmer, know that something wasn't right."

"What about it?"

"I think that was legit. But what evidence is there that Domm was in the same corps as Loftis?"

"Then who—"

"Who would normally conduct such an investigation?"

"Uh . . . I don't remember. That group that reports to Indus?"

"Right. The Surveillance group. And there almost had to be someone from that group involved, just because it would look funny if there weren't."

"But now we're implicating Indus."

"So? As far as I can tell, Vlad, we're implicating everyone in the Empire with the possible exception of Her Majesty and Lord Khaavren."

"I—"

"I don't think you realize what we're dealing with here, Vlad."

"You mean it's that big?"

"No, I mean it's that—I don't know the word—*pervasive*. We've been looking for corrupt officials, and checking them off our list when we decided they weren't corruptible. But that isn't the point at all."

"Go on," he said, frowning.

"Corruption doesn't enter into it. Oh, maybe Shortisle, or someone on his staff, is lining his pocket. But that's trivial.

What's happening here is everyone involved in the mechanism of the Empire is working together to do his job just the way he's supposed to."

"Come again?"

"The Empire is nothing more than a great big, overgrown, understaffed, and horribly inefficient system for keeping things working."

"Thank you," he said, "for the lesson in government. But—"

"Bear with me, please."

He sighed. "All right."

"By things," I said, "I mean, mostly, trade."

"I thought putting down rebellions was the big thing."

"Sure," I said. "Because it's hard to trade if there's a rebellion in progress." He smiled, and I shook my head. "No, I'm really not kidding. Whether a certain piece of ground is ruled by Baron Wasteland or Count Backward doesn't make a difference to much of anyone, except maybe our hypothetical aristocrats. But if the trees from that piece of ground don't reach the shipwrights here in Northport, then, eventually, we're going to run out of that particular lime they have in Elde, which we use as an agent mixed with our lime to make mortar to keep our buildings from falling down."

"Reminds me of the couple who didn't know the difference between—"

"Hush. I'm being grandiloquent."

"Sorry."

"And we'd also, by the way, run out of that lovely Phoenix Stone from Greenaere that I think you know something about. That's one of the simplest examples. Do you want to hear about how a dearth of wheat from the Northwest shuts down all the coal mines in the Kanefthali Mountains? I didn't think so.

"The point," I continued, "is trade. If it weren't for the

Empire, which controls it, everyone would make up his own rules, and change them as occasion warrants, and create tariffs that would send prices through the overcast, and everyone would suffer. If you need proof, look to your homeland, and consider how they live, and think about why."

"Life span has something to do with that," he said. "As does the tendency of the Empire to invade whenever it doesn't have anything better to do."

"Trade has more to do with it."

"Maybe." He shrugged. "I suppose. But how does all of this relate to corruption among the great and wonderful leaders of our great and wonderful—"

"That's what I'm saying, Vlad. It isn't corruption. It's worse—it's incompetence. And, worse than that, it's inevitable incompetence."

"I'm listening, Kiera."

"Why does a banker go into business?"

"I thought we were talking about the Empire?"

"Trust me."

"All right. A banker goes into business because he's an Orca and he doesn't like the sea."

"Stop being difficult."

"What do you want?"

"Obvious answers to stupid questions. Why does a banker go into business?"

"To make money."

"How does he make money."

"He steals it."

"Vlad."

"All right. The same way a Jhereg moneylender does, only he doesn't make as much because his interest rate is lower and he has to pay taxes—though he does save some in bribes."

"Spell it out for me, Vlad. How does a banker make money?"

He sighed. "He makes loans to people and charges them for it, so they pay him more than he loaned them. In the Jhereg, interest is calculated so that—"

"Right. Okay. Here's another easy one: what determines how much profit a banker makes?"

"How much money he loans, and at what interest rate. What do I win?"

"So what keeps him from running up the interest rates?"

"All the other bankers."

"And what keeps them from getting together and agreeing to raise the rates?"

"Competition from the Jhereg."

"Wrong."

"Really? Damn. And I was doing so well. Why is that wrong?"

"I'll put it another way: what keeps them from getting together, *including* the Jhereg, and fixing interest rates that way?"

"Uh . . . hmm. The Empire?"

"Congratulations. The Empire sets limits on the rates, because the Empire has to take loans out, too, and if the Empire got rates that were *too* much better than everyone else's, the Great Houses would object, and the Empire has to always play the Houses off against each other, because, really, the Empire is just the sum of the Great Houses, and if they all combined against the Empire . . ."

"Got it. No more Empire."

"Exactly."

"Okay, so the Empire fixes the maximum loan rate."

"Rates. There are several, having to do with, well, all sorts of complicated things. That's Shortisle's job."

"Got it. Okay, go on. So, in effect, the maximum profit a banker can get is set by law."

"Nope."

"Uh . . . okay, why not?"

"Because there's another way to maximize profits."

"Oh, right. Loan more money. But you can't make loans if people don't need the money."

"Sure you can. You can create the need."

"You mean the land swindle?"

"No. That's trivial. Oh, I'm sure that's why it's being done, but it isn't happening on anywhere near the scale that would pull the Empire into it."

"All right. Go on, then. How?"

"Undercut the Jhereg."

He shrugged. "They always do that. But the Jhereg moneylenders stay in business, anyway."

"Why?"

"Because we aren't as fussy about making sure the customer can pay us back, because we have our own ways of making sure we get paid back."

It was interesting that Vlad still thought of the Organization as "we," but I didn't choose to comment on that. I said, "Exactly. And so . . . ?"

He frowned. "You mean they start making it easier to get loans?"

"Precisely."

"But then, what if the loans aren't paid back?"

"Vlad, I'm not talking about small stuff, like someone wanting to buy a house. I'm talking about big finance, like someone wanting to start a major shipping firm."

He smiled. "Just to pick an example by random? Well, all right. So then what happens?" He answered his own question. "Then the banks go under. That's stupid business."

"Maybe. But what if you don't have any choice?"

"What do you mean?"

"If you had a pile of cash—"

He smiled. I'd forgotten how much money he had.

"Let me rephrase. If you had a pile of cash that you wanted to put into a bank—"

"Ah!"

"Which bank would you choose?"

"I wouldn't. I'd give it to an Organization moneylender."

"Work with me, Vlad."

"All right. I don't know. I guess the one that had the best rates."

"What if they were all the same?"

"Then the one that seemed the most reliable."

"Right. What makes a bank reliable? Or, more precisely, what would make you *think* a bank was reliable?"

"I don't know. How long it's been around, I suppose, and its reputation, how much money it has."

"How do you know how much money it has?"

"The Empire publishes lists of that sort of thing, doesn't it?"

"Yes. Another of Shortisle's jobs."

"You mean he's been lying?"

"Not exactly. Don't get ahead of me. What determines how much money the bank has, or, rather, how much money the Empire reports the bank as having? I mean, do you think they go in and count it?"

"Well, sort of. Don't they do audits?"

"Yes. And do you know how the audits work?"

"Not exactly."

"They look at how much gold they claim to have on hand and compare it with what they find in the vaults, and then—here's the fun part—they look at their paperwork and add the amount they have, as we'd put it, on the street.

And the more money they have on the street, the richer they are. Or, rather, the richer they *look*."

He frowned. "So, you mean, if they start making risky loans, it looks like they're doing really well, when in fact they may be—"

"Tottering on the edge of ruin. Yes."

He didn't speak for a moment. Savn was snoring in a corner, Buddy curled up on one side of him, Rocza on the other, with Loiosh next to her. There were occasional sounds from the predators outside, but nothing else. I gave Vlad some time to think over what I'd told him.

Eventually he said, "The Empire—"

"Yes, Vlad. Exactly. The Empire."

"Aren't they supposed to check on things like that?"

"They do their best, sure. But how many banks are there making how many loans? Do you really thing Shortisle has the means to inspect every loan from every bank to make sure it isn't too risky? And, even if it is, it has to be pretty extreme before the Empire has the right to step in."

"But—"

"Yes, but. But if several banks fail all at once, then what happens to trade?"

"It falls apart. And they can't allow that."

"So what do they do?"

"You tell me," said Vlad.

"All right. First of all, they curse themselves soundly for having allowed things to get into that sort of mess in the first place."

"Good move. Then what?"

"Then they try to cover for the banks as much as they can."

"Ah ha."

"Right. If word get out that Fyres was murdered, then they'll have to find out why, and then—"

"Right," said Vlad. "Then word will get out that lots of big banks, starting with the Verra-be-damned bank of the Verra-be-damned Empire, are very rich on paper and, in fact, are on the edge of taking that big tumble into oblivion. And if that happens—"

"Panic, bank runs, and—"

"Trade goes overboard in a big way."

I nodded. "That's what I didn't see right away. This isn't a few slimebags in the Empire lining their pockets, this is the Empire doing what it's supposed to do—protecting trade."

He shook his head. "And all of this starting off just because somebody knocked a big-time scam artist in the head."

"A big-time, extremely wealthy scam artist."

"Yes. Only one thing."

"Yes, Vlad?"

"Why?"

"Why what?"

"Well, this sort of mess isn't good for anyone, right?"

"Right."

"So if all this was set off by Fyres's death, why was he killed?"

I stared off into space for a moment, then I said, "You know, Vlad, that is a very, very good question."

"Yeah, I thought so. So what's the answer?"

"I don't know."

"And here's another question: with Stony dead, is the Jhereg still onto me? I mean, are they still breathing down my neck, or do I have a little time to find the answer to the first question?"

I nodded. "That one I think I can find the answer to."

"I'd appreciate it. What about the other one?"

"We'll see," I said. "I'll be back."

"I'll wait here," he said.

Chapter Fourteen

I LEFT THE cottage and was instantly in Northport; a quicker teleport than was my custom, but I realized after I performed it that there was a feeling of urgency within me that was still growing.

So I deliberately teleported to a place more than a mile away and made myself walk the rest of the distance so I could calm down. I strolled casually—at least, I did my best to stroll casually—through the narrow, winding streets, where the second-floor balconies almost touched each other and the roofs all but hid the sky, until I arrived at a place I knew. This time Dor was in.

He looked up when I came in, and he seemed afraid. That made me sad. The last thing I want is to inspire fear. I said, "What's wrong, Dor?"

His brow furrowed, and he said, "You don't know?"

"No, I don't, unless it's about Stony's death. But I had nothing to do with that."

"That Easterner did."

"Perhaps."

"No perhaps about it. We were able to revivify Raafla, and he told us."

"I imagine Stony hasn't been saying much."

He glared at me. "That isn't funny. I liked him."

Liked.

Past tense.

"What do you mean?" I said. "Hasn't he been revivified?"

"You know damned well—"

"Dor, I know very little 'damned well'; even less than I'd thought. What are you telling me?"

"He wasn't revivifiable."

"He wasn't? What happened?"

He stared. "You really don't know?"

"Please tell me, Dor. What happened?"

"The kind of spells assassins always use, that's what."

If Vlad had ever used those sorts of spells, I sure didn't know about it. And he hadn't said anything. . . .

"You'd better tell me all about it," I said.

"Why?"

"Because I'm curious, and because I need to know."

"If you're looking for your friend," he said bitterly, "he'll be long gone by now."

"Tell me, please," I said.

He did so.

His story shook me up enough that I had trouble believing it, so after leaving him there, I used some of my other contacts in Northport to verify it. The details aren't important, but the story stayed the same. I was convinced, and also confused, but I'd at least answered Vlad's second question, about whether the Jhereg thought he was still in town.

About Vlad's first question, why was Fyres killed, I still

had no clue, but I returned at once to tell Vlad what I'd learned. When I arrived at the blue cottage, and had said hello to Buddy, I found Vlad sitting near the hearth having a one-sided conversation with Savn.

Vlad looked at me, blinked, and stood up. We moved over to the table in the kitchen and I sat down. Vlad brought me some klava. "The honey is almost gone," he said. "And we haven't been stung too badly."

"Yet," I said.

He raised his eyebrows.

I said, "Well, Vlad, it goes like this."

He poured himself a cup, sweetened it, and said, "Not here."

"All right," I said.

Vlad and I stepped outside. Loiosh rode on his shoulder and seemed better, but I hadn't seen him flying yet. Vlad leaned against a tree and said, "Uh-huh?"

"The first item is that, while everyone knows you shined Stony, no one has any idea of the circumstances. They figure he somehow found you and wanted to be there personally for the kill, and you were too quick, or too tough, or too nasty for him. Which means, I suppose, that next time they'll be even more careful."

"Next time," said Vlad, smiling wryly. "I can hardly wait."

"Yes."

"Are you sure they told you the truth? I mean, we're known to be friends, and—"

"Vlad, I didn't come right out and ask, you know. Trust me."

"All right."

"There's more. Everyone is pretty sure you've left town."

"Really?"

"Yeah. It's what any of them would do."

"So, for the moment, I'm safe."

"Yes. Until you do something stupid."

"Right. So I'm safe for another five minutes, anyway. All right. Anything else?"

"Yes," I said. "One more thing: there's also some speculation that you had it in for Stony personally, and no one knows why."

He shrugged. "They're wrong. So what?" Then he looked at me again and said, "All right, let's have it. Why do they think so?"

"Because otherwise why, in the middle of a fight, would you have taken the time to put the spells on him that make him unrevivifiable?"

"Huh? Oh."

"Right."

"Well, now, isn't *that* interesting."

"I thought so."

"I take it you didn't disabuse them of the notion?"

"How could I?"

"Good point. Not that it matters; they don't like me, anyway. What about his associates?"

"All four were extremely dead, as were three of Vonnith's personal guards who, as they suppose, got in your way. And so was her servant."

"Shards! All unrevivifiable?"

"Not all, but there's another interesting point."

"Go on."

"Stony was unrevivifiable, and so were all three of the Orca guardsmen, but the Jhereg weren't, and there were another three of Vonnith's private guards who weren't even touched."

"Did they see what happened?"

"No. It was all inside. Some of the guards were summoned in, and then . . ." I let the sentence trail off with a shrug.

"My word," said Vlad. "What a bloodbath! Jhereg don't kill like that, Kiera, at least not since prehistory. Only Dragons kill like that, and Dzur, I suppose."

"You're right," I said. "Dragons and Dzur. And also Orca, if there's a profit in it."

"Good point," he said. "Orca. Yes."

"What are you thinking now?" I said.

"Thinking? I'm not thinking; I'm being angry. I'll get over it."

"Vlad—"

"I've been hanging around Orca quite a bit lately. Usually, when I get to know people I begin to be more sympathetic with them. You'd have thought that, now that I've gotten a chance to know these Orca, I'd have a little more understanding of them. But I don't. I hate them, Kiera. I hated them when I was a kid, and I hate them now, and I think I always will hate them."

I started to defend them, then shrugged and said, "So you don't invite Shortisle to dinner. We still need to—what is it?"

"Shortisle to dinner," said Vlad. "That's what's odd about it—to *dinner*."

"Huh?"

"Those notes you stole from Fyres. Here, just a minute."

He walked into the cottage and emerged with Buddy and the sheaf of notes I'd stolen from Fyres's place. He looked through them for a while, then held one up triumphantly. "It says, 'Shortisle to dinner.' "

"What's your point?"

He waved the papers in front of my face. "My point, Kiera, is that it was included in his financial notes, not his personal notes."

"I'm sure it was a business meeting, Vlad. What does that tell you?"

"Everything," he said.

"Huh?"

Vlad shook his head and was quiet for several minutes, and, once more, I could almost watch him working things out. It was like seeing someone assemble a puzzle, but not being able to see the puzzle itself; it was a trifle annoying. Eventually he said, "One question."

"Yes?"

"When Stony told you he wasn't in debt to Fyres, did you believe him?"

"Well, at the time I did, but—"

"That's good enough for me."

Then he frowned, and Rocza flew out of the house, landing on his other shoulder. "I'll see you in a bit, Kiera," he said abruptly, and started walking away from the cottage.

"Wait a minute—"

"No time," he said.

"What about your sword?"

"It'll just get in the way."

"Where are you going?"

"To town."

"But—"

"Keep an eye on Savn," he added over his shoulder as he headed down the road toward Northport.

I watched him go, hoping he wasn't going to do anything stupid. I had the sudden realization that we hadn't talked about my decision to let myself be a target in hopes of flushing out whoever was behind it—back when we'd thought there was someone behind it. This mattered because, although he would come up with some reason for justifying it, especially to himself, Vlad might well feel it necessary to go and do something equally dangerous, and if

I let him get himself killed, I'd never be able to explain it to Cawti.

On the other hand, I couldn't insult him by following him. Nothing to do but worry, I suppose. Savn was awake, and looking at me.

"Hello," I said. "My name is Kiera."

He looked away, then closed his eyes as if he were going back to sleep. On impulse, I stood up and said, "Come on, Savn. We're going for a walk."

He dutifully stood, and I led the way out the door, into air that was crisp with that indefinable smell of snow that hasn't arrived yet, but is coming, coming; and all overlaid with the ocean, fainter than it smelled in my Adrilankha, but still there.

Buddy got up and padded along after us, a few paces behind. It was odd, not having Rocza there—I'd begun to associate her with Savn even more than with Vlad; I kept expecting to see her on Savn's shoulder. I wondered if he had a future as a witch. Odd how the jhereg seemed to be so protective of the boy. I wondered if there was a story in it.

What now, Kiera? I'd gotten him moving; should I try to get him talking? I didn't particularly want to talk about knives.

"The jhereg, Rocza, seems very attached to you," I said. "She spends a lot of time watching over you. I wonder why that is?" Buddy came up beside us, then suddenly lunged ahead to chase something or other through the leafless trees. After a while he came back. He'd missed whatever it was, but didn't seem to mind, having enjoyed the chase.

"Although I suppose it's reasonable to wonder why anyone watches over anyone. Vlad still doesn't know why I watch over him, you know." Savn kept walking along, oblivious to me and everything else, but at least not tripping over tree roots. "Come to that," I added, "I'm not altogether certain myself." The ground dropped a bit, not like a hill, but more like a small depression, and the trees here were a little more sparse. There are many things that can cause this sort of land formation; even the ground has its story to tell. Not all stories are worth listening to, however.

"Guilt, I suppose," I said. "At least, that's part of it." We rose up again and were back in a part of the forest that was thicker; we splashed through a tiny brook, perhaps four meters across and two or three centimeters deep, running back past us toward the depression. "Though I doubt that Rocza has anything to feel guilty about. And I shouldn't still feel guilty toward Vlad. It was a long time ago, and, well, we all do what we have to.

"Vlad, too," I added. "He's a good person, you know. In spite of many things, including his own opinion, he's a good person. Maybe a bit conceited, overbearing, and arrogant, but then, people without a trace of these diseases aren't usually worth one's time." I heard myself chuckling. "Or maybe I'm talking about myself, there.

"It's odd, Savn, addressing someone who doesn't respond. It's uncomfortable, but it also frees you up in a way: you can say things and pretend it doesn't matter, that no one is really hearing them, but, at the same time, you've said them, and you don't really know what you think until you've found a way to get your thoughts outside of you, in words, or some other way. And so, my friend Savn, while it may seem that I am speaking for your benefit, to help you overcome whatever it is that pulls you away from us and from the world outside of your head, in fact, I should be thanking you. And I do.

"But enough self-indulgence. We have a problem, Vlad and I, and I'm not certain what to do about it." We had been moving in a large circle because I didn't want to get too far away from the cottage; now I caught a glimpse of it, blue and ugly, through the trees. Savn didn't look at it, he just kept walking, one foot in front of the other, careful not to trip. He was doing fine, I suppose. If there was nothing more to life than walking without tripping, I'd pronounce him cured on the spot.

I headed us away from the place, though not quite so far this time. I wondered what Vlad was doing. Buddy bounded about here and there, energetic for as old as he was. A good dog, probably a good companion for a woman like Hwdf'rjaanci, just as Loiosh was a good companion for an assassin. Or an ex-assassin, or whatever he was now.

Game, that's what he was. Hunted game. The target of the Organization he'd worked for and been a part of, but, in my opinion, never really belonged in. It's not his fault, but he's not human, and he doesn't have whatever it is within the genes of a human being that makes a Jhereg.

But whether he had ever belonged or not, now they were hunting him, and he was off doing something improbable that might make it easier for them. What? "What do you think he's up to, Savn? I doubt he'd go after Vonnith again, after how close it was last time. Endra? Reega? I just don't know. And there's nothing I can do about it, anyway, except wait and see what he comes up with. I don't like being responsible for other people, Savn; present company excepted. I don't like having to rely on them. I think that's the big difference between me and Vlad: he's always liked people, and I've always liked being by myself. So, of course, the way things worked out, he's the one who has to take off and spend his short lifetime away from everyone he cares about. Feh. No sense complaining about fate, though, Savn; it never listens. When there's nothing you can do except worry, that's a good time to worry. I don't remember who said that. Maybe me."

We made our way back to the house, Buddy preceding us through the door. Hwdf'rjaanci was washing some sort of tuber that would probably feed us later. Savn sat down near the hearth, facing out, rather than looking at it. Buddy poked his nose at Hwdf'rjaanci's leg, was petted, wagged his tail, and sat down by Savn. I said to Savn, "Are you hungry?"

He shook his head.

I nodded, pretending that having him respond to a question was the most natural thing in the world, but I realized that my heart was pounding. There was no question, we'd made progress. On the other hand, we deserved to, because we had paid for it. Or, more precisely, others had paid for it.

Fyres was dead.

Stony was dead.

Loftis was dead.

I looked at the boy, who had closed his eyes and was resting easily. At least Vlad wasn't dead. But there was still too much death. Death follows Vlad around like another familiar, and sometimes I wondered if he even noticed, much less cared. I knew what that felt like, and what it could do to you, but it wasn't supposed to happen to Kiera the Thief, who had never killed anyone, and who didn't enjoy being around when things like that were going on, and who especially hated it when she couldn't do anything about it. But this was too big for Kiera the Thief. Much too big for Kiera. And much, much too big for Vlad.

On the other hand, it was clear he had figured something out, there at the end. What? And why hadn't he told me? I hate it when he does that. If he managed to return in one piece, though, I'd be able to tell him that there was progress—that the boy had responded to a question that had nothing to do with knives, and that there was probably hope for him. Vlad would think it worth whatever trouble he'd been through; oddly enough, I thought so, too.

Buddy's head came up, and he padded out the door, his tail giving a couple of perfunctory wags. I heard the sound of a familiar walk, and something in me relaxed, and I was able to look entirely normal an instant later when Vlad walked in, looking smug.

"What?" I said.

"It's done," he said.

"What, everything?"

He glanced quickly at Savn and said, "Almost everything. Everything we can take care of, at least."

"I have good news on that front, too," I said.

"Tell me," he said, almost snapping out the words.

"You first."

"No, you."

"I—all right." So I told him about Savn not wanting to eat, and Vlad was every bit as pleased about it as I was. Then Hwdf'rjaanci came in, and I had to tell her, too, and she grew a smile, too.

When I'd waited as long as I could, I said, "All right, Vlad. Your turn."

"Sure," he said. "Let's go outside."

Hwdf'rjaanci sniffed, and Vlad winked at her. Then we went outside and he told me about his day.

Chapter Fifteen

I HID AS best I could, which was pretty well, in a doorway across the street from City Hall—maybe the same place you hid, Kiera—and I waited for the day to fade. I didn't feel especially safe. Loiosh wasn't fit to fly, so Rocza was doing the watching, and I was getting the information from her through Loiosh, which is too indirect for my taste, and Rocza wasn't trained for this kind of work. Loiosh attempted to reassure me, without much success.

Eventually Domm left the building. I gritted my teeth and watched him go by. He took a few steps away from the door and teleported. I kept waiting. Things were shutting down and people were going home from work. Had I missed her? Had she gone out a back way, or not been there at all, or teleported from inside the building? These are the questions that inevitably go through your head when you're doing what I was doing, and you don't have a partner. When I was with the Jhereg, I made sure people doing this sort of thing always worked in pairs, at least one of whom was a competent sorcerer. I was a competent sorcerer, but as long as I wore the gold Phoenix Stone, it didn't help a bit, and whenever I removed it, even for an instant, I was risking rather more than my life—the Jhereg are tenacious, I know because I was one, and I was as tenacious as any of them, damn them to Verra's coldest hell.

Timmer came out, walked a few steps down the street, paused, no doubt to teleport, then stopped as Rocza flew down, almost into her face, then away. She reached for a weapon, frowning, and looked for her; then she saw me walking toward her, hands in front of me and open.

Rocza landed on my shoulder. Timmer waited, her hand still on her blade. "Let's talk," I said.

"We have nothing to talk about."

"Oh, no, my lady. We have a lot to talk about. If you try to arrest me, which I know you're thinking about, you'll get nothing. If you don't, you'll find out who killed your associate, and why."

She looked like she was starting to get angry, so I added, "I didn't do it. I had no reason to do it. I suspect you don't know who did. I do. Give me a chance and I'll prove it, and what I want in return is something I don't think you'll mind giving me at all."

"Who are you this time?"

"Someone who's all done playing games, Ensign. I'm not asking you to trust me, you know. Just to listen. Can you afford not to?"

Her face twitched, and she said, "Inside, then."

"No, not there. Anywhere else, as long as it's public."

"All right. This way, then."

We walked about a quarter of a mile, past two or three public houses, and then we entered one; she was being careful, which I approved of. The place was just starting to fill up, but we found a corner, anyway. She didn't drink anything, or offer to buy me anything, either. She took out a dagger, set it on the table. She said, "All right, let's have it. All of it."

"That's my intention," I said.

She waited. Loiosh and Rocza sat on my shoulders like statues, drawing stares from everyone in the place except her. That was all right. I said, "I'm betting a great deal on a single glance, Ensign."

She waited.

I said, "The Surveillance Corps and the Tasks Group. I'm betting that you're with the latter and that Lieutenant Domm is in the former, and I'm basing this guess just on the way you looked at him that time at the Riversend. Care to tell me if I'm right?"

"You talk," she said. "I'll listen."

"Okay." I was beginning to think she didn't like me. "My name is Vladimir Taltos. I used to work for the Jhereg, now I'm being hunted by the Jhereg." I stopped to give her a chance to respond, if she cared to.

"Keep talking," she said.

"There's a boy, a Teckla boy. He has brain fever—"

"Stay on the subject."

"If you want to know what's happening, Ensign, don't interrupt. He has brain fever. I've arranged for him to be cured. The woman who's working on him is a victim of a very minor land swindle that you may or may not know about, but it's what led me into this. I believe I need some wine."

She got the attention of the host, who had a servant bring a bottle and two glasses. I poured some for myself, Timmer declined. I drank and my throat felt better. "The land swindle isn't really important," I said, "but it is, as I said, the piece of the whole thing that got me involved. And it isn't even a swindle, really—I'm not certain it's illegal. It's just a means of putting some pressure on a few people and raising prices a little—inducing panic. In an atmosphere of general panic, where everyone is wondering how bad he's going to be hit, everyone is susceptible to—"

"Go on, please."

"You know how the land thing works?"

"Go on."

"I don't think she likes you, boss."

"What was your first clue, Loiosh?"

I collected my thoughts. Someday I hope to have them all. I said, "Let's start with Fyres, then. I assume you've heard of him."

"Don't be sarcastic with me, Easterner."

Her hand was casually near her dagger. I nodded. "Lord Fyres," I said, "duke of—of whatever it is. Sixty million imperials' worth of fraud, left to a not-grieving widow, a son who probably doesn't even notice, a daughter who intends to continue the tradition, and another daughter who—but we'll get to her. Fyres was worth about sixty million, as I said, and almost none of it was real, except for a bit that he'd put into legitimate shipbuilding and shipping companies, most of whom have now gone belly-up, as the Orca say.

"Now, Ensign, allow me to do some speculating. Most of what I have is based on fact, but some of it is guesswork based on the rest. Feel free to correct me if I say something you know is wrong."

"Go ahead."

"All right. Fyres was getting fatter and fatter, and more and more large banks were involved, and many of them—many of the biggest—were so heavily involved that, when he came to them and said he'd need another fifty dots—excuse me, fifty thousand imperials—or he'd go under, they had no choice but to give it to him, because if he defaulted on his loans, the banks would go under, too, or at least be pretty seriously crippled. This included the Bank of the Empire, the Orca Treasury, and the Dragon Treasury, as well as some very large banks and some extremely powerful Jhereg about whom I suspect you don't care but you ought to."

"Stony?"

"No, oddly enough. As far as I know, he wasn't directly in debt to Fyres at all. But, yeah, he's in this—mostly because he wasn't in debt."

"How is that?"

"Wait. I'll get to it."

She nodded. I tried to read her expression, to see how she was taking this, but she wasn't giving me anything. So be it, then.

"Eventually Lord Shortisle realized what was going on. One of his accountants found out first, but agreed not to say anything about the bank he knew was in jeopardy. He did this, you understand, in fine old Orca tradition, in exchange for having his pocket lined." I considered, then said, "Maybe several of them did this, but I only know about one. And that poor bastard had no idea what scale this was on, or he wouldn't have tried it. For all I know, this was happening all through Shortisle's department, but it doesn't matter, because eventually Shortisle found out about it."

"How?"

"I don't know, frankly. I suspect he has ways of knowing when his accountants are spending more money than they ought to; it was probably something like that."

She shrugged. "All right. Go on, then."

I nodded. "So Shortisle spoke to this mysterious accountant. I'm speculating now, I don't know the accountant's name, but I'm sure he was important in Shortisle's organization because Vonnith always referred to him as a 'big shot.' At a guess, then, the conversation went something like this: Shortisle bitched him out, and informed him he was dismissed from the Ministry and was probably going to face criminal charges. The accountant said that if he was dismissed, the news would come out about why he was dismissed and the bank would fail. Shortisle asked why he should care about one bank. The accountant, who by now had at least a glimmer of what was going on, pointed out that, once that bank failed, others might, and maybe Shortisle should find how big the problem was before creating a scandal that would result in a general loss of confidence. Shortisle was forced to agree that this was a good idea.

"So our man from the Ministry of the Treasury starts looking into things, and finds Vonnith, or maybe someone like her, and discovers that every bank she owns or runs is in danger of collapse because everything she has—on paper—is tied into someone named Fyres. So he checks on Fyres to see who else is into him, and discovers that everyone and his partner is in the same position, and that it's getting worse." I paused. "The only reason I know about Vonnith is that she happens to own the bank that the old woman I'm trying to help saved at. There are probably scores of bankers in the same position she's in, and she only gained importance because of me."

"I don't follow you," she said.

"Never mind. You'll see."

"Continue, then." Her hand was still resting near the dagger, but she seemed interested now.

I nodded and said, "So Shortisle pays Fyres a visit—"

"How much of this do you know?" she said. "Are you still speculating?"

"Yes. This is almost all speculation. But it holds up with what's happened. Bear with me and I'll try to draw all the connections."

"All right. Go on, then."

"He pays Fyres a visit to find out what can be done. Fyres is intractable. He tries to bribe Shortisle, he tries to dazzle him, he tries to sell him. He doesn't get away with it, because, by now, Shortisle knows Fyres's history, and he also knows, or is starting to know, how big this is. So he threatens to have Fyres brought down. Now, this is a bluff, Ensign. Shortisle *can't* bring Fyres down, because it would bring down too many others and create chaos in the finances of the Empire, and it's Shortisle's job to prevent exactly that. What Shortisle wants is for Fyres to work with him in trying to ease out of this with as little damage as possible, and the threat is just to get Fyres's attention so they can start negotiating. But the threat backfires—"

"Still speculation? It almost sounds as if you were listening to them."

"Just bear with me. I may have a lot of the details wrong, but I know that Shortisle paid Fyres a visit. Chances are the conversation didn't go like that, but the results are the same as if it had, so I'm trying to show you how it might have ended up the way it did. And, by the way, with what I know about Shortisle and Fyres, I might not be all that wrong."

She shrugged. "Okay."

I nodded. "Fyres gets scared by the idea of losing everything, because he's done that twice before. If he, Fyres, is going to help Shortisle, he wants guarantees that he's going to come out of this rich and powerful. Shortisle makes a counteroffer, saying Fyres will come out of this a free man, instead of spending the rest of his life in the Imperial prisons. That's not good enough for our man Fyres—he's on top now, and he sees no reason why he shouldn't stay there. So he does something stupid: he threatens Shortisle. He tells him that he has contacts in the Jhereg—which he does—and that he, Shortisle, had better leave him alone.

"But Shortisle has a friend in the Jhereg, too; a fellow named Stony. Remember him? I promised we'd come back to him. Now, our dear friend Stony is extremely powerful in the Jhereg, and, just as important, he's not directly in debt to Fyres, and, most important of all, he's always, always, *always* willing to help out the Empire, because the Jhereg can't function without help from the Empire."

Timmer opened her mouth then, but I said, "No. I know what I'm talking about here. When I was a Jhereg, I regularly bribed the Phoenix Guards to overlook small illegalities. Nothing big, and nothing violent, you understand, but the little stuff that keeps the Jhereg earning, and keeps the Phoenix Guards in pocket change. It didn't occur to me that the same thing was happening on a much larger scale all the way to the top until I messed with the official Jhereg contact to the Empire and I saw the heat that came down on me for it—that's the main reason I'm on the run right now."

She didn't like it, but she said, "All right. Go on, then."

"So one week later—"

"A week? What is this, a hard date, or more guessing?"

"A hard date. One week after Shortisle and Fyres have dinner together, Fyres goes out on his private boat to have a nice, relaxing sail with some business associates—how many of those aboard the boat were Jhereg, by the way?"

"Three," she said.

"Okay. So he goes out sailing, and, late at night, he slips on the deck and—"

"Yes. I know that part."

"Right. Okay, so Fyres is dead. Shortisle goes into action right away. Or, in fact, he's probably ready to go into action before it even happens. He talks to Indus, explains the problem, and says they have to minimize the damage or everything falls apart, and there's major chaos, and, just incidentally, Shortisle loses his job, because the Empress is a reborn Phoenix and doesn't take people's heads for incompetence.

"So someone—probably Indus—tells Domm, who works for her, that he has to just go through the motions of investigating Fyres's death and conclude that it was an accident. Domm comes in, and, a week later, announces that everything is fine. The Empress hears about this, and the Warlord, and probably Khaavren, and they all immediately smell something funny, because there's no way you could conclude something like that in a week. So, what do they do when there's something fishy from one of the special Imperial groups? They send in the Tasks Group—yours, isn't it?" I stopped and looked at her. "That's what I'm betting my life on, you know. And I'm betting on it based on that one look you gave Domm. I don't think you're from Surveillance."

She nodded once, quickly.

"Okay," I said. I relaxed. "Good."

"Keep talking," she said.

I nodded. "So Khaavren tells Loftis to get a group together and find out what's going on. Shortisle, who always knows what's going on with the Empire, finds out about this and, instead of panicking, does something smart—he tells Indus about it."

"Do you know that? I mean, couldn't it have been Indus who found out about it in the first place, and she told Shortisle and it went from there?"

"Actually, yes," I said. "I was just enjoying putting the story together my way. But it could well have happened the other way, and probably did, because the Minister of the Houses hears even more than the Minister of the Treasury."

"It doesn't matter, anyway," she said. "Go on with your story."

"Okay. However it worked, Indus knows about the problem, and she knows how much trouble there will be, for her, too, now, if word gets out about what's going on. I'm pretty sure that the Warlord or the Empress or both were involved in sending your group in, because if it was just Khaavren, Shortisle would probably have had him killed."

Timmer looked shocked at that, and opened her mouth, but then she closed it again and nodded for me to continue.

I said, "Now, Indus, as we know, is very persuasive; she's an Issola, after all. She finds Loftis, whom she knows somehow or other—"

"They worked together when our group was called in to find a security leak in Division Six during the Elde Island war."

"Okay," I said. I still wanted to wince every time someone mentioned the Elde Island war, but that wasn't important now. "She persuades him to help behind Khaavren's back, because they both know Khaavren wouldn't go for anything like this, and they both know that, however much they dislike it, it's the only way to keep the financial roof of the Empire from collapsing and to save both of their metaphorical heads.

"So you and Loftis show up in Northport, just the two of you, with three others in reserve. Is that right?"

"Why?"

"It doesn't matter. Loftis told me there were six of you and three in reserve, and I think he was telling me a half-truth by including Domm and his people, just to test me."

"Yes," she said. "It was he and I, with some others on call if we needed them."

"Okay," I said. "Anyway, Domm is already here with Daythiefnest and three others, and they've bungled things up nicely. You and Loftis know the score, and Domm knows what's going on, but no one else does. You and Loftis have probably done a lot of things you didn't enjoy, but this has to be one of the worst—when Loftis and I were pumping each other for information, I got that out of him and I think he meant it. Your job was to cover up a murder, and, at the same time, cover up for the fact that the guy whose job it was to do the cover-up—Domm—had bungled it horribly by being impatient. That meant tracing every little indication that people thought the investigation wasn't real, while, at the same time, keeping up the appearances of making the investigation, and still coming up with enough to convince, among others, the Empress, the Warlord, and your own chief that, no, really, Fyres's death was an accident. Have I got that right?"

"Go on," she said.

I wetted my throat again. "Just about this time, Loftis learns that Fyres's home has been burglarized and his private notes taken. I'm sure he had words about that. Why didn't Domm take those notes in the first place? And why wasn't the house better protected against burglary? Answer: because Domm didn't care. Maybe—I'm speculating again—maybe it was then that Loftis realized he only had one way to go: he had to throw Domm to the dzur. That is, he was going to have to make it look like Domm was just plain incompetent—which he is—and then do the investigation himself and come up, with a greater appearance of honesty, with the same results Domm got.

"The trouble was, Domm, whatever else he is, isn't stupid. He figured that out, too."

Timmer's eyes got wide.

"You mean *Domm*—"

"Wait for it, Ensign. I'm not going anywhere, and neither is Domm."

Her eyes narrowed then, but she said, "All right." Then she said, "About Fyres's death—"

"Yes?"

"How was it arranged?"

"It was a Jhereg assassination."

"I know that. But how?"

"Huh? You should know that. Making it look like an accident—"

"No, not that. I mean, how could a Jhereg assassin get close to Fyres on his private boat, especially when he knew—when he must have known—that he was messing with dangerous matters and dangerous people?"

"Ah," I said. "I'm glad you asked. Stony set it up, and he had Shortisle's cooperation. Between the two of them, they were able to get inside help. Again, I'm guessing, but it does all fit."

"Inside help?"

"Yep. Someone Fyres trusted, or, at any rate, was willing to let onto the boat, along with a friend. Who was on the boat, Ensign? That's something you know but I don't. I think I can guess, though."

"Go ahead," she said. "Guess."

"I'd say that at least one of his daughters was there, and had a date with her. In particular, I think it has to be Reega, judging by the way she reacted when I suggested to her that the investigation wasn't entirely honest."

I waited.

"Yes," she said, after a moment. "Reega. We know she brought a date, and the guy she was with . . . yes, he could have been a Jhereg. We can still find him—"

"Three pennies that you can't."

She shrugged. "All right, then: why would she go along with that?"

"Remember the land swindle I mentioned?"

"Yes."

"That was the price. Shortisle put her in touch with Vonnith and some others, or maybe they all knew each other, anyway; they probably did. They cooked it up among themselves, with Shortisle's help, in exchange for Papa's life. That way, however things went, they each knew they'd still have enough wealth for what they wanted: Vonnith to keep her lovely house and Reega to be able to live alone and do nothing, which seems to be her goal. Of course, it could have been the wife, the son, or the other daughter; as far as I can tell they all had reasons."

"Nice family."

"Yeah."

"All right. Go on."

I nodded. "Then my friend and I enter the arena. First, there's the burglary."

"Yes. Loftis was, uh, not happy about that."

"Right. Okay, but Loftis finds himself having to work with the Jhereg, right? So he tells Stony about it, and then my friend—"

"Who?"

I shook my head. "You don't get that."

She started to object, then shrugged. "All right."

"My friend starts asking Stony questions, which information he passes on to Loftis, and then I show up, and Loftis passes that information to Stony, and then I go leading you and Domm all around the countryside, and, at about the point my feet are getting ready to fall off, we wind up at the Riversend, and Loftis gets hold of you or Domm, probably you—"

"Me."

"With orders to question me."

"No, with orders to bring you in."

"But—"

"Domm wanted to question you first. I objected, but he outranked me." Her face twitched and contorted just a bit as she said that.

"I see." I nodded. "He was nervous about what Loftis intended, and wanted to know where I fit in, and if I could be used."

"Yes. What was your game?"

"Trying to learn what was going on. Remember, all I really knew about was that our hostess was having problems with her land; I didn't even know that the investigation into Fyres's death was phony."

"And that's what you were trying to find out?"

"Yes. And I did, both from Domm's reaction and from yours, although I misread a look you gave him as indicating that you didn't know what was going on, when in fact the look was just one of contempt for him being such an idiot as to let me pump him like that. That was the last thing I got, and what made me decide to come to you now."

She nodded. "Then what?"

"Then we come back to Reega. If it *was* her who set up Fyres, and, from what you say, I'm sure it was, then it fits even better. When I showed up at her door, she panicked. She thought it was all going to come out, and someone— namely Loftis—would *really* investigate dear Papa's death, and she'd get caught. So she—"

"Arranged with Domm to kill Loftis," said Timmer, very slowly and distinctly.

I nodded. "That's how I read it."

"So why did you kill Stony and all those others?"

I smiled. "Well, actually, I didn't."

She frowned.

I shook my head. "I did kill Stony, but I put no spell on him to prevent revivification. I had no reason to, and, even when I did that sort of thing, I didn't use spells because I'm not fast enough with them. And I certainly had no time then."

"But who—"

"Think it through," I said. "Domm has killed Loftis. Stony and Loftis know each other, and Stony is in touch with powerful people in the Empire."

"Does Domm know that?"

"He has to at least be pretty sure about it. So Domm uses me to set up Stony, knowing that, eventually, I'll be sure to go blundering into Vonnith's place, or Endra's, or Reega's."

"Wait. He used *you* to set up *Stony*?"

"Yeah. That's how I read it. He probably thought I'd be killed, too, which would have been fine, but he had some of his people there to make sure Stony didn't get out alive in any case."

"Did you spot them?"

"No. But I got away."

"I don't understand."

"I shouldn't have been able to escape. My familiar here"—I gestured to Loiosh—"was injured, and that slowed me down. And, for various reasons, I can't teleport. And the Jhereg wants me *bad*. So how could I go tromping away from there through the woods and escape without even having to draw my blade? Answer: because Domm arranged for a teleport block around the house and grounds to seal Stony and his people in, then—"

"Did you feel a teleport block?"

"No, but I wouldn't, for the same reason that I don't teleport myself." She looked a question at me. I said, "I, uh, I have a device that prevents anyone from finding me with sorcery, and it has the side effect of preventing me from detecting it. Loiosh here usually lets me know if there's sorcery happening around me, but, as I said, he wasn't in any shape to do that then."

"Sorry about that, boss."

"Don't sweat it, chum."

"When did you work all this out?"

"Just a little while ago, when my friend informed me that Stony was unrevivifiable and that there'd been a mass slaughter in the house. My first thought was that it was being done so I'd be blamed, but that didn't make sense. The Jhereg were after me already, and they, frankly, have better resources for that sort of thing than the Empire, so what was the point? The point, of course, was Domm."

"Yes."

"And now, Ensign, can you figure out why it was not only Stony whose death was made permanent but also three of those Orca who are Vonnith's private guards?"

She nodded. "Three of the four who killed Loftis." She frowned. "What about the fourth?"

"I would imagine," I said, "that he died of the wounds I gave him, and was given to Deathgate Falls. And, as far as I'm concerned, you now know everything."

She nodded slowly. Then she said, "Why did you tell me all of this?"

I shrugged. "A number of reasons. For one thing, I rather liked Loftis." She frowned, but didn't speak. "For another, it annoys me to see these people tromping over lives like that—Loftis, Stony, all of those people whose lives have been messed up by the shipwrights closing and by the banks closing. And, for another, I want something in exchange."

Her eyes narrowed. "I believe that, Jhereg. What do you want?"

I said, "There are not witnesses who can implicate Domm, you know."

"Except Vonnith."

"Yes. Except Vonnith and Reega. Will you be going after Vonnith?"

"Maybe. I don't know if I can touch her. I'll have to check with—" She got a look of distaste on her features. "With Shortisle and Indus."

"Reega?"

"Not a chance. She gets away with it."

"I thought so. Well, that's fine. I don't care. Everyone involved in killing Fyres deserves an Imperial Title, as far as I'm concerned. But I do care about Vonnith."

"As I say, I don't know if I can—"

I held up my hand. "You can put pressure on her, and a little pressure is all it should take."

"For what?"

"To get her to cough up the deed to a small piece of property on the north side of town. A very small piece, a couple of acres, with a hideously ugly blue cottage on it. There's an old woman living there. I can't pronounce her name, but here it is." I passed it to her and enjoyed watching her lips move as she tried to figure out how to say it.

Then she said, "That's all you want?"

"What do *you* want, Ensign?"

She glared at me. "I want . . ." She stopped glaring, but continued staring, if you know what I mean.

"What do you want?" I repeated. "What would please you right now?"

"I . . ."

"Yes?" I said.

"Are you—?"

I looked away and waited.

Presently she said, "You used to be in the Jhereg?"

"Yes," I said.

"And what, exactly, did you do?"

I turned back to her. "You know what I did."

She nodded slowly. "The deed to the land for the old woman—that's what you're getting out of this?"

"Yes."

"That's all?"

"That's all."

"What about Fyres's personal notes?"

I extracted them from inside my cloak and put them on the table. She looked at them, riffled through them, nodded, and put them in her pouch.

She said, "Are you, uh, going to be somewhere for a while?"

I remembered the area and said, "This is as good a place as any, I think."

"Yes," she said. "I suppose it is."

She looked at me for a long time, and then she picked up her dagger and sheathed it. She reached for the wine, poured herself a glass, held it up to me, and drank. She held out her hand to Loiosh. He hesitated a moment, then hopped over to her wrist. She studied him for a moment, looking closely into his eyes and showing no sign of fear at all.

"I've never been this close to one of these before. It looks very intelligent."

"More intelligent than me sometimes," I said. *"That's just banter, Loiosh. Forget I said it."*

"No chance, boss. You're stuck with that forever."

She held her hand out and Loiosh hopped back over to my shoulder. She took out a handkerchief and wiped her wrist, then folded the handkerchief and put it away.

Then she looked at me and nodded.

"You got it, Easterner," she said.

Chapter Sixteen

AND THEN, KIERA, I waited. And, as I waited, I was just a bit nervous.

I mean, you speak Jhereg—You know what we were talking about, or, rather, *not* talking about; and of course I knew, but I wasn't sure if Timmer knew. I thought she did, I hoped she did, but I didn't know, and so I sat there and waited and was nervous, in spite of Loiosh's comments designed to irritate me into relaxing.

No, don't ask me to explain that.

By this time I had blended into the background of the public house, and no one was really looking at me, so at least I didn't have that to worry about. In fact, Kiera, while I was nervous about Timmer, I wasn't really *worried* about anything; it seemed that the time for worrying was well past; besides, I had plans to make, and the time to worry is when you don't have anything else to do. I'm not sure who said that; I think it was you.

An hour later she came back and sat down. She looked at me. There was no expression on her face.

I said, "Well?"

She said, "I've asked the local magistrate for a seizure card. Just temporary, of course; until the investigation is over."

"For me?"

"Yes, for you. Of course," she added, "I don't know your real name, so I had to mark it 'name unknown,' but I know that you have information about Fyres's death, and that's what we're investigating."

"I understand. When will it go into effect?"

"In about fifteen minutes."

"Fifteen minutes," I repeated. "All right."

"Until that time," she said carefully, "I cannot legally stop you from leaving the city, or even this public house; but I would ask, from one loyal citizen to another, that you consider your duty to the Empire and remain here, as a gesture of cooperation."

"Here?"

"Yes. The card will be served here."

"Will you be remaining here as well, to serve the card?"

"I'm afraid that's impossible; I have to act on the information that you've given me. But, ah, someone will be by to serve it as soon as it's ready."

"About twenty minutes, then."

"Or less." She stared off at nothing. "Someone will be arriving with it, directly from the magistrate."

"And where is the magistrate?"

"A quarter of a mile away. To the east."

I nodded. "All right," I said.

I started to drink some more wine, then thought better of it. Wine sometimes affects me very quickly. "I'm afraid," I said slowly, "that I'm going to have to decline. I'll be running from the seizure, so you will have to send someone after me to serve it."

"I thought you might," she said. "Unfortunately, I cannot, at this time, detain you."

"I'm already being hunted," I pointed out.

"Not by the Empire."

"No," I said. "That's true. Not by the Empire."

"With some crimes, the Empire looks for the fugitive harder than with other crimes. And there are even some crimes, some very serious crimes, that never get properly handled, and where descriptions are lost or mixed up."

"I understand," I said.

She rose to her feet. "Too bad I can't stay to serve the card," she said. "But duty calls."

"In a very clear voice," I said.

"I'll see you again," she said.

"Why, yes. If I'm arrested—"

"Detained."

"Detained. Right. If I'm detained, then, no doubt, I'll be at City Hall tomorrow, being interrogated."

"And if you're not?"

"Who knows?" I said. "You know, I rather like this place. It's especially nice at this time of the evening."

"Yes," she said. She opened her mouth as if she had something else to say, but closed it again, leaving whatever it was unsaid. Then she stood and left without any ceremony whatsoever.

I waited a decent interval—say, about a minute—then I settled the score, got up, and went outside. It was a lovely, crisp day, with the winter not yet arrived. The street was almost empty of people. I looked around carefully, as did Loiosh, and we consulted.

There were about a hundred places to choose from in an area like this, but I settled on a doorway right next to the public house—it was deep, and quiet, and didn't look like it got much use. I slumped against it and sent Rocza into the air.

I stood there for perhaps twenty minutes. A few people walked by but none of them noticed me. One elderly Teckla walked past me to go into the building whose doorway I was occupying, but even he didn't appear to notice me as I stepped out of his way. You taught me how to do that, Kiera; you said it's more attitude than anything else. Maybe you're right.

"Rocza says he's coming, boss."

"The right way, or the wrong way?"

"The right way. From the east."

"Can't ask for better than that."

I let a dagger fall into my hand. It was one of the new ones. I wiped the hilt on my cloak, as much for luck as for any other reason, then took my position.

Domm walked right past me. There was a rolled-up piece of paper in his hand, no doubt the seizure card, naming some nameless person who happened to be me as a witness wanted for questioning in an Imperial investigation.

Pretty serious stuff.

I fell into step behind him, and I left nothing to chance, nor did I speak. Afterward, I continued past, walking easily, as if nothing had happened. I turned a corner, and then another, and Rocza informed Loiosh, who informed me, that no one was following me.

INTERLUDE

"DID IT SEEM to bother him?"

"Killing Domm? I don't think so. Should it have?"

"I'm not sure. I suppose I would have been happier if it had, but—"

"You've changed, Cawti."

"So has he."

"Not as much as you have."

"From what you've told me, I'm not sure that's true."

"Come to think of it, neither am I. But . . ."

"Yes?"

"There's so *much* you're leaving out. I can see the gaps in your story."

"I told you—"

"I know, I know."

"In any case, that was about it."

"And there's another gap."

"Cawti—"

"Sorry. You mean, you just left after that?"

"Pretty much, yes. There was a bit of excitement that proved to be nothing, and we got some reassurances, and then Vlad took Savn and went away for parts unknown, and I came back home where I found your letter waiting for me."

"Tell me about the excitement that proved to be nothing, and about the reassurances."

"All right. What is it?"

"I don't know, Kiera. It's good to hear this, but it just makes me want to find out more."

"Are you going to try to?"

"Not if you don't want me to."

"I don't want you to."

"All right."

"Should we have more tea?"

"I think something stronger."

"Good idea."

"And then some food. I'll buy."

"Thank you."

"It's the least I can do."

"Is there a hint of irony there, Cawti?"

"No, actually, I don't think there is."

Chapter Seventeen

"AND THEN I came back here," he concluded.

"What next?"

"As I said, we arranged that I'd meet her tomorrow evening at that same place, and she'll give me the deed to this chunk of land. And that is the story of my latest triumph."

"Triumph," I repeated. "Will it still be a triumph tomorrow, when you walk into that public house to find yourself arrested, if you're lucky, or surrounded by Jhereg if you're not?"

"She promised," said Vlad smugly.

"And what," I said, "makes you think you can trust her?"

"Instinct," he said.

I bit back a nasty reply. As much as we'd both bungled these last few days, I still trusted my own instincts, so I could hardly blame him for trusting his. The thing is, *I* didn't trust his.

He said, "Okay, maybe that was one more screwup. But,

Kiera, it felt right. Loftis was her friend, and her superior officer, and an associate. I don't know, maybe she hated his guts. But—"

I shook my head. "No, you're probably right, only—" I stopped.

"What is it?" he said.

"I don't know. A spell of some kind, centered around here."

"Aw nuts," said Vlad.

"Perhaps," I said slowly, "we had best gather up Savn and Hwdf'rjaanci and head into the woods while we can."

"I don't believe it," he said.

"I think," I said carefully, "that it was a location spell."

He gave me an odd look and said, "The Jhereg?"

"Maybe."

"Where can we go?"

I cursed softly and didn't answer.

He said, "You take the old woman and the boy and make tracks. It's only me they want."

"Wrong answer, Vlad."

"Heh."

He walked into the house, emerging a minute later with his sword belt. He wore no cloak at all and had several knives strapped to his body. He said, "Go, Kiera."

"Not a chance."

He indicated the house. "What about them? Can't you stash them someplace and then retrieve them later, if there is a later?"

Well, in point of fact, I could. Then something else happened. "Someone has just teleported into the area," I said. "About a quarter of a mile away."

"How many?"

"One."

"One?"

"That's right."

He shook his head. "If it's Mario, there's no point in trying to run, and if it isn't, well, there isn't any other one person I'm particularly afraid of."

I nodded. I felt the same way, except that I didn't have his superstitious dread of Mario.

He drew his blade and waited. "May I borrow a knife?" I said.

"You don't want to use your own?"

"I'm not armed," I told him.

"Oh, yes. I forgot." He handed me a weapon. I tested the feel, the balance, and the edge, and then we stood back-to-back and waited. Loiosh and Rocza sat on Vlad's shoulders. Buddy came out of the house, sniffed curiously, then sat down next to us; it was somehow comforting that he was there, though I didn't know if he'd be useful.

Vlad saw her first. He said, "There she is."

I turned. She was walking through the woods toward us, a sword at her side, but her hands were empty. Buddy stood up and started growling, and a glance told me that his teeth were bared. Well, well.

The woman ignored Buddy, and ignored the fact that Vlad and I were holding weapons, but nodded hello to each of us as she stopped about five feet away and looked at the cottage.

"It *is* blue," she said.

"You thought I lied?" said Vlad.

She shrugged. "It was a possibility. But you told the truth about everything else, so—"

"How did you find me?"

"In the public house," she said. "With the help of your uh, familiar, is that the right word?"

Vlad used a word he wouldn't have wanted Hwdf'rjaanci to hear. "A bit of Loiosh's skin on the handkerchief," he said. "And then you went to a sorcerer with it, and located him, because you knew you couldn't locate me."

She nodded. "Shall we go inside?"

"Let's settle it out here," said Vlad.

"Settle what?" said Timmer.

"Aren't you here to arrest me?"

"No."

"But—"

"I wanted to meet the rest of this little troupe that's caused so much trouble, and I thought you'd want to hear how everything came out."

For a moment no one spoke. Then Vlad said, "Oh."

He put his sword away, then the knife I handed him. Then he petted Buddy, who took that as a clue that everything was all right, and introduced himself to Timmer. The old woman came out as this was going on.

"Who are you?" she snapped. "And what are you doing here?"

"Ensign Timmer," said Vlad, "this is the woman we call Mother, because her name sounds rather like a sneeze and no one but Kiera here can say it. Oh, and this is Kiera—I don't think you two have been introduced yet. And this is Buddy, who I think is, really, the intelligent one of the bunch—at least, he's the one who hasn't made any mistakes yet."

Rocza hissed. Vlad laughed and said, "One of the two, then."

"A pleasure, my lady," said Timmer. "I have something for you." I heard a quick intake of breath from Vlad.

"You got it?" he said.

She smiled. "Of course. I said I would."

"That was quick. What's it been, three, four hours at the most?"

"Yes. Shall we go inside?"

"By all means," said Vlad. "After you."

We trooped into the cottage, Hwdf'rjaanci leading and Buddy bringing up the rear. Once inside, Timmer looked around the place, then licked her lips, probably because biting them would have been too obvious. We introduced her to Savn, who almost, maybe, just a little bit, might have given a flicker of acknowledgment. Or maybe not.

"Brain fever, you said?" asked Timmer.

"There is no such thing as brain fever," said Hwdf'rjaanci.

Vlad shrugged. Hwdf'rjaanci sat next to Savn, Vlad and I sat at the table. Timmer declined a chair, preferring to lean against the wall. Buddy curled up near Savn and Hwdf'rjaanci and tried to insinuate himself between them. Savn absently stroked Buddy's head. That was, as far as I knew, another first. I caught Vlad's eye and saw that he had seen it, too.

"Where shall I begin?" said Timmer. "Does everyone know what has been going on?"

"Kiera knows everything up through our conversation today. The old woman doesn't know much of anything about the affair," said Vlad.

"That's because I don't want to," she snapped. "And I won't thank you for telling me."

Timmer nodded. "All right," she said. "Do you want us to go somewhere else, then?"

"No. Say what you want, and I'll listen, but don't bother explaining it."

"Very well," said Timmer.

She turned to us. "There isn't all that much to tell, truly. Domm was found murdered, just a few hours ago. A dagger was driven into his head."

"Oh?" said Vlad with that assumed casualness he does so badly. "Any idea who did it?"

"A fugitive. Someone we wanted in connection with our

ongoing investigation into the death of Lord Fyres. We think he was a Chreotha," she added.

"I see," said Vlad. "What else is new?"

"I spoke to, uh, to certain persons in the Empire, and was told to leave well enough alone." She looked like she'd just eaten a jimmberry thinking it was a rednut.

"So Vonnith goes free?" said Vlad.

"Free? Yes. Free and clear. And still rich. And still the owner, or manager, of three or four banks. We can't touch her."

"And Reega?"

"The same." She shrugged, as if Reega didn't much matter to her, which was probably true; Reega hadn't been involved in Loftis's death.

Vlad shook his head. "Not the way I'd have preferred them to end up."

"Nor I," said Timmer. "But then"—she spread her hands—"it isn't my choice."

"And?" said Vlad. "In exchange?"

She nodded. "Cooperation. They're both going to do what they can to minimize the damage to the Empire. That, after all, is what's important." In her voice was a trace of the same bitterness that Vlad had described in Loftis's voice when he spoke about having betrayed his chief.

"What else?" said Vlad.

She nodded, and, from a pouch at her side, pulled a rolled-up piece of parchment, which she handed to Hwdf'rjaanci. She took it hesitantly, looked at Timmer, then at the document. Her hands trembled a bit as she undid the ribbon with which it was tied and broke the wax with which it was sealed and unrolled it. She read it slowly and carefully, her lips moving, and I saw that there was a tear in her eye.

Vlad loudly cleared his throat, stood up, and said, "Does anyone want klava?"

No one did. Vlad sat down again.

I said, "Timmer."

"Yes?"

"Vonnith and Reega now know, or can easily learn, who it was who—"

"No," she said. "Don't worry about it. This old woman's continued health is now my business."

Hwdf'rjaanci looked up and said, "What was that? My health?"

"Never mind," I said.

She looked at the three of us one at a time, harrumphed softly, and went back to reading the deed to her land.

"Okay," I said. "I trust you."

"So do I," said Vlad. "Only . . ."

"Yes?"

"Do me a favor, and don't tell anyone how you found me. I don't think the Jhereg would figure it out on their own in a million years, but—"

"Right," she said. "Don't worry." She stood up. "I think that's it, then."

"Yes," said Vlad. "Good luck."

"And to you," she said. She looked at me and we nodded to each other, then she turned and left and it was over.

"It's over," said Vlad.

"Not quite," I said.

"Oh?"

"Care to take a walk with me?"

He frowned, then he shrugged and stood up. We stepped outside. Buddy followed us, and Loiosh was on Vlad's shoulder, but there was no one else there. We walked into the woods near the house. "What is it, Kiera?" he said.

"How long have you known?"

"Know what?"

"I'm not stupid, Vlad, and I don't think you are, either."

"I—"

"Vlad, how long have you known?"

"I hadn't been planning on talking about it," he said. "What gave me away?"

"That's *my* question."

He laughed. "I suppose it is. But you go first. When did you know that I knew?"

I shrugged. "Just now, a few minutes ago. You're sometimes very careless with your life, Vlad—especially when you're annoyed. But you're never careless with other people's. Even when you were in the Jhereg—"

"Who's life was I careless with?"

"No one's. That's the point."

"I don't understand."

"Don't you? Think about it."

He did, and I could see him going back over the last hour in his mind; then he nodded. "I see."

"Yes. You told me to get the boy and the woman somewhere safe. You asked me to, uh, *stash* them somewhere. Where could Kiera the Thief stash anyone that would be safe? It didn't occur to you to ask if there was a teleport block up, you just assumed there was, because the Jhereg, or the Empire, was coming to get you, and you can't tell if there is one or not with the Phoenix Stone you wear. So how could Kiera the Thief break through a teleport block?"

"Right," he said. "I was scared—"

"Sure. For Savn and Hwdf'rjaanci. And then there was the remark about the knife, which is what really convinced me."

"Yeah. I was panicking, I guess."

"I guess. So, your turn. How did you find out, when did you find out, and who have you told?"

"I haven't told anyone, Kiera."

"You may as well call me by my real name."

"All right, Sethra. I haven't told anyone. You should know that."

I nodded. "Yes, I guess I know that. When did you figure it out?"

He shrugged. "I've known you in both guises, you know—I mean, known you well. And there can't be many of us who have."

"No one. Only you."

He bowed his head as if he felt he had been honored; which he had been, of course.

"How long have you known?"

"Not long. Since yesterday. No, today, I guess. I don't know."

"What did I do yesterday?"

He shrugged. "It was an accumulation of little things."

"What? I'm curious. You know, I never cheat. I mean, when I'm Kiera, I only do Kiera things—"

"You almost cheated tonight."

"Oh, you noticed that?"

"I sort of guessed, at any rate—just before we realized there was only one person coming, I was expecting to see Iceflame in your hand."

I nodded. "And you almost did, especially since I knew that you knew. Which brings us back to the question: how did you know? What were these little things that accumulated?"

He spread his hands. "I'm not sure if I can even identify them all, Kie— Sethra."

"No, call me Kiera. It'll make it easier."

"Are you trying to confuse me? Don't answer that. Kiera. Yes. As I say, it was a lot of little things. This is the first time we've worked this closely together, but we've known each other for a long time, and I've always wondered why you gave a damn for a little Easterner kid. Now I know, of course."

"Of course."

"And I'm still grateful. Only . . ."

"Yes?"

"I don't know. I keep thinking of things, like the way you recruited me to find Aliera."

"There was no other way, Vlad."

"I understand that, but still. And what was that whole business with the blood of the goddess? Not that I haven't figured out who the goddess is."

"I can't tell you that, Vlad. She said it was important for you to have that vial, and that she, herself, didn't know why."

"The ways of the gods are mysterious."

"Don't be sarcastic."

"Why not?"

I shrugged. "I want to know what gave me away, Vlad."

"It was simple, really. You see, I've known you and Sethra for a long time, but I've never seen you at the same time or in the same—"

"Cut it out. I'm serious. This matters to me. I want to know."

He nodded. "All right." He got his considering look on his face and said, "Well, for one thing, you got upset once, when you were talking about how we'd been fooled, and your speech patterns changed. Come to think of it, that happened more than once. I remember when I first told you things that implied that the Empire was involved, you, uh, you talked different."

"My speech patterns slipped," I said, shaking my head.

He nodded. "Not very often, or for very long, but it was one of the things that got me thinking."

"I suppose it would be. Damn. After two thousand years, you'd think . . . never mind. What else?"

"What else? Oh, how little you ate was probably part of it, though by itself it didn't mean anything. But I know that Sethra is undead, and lives on, well, on other things, so she doesn't eat much. And, by the same token, there was the way the dog reacted to you, and—how did you fool Loiosh, by the way? He can usually tell the undead with one sniff."

"He's not as good at it as Buddy, apparently," Loiosh hissed and I heard myself chuckle and I suspected that Vlad was never going to let Loiosh forget that. "But," I continued, "there are ways to conceal the fact that one is undead. It's difficult, but—"

"But you're Sethra Lavode. Right. I keep forgetting that."

"How else did I give myself away?"

"I heard you muttering something about battle shock when you first saw Savn, and I thought it was odd that Kiera would recognize battle shock."

"Cracks and shards. I'm an idiot."

"No, I just know you well."

"Okay, keep going."

"Well, you knew stuff that I couldn't see how Kiera knew."

"Like what?"

"Like what 'he didn't break the stick' meant, and, more than that, what it feels like to have a spell-stick discharge in your hand. And you knew more about Imperial Signets and secret Imperial organizations than seemed reasonable for your basic thief. Or even your extraordinary thief."

"Oh." I shook my head. "It's starting to sound like a miracle that no one else has figured it out. That must have been what you meant when you said you got more than you wanted."

"Did I say that?" He shrugged. "But remember: no one else knows both of you. And you *are* a very effective Jhereg—I've known you since I was a child, and I never suspected that you were anything but what you seemed to be. But then, as I said, we've never worked together before. You, Kiera, have never worked closely with anyone, have you? And that's the reason, isn't it?"

I nodded. "Continue, then."

"Okay." He was getting warmed up now. "When you first met with Loftis, there was something odd in the way you reported the encounter."

"Odd? How?"

"Like you left something out—like you didn't tell me everything that happened."

"What didn't I tell you?"

"The part where you were first bluffing him, you talked about mentioning a few details about some activities the Tasks Group had done, but you wouldn't tell me what the activities were. Later, when I was putting things together, it occurred to me that maybe that was because they were things that would make you seem knowledgeable to him, but would connect Kiera with someone else for me—like something Kiera couldn't know about, but Sethra could. Am I right? Or maybe just things Kiera couldn't know about. I don't know. I think it was one of the things that first made me think there was something funny going on, although I didn't really pay too much attention at the time. But it was a hole in your report and it only made sense later."

The Jenoine at Dzur Mountain. I nodded, while trying not to think too much about the experience itself; it was one I hadn't enjoyed, and I'd been damn glad to have the help of the Tasks Group at the time. And, of course, I'd had to leave out all the other incidents that Sethra knew about from having been Warlord, but Kiera couldn't. Damn.

"All right," he continued. "What else gave you away? It's hard to think back on it this way, because I wasn't really trying to put it together; it just happened. Oh, well, I remember one thing. You—that is, Sethra—once told me that you were originally from the Northwest."

"So what's your point?"

"How easy you found it to say the old woman's name."

"Hwdf'rjaanci? That's a Kanefthali name. There are lots of people who can pronounce Kanefthali names."

"Maybe," he said. "But there are even more who can't; you'll notice that Timmer didn't try." I started to speak, but he held up his hand. "Okay, maybe it didn't mean anything by itself, but it was another piece, all right?"

I scowled at him.

"And you were too sensitive to magic—you kept reminding me of Aliera, the way you'd pick up on spells. In fact, I wasn't really convinced until you detected that teleport just now, and knew right away how many there were."

"That was stupid, too," I said, or, I suppose, growled.

He said, "Tell me something."

"What?"

"Why, Kiera? Or, rather: Sethra, why Kiera?"

"You mean why the name? In the old form of the language there are female endings of—"

"No, not the name. Although, now that I think of it, that should have tipped me off, too—a very, very old feminine version of 'Kieron.' But, no. I mean, why does she exist at all?"

"Oh, why did I invent her?" I shrugged. "At first, to keep in touch with the Underworld—it was part of the job of the Lavodes to keep track of what the Jhereg and various others were up to. After that, well, I got to like it. It was different, it was a challenge, it was scary at a time when it was hard for anything to frighten me—"

"Yes," said Vlad, his face twisting into part of a smile. "You'd hate never being frightened, wouldn't you?"

I smiled back. "As I say, I never cheated when I was being Kiera. I never used, well, anything that Kiera didn't come by herself, or any skill that wasn't Kiera's own. I've gotten to like her."

"And no one knows?"

"Only you."

He licked his lips. "Uh, Sethra—"

"Don't worry about it."

"Okay."

I smiled. "I still like you, you know."

"That's a relief."

"Kiera has never killed anyone, and I decided long ago that keeping that secret wasn't worth a life."

He shook his head. "Sethra doesn't value life as much as Kiera does, I think."

"I don't think you know Sethra as well as you know Kiera," I said.

"Maybe not, maybe not."

He didn't say anything for a while. Trying to keep my voice casual, I asked, "What now?"

He pointed to his upper lip.

I said, "Right. In addition to growing your facial hair back."

He shrugged. "I don't know. I think I'm going to bring Savn back home."

"Teleport?"

He shook his head. "It'll take a long time to get back there, and, with any luck, by the time we make it he'll be better. Some better, anyway. Better enough that he can see his family again."

"How will they react to you?"

He smiled. "I don't think I'll want to settle down there. Although, come to think of it, there is an Issola minstrel in the area I could stand to see again."

I shook my head. "I wish . . ."

"Yeah. Me, too. Wait here," he said. He went back into the cottage and returned a few minutes later with his backpack, Savn trailing along behind.

"That was a short goodbye," I said.

"I don't think the old woman likes me," he said. "But don't tell her I know. I think it would hurt her feelings."

"Vlad—"

"And, look, give my regards to, uh, to people, all right? And look in on Noish-pa when you can."

"I will," I said.

"Then that's all," he said.

"I doubt it very much," I told him.

He smiled, nodded, and began walking down the road, Savn keeping pace. Buddy and I watched them. I petted Buddy, who didn't seem to mind.

Being Vlad, and thus needing to get in the last word, he turned around just before reaching the road, and called back, "We all need work on our disguises, don't we?"

They were gone before I could think up a good answer.

EPILOGUE

My Dear Cawti:

   It was delightful, as always, seeing you, although perhaps you don't feel the same way. If not, I can certainly understand. Maybe you were upset by what I didn't tell you, yet you know there are things that I had to leave out, both on Vlad's behalf and on my own. I had hoped I told you enough for your peace of mind. On the other hand, perhaps it bothers you not to tell Vlad those things you have chosen to keep from him, and perhaps it should bother you; I am hardly one to judge what another person's secrets ought to be.

   You seemed concerned about the boy. I know no more than I told you, but do not be discouraged. You cannot expect such a complex ailment to be cured at once in its entirety. There has been clear progress, and I feel confident that, in time, his cure will be ef-

fected. As for what will become of Vlad—that is a more difficult matter to judge.

And yet, as I said yesterday, he is well, and in this matter he emerged unscathed. You cannot reach him, and I cannot reach him, and we accept this because we also know that the Jhereg cannot reach him. Of course, he always takes chances, yet he is being very careful and that is a consolation to us; and Loiosh is watching over him, and that is another consolation to us; and now I believe there may be another, of whom I cannot speak, who has found a way to watch over him. No, you must not ask what I mean, Cawti, you must simply trust me. That is what trust is, you know: if we never had secrets from our friends and loved ones, there would never be any need for them to trust us.

There is little more I can say, my dear, except that I'm sorry to have caused you any distress, and I hope you can understand that I have done my best in a very difficult situation.

Let us give it some time, and then we'll meet again, and if you have any more questions you may ask them, and if you feel the need to berate me, well, I will listen and take it like a trooper. In the meantime, you know that you can always call on me if you are in trouble, and I will repeat that it was a joy to me to see you and Vlad Norathar, who seems to already have the good looks of his father and the iron will of his mother.

Faithfully,

Kiera